I0713331

SHIFT

By
Frank Darbe

JaCol Publishing Inc.

ISBN: **978-1-946675-10-1**
For information regarding permission, write to:

JaCol Publishing Inc.
195 Murica Aisle
Irvine, CA 92614
818-510-2898
Editor-in-Chief: Randall "Jay" Andrews
Managing Editor: Jessica Collins
www.jacolpublishing.com

Acknowledgment

Writing Shift used every iota of knowledge I learned of writing. Sadly, much of it was wrong or untaught in formal schooling. So for that informal schooling, the boot camps, the patience while retraining, the hand holding, and the occasional kick in the ass, I want to thank my editor and publisher, Randal Andrews.

For the cover that graces this book, I want to thank Karen Brosinsky Edwards, who is an excellent artist, and part of the JaCol team.

I want to thank my family, my wife Eva Brzezinski, my sons Szymon and Allan, my mother in-laws Joan and Szymon Brzezinski for their support and generosity over the years. My friends, Nadin and Tom Abbot, contributed patience and the inspiration of their incredible work ethic. To my dear friend, Jean Goldstrom, I want to thank the farm team writers, and years of friendship and the privilege of learning from her.

I want to thank the members of Writers World, in and out of the boot camps. The excellent writers who critiqued my work and whose work I critiqued, you served as teachers, fellow students, and Jedi master's on the road to publication.

Finally, I want to thank all those unnamed who served as sources of inspiration and support.

Table of Contents

CHAPTER ONE

Five Days Ago Last Week

Light, bright enough to blind, to wince away from with sufficient violence that Aranea Gekas dropped her smart paper.

Hamilton North caught the paper like his right fielder days in college. "Careful Ms. Gekas." His voice boomed in the elevator.

She blinked away residue of light and tears. After everything they had meant to each other, Hamilton called her Ms. Gekas. "What was that?"

"Your paper, you dropped it."

She shook her head. "No, the light."

"Light?"

She jerked her head up. "It blinded me. You didn't see it?"

"You mean something like a phosphene flash? A bit deep in the earth for cosmic rays. The Lux isn't Lagrange Four."

"No, no," she paused. "Much brighter."

Hamilton tilted his head. "You Okay?"

"It's nothing."

Together for less than a minute, and she had already slipped into the fallback answer developed over the two years they had lived together.

He frowned. "Am I failing to understand you again?"

"Not again, Ham, still."

His eyes widened. "So, what're you reading?" The maladroit change of subject fit their pattern of avoidance. Love doesn't always find a way.

"The breakup of 1709 Ukraina."

He nodded. "I saw it on the news."

His face took the stern, serious look of a media commentator, and his tone dropped an octave. "The Near-Earth Observatory reported with high confidence that there is no real danger of a humanity-ending cataclysm from the asteroid 1709 Ukraina."

She rolled her eyes. "As if you could trust anything Bezrukov says." But Ham's bit of humor relaxed her. They were just old friends catching up after a separation of several years.

"The physicist you worked with on the Stellar One Station?"

She nodded. "Bezrukov took over the Near-Earth Observatory 48 hours before I left, but I knew him when we worked at the Yevpatoria RT-70 Radio Telescope in the Crimea."

Ham nodded in recognition. "As I recall, you collaborated there with Vasyl Petrenko. I've seen his work. He's brilliant."

She did not want to speak of, or even think about, Vasyl. "Vasyl *was* brilliant. He suffered a breakdown in 2018. Last time I saw him, he could not remember his name, called himself Vin."

"I had heard that you and Vasyl were two of five survivors after the asteroid strike in 2018. That was an ugly bit of business."

Aranea's memory flashed back to the faces of the others; Toss Bonneteau, Vasyl, and the sisters, Yume and Shiso de Guzman. She had managed not to think about them for five years and saw no reason to start now.

"Bezrukov took Vasyl's place at the observatory."

The elevator doors opened. The icy air swirled, freezing moisture from the air. Yellow signs pointed to the changing rooms and the LUX Control Room.

Aranea rubbed her forehead. "We've hit bottom."

Ham nodded. "Time to put on our suits. Dark matter waits for no one."

Aranea undressed and walked barefoot across the rubber tiles to enter the cleanser. Steam, sharp and medicinal, burned her skin and nose. Blasts of water scoured her clean, and bursts of air blew away every drop.

She slipped into the utilitarian underclothing provided to staff members and eased into a coverall and facemask. With the suit sealed, Aranea took the lift down to the control room, braced against the cold and the sight of Ham.

The door opened, and Aranea paused just inside the central control room of the large underground Xenon Observatory. Half a dozen controllers, dressed in anonymous, clean gray suits, moved from station to station and observed lights flashing and data scrolling in endless streams.

SOP called for two operators on watch at any one time at the heart of the most advanced dark matter telescope on earth.

"Doctor Chekhov?" She addressed the group.

A short woman raised her head. "Take station five, Doctor Gekas."

"What's happening?"

"We've had seventy-six events since 1632. It's accelerating."

Aranea ran to the console at station five, all professional, looking for details, for problems. Seventeen liquid Xenon detector strings fed data to her console, one of six in the observatory. In theory, dark matter particles passing through the Earth, on rare occasions, struck a Xenon nucleus, releasing photons and other high-energy particles. Results relied on keeping the Xenon within a narrow temperature range.

She glanced up to catch Doctor Chekhov's eye. "Temperatures are high."

From another part of the control room, Ham called. "Same here."

"I said we had seventy-six events." Doctor Chekhov stood at the center of the control room, watching.

Aranea initiated an emergency pressure release and observed the temperature. "In which strings?"

"All of them," Chekhov answered.

"What?" How could that happen? Dark matter rarely reacted with ordinary matter. In a week, they might find one or two positives in the string detectors, and most of those false positives. In 2018, during the most significant single Dark Matter event in history, only seven positives occurred.

The heat sensors in the Xenon string detectors spiked. Alarm lights flared. The xenon had melted, and pressure in the containers exceeded the maximum limits.

An explosion shook the floor, and a section of her console darkened.

"I've lost power to three strings," She said.

A klaxon blared. Xenon flooded the chamber from below.

Chekhov screamed, "Out!"

Aranea hit the emergency shut off switch. She ran to the lift. A second explosion shook the floor. Metal shards sprayed up from the string containers. A gray-suited scientist collapsed beside her, blood gushing from the woman's neck and chest.

Aranea bent to help. Blood pulsed from a tear in the woman's throat.

Her name is Smith, Doctor Ellen Smith of London.

"Run!" Ham grabbed Aranea's shoulders and pushed her toward the lift.

He hoisted Doctor Smith onto his shoulders and followed.

Seven explosions, like a string of giant firecrackers, blasted debris through the control room. Aranea tumbled into the lift. Her hood caught on the edge of the door and tore free. She inhaled. Her lungs filled but gave no relief. Unbearable light burst around her.

Ham staggered outside the elevator; blood flowed down his chest. He leaned against the edge of the door, silhouetted by the hard, brilliant light. His bones cast shadows visible through the gray suit.

He reached out. His hand hit the elevator button. Light filled her, emptied her, and left her dark and cold.

****

Vin pointed to the stars and glanced at the rat on his shoulder. "They fall."

The rat stood on its hind legs and nuzzled Vin's ear.

Vin spread his arms wide, tilted his face to the sky, and screamed. "Comets, meteors, asteroids, planetoids perturbed by the gravitational influence of a massive dark body moving near the outermost edge of the Kuiper belt have fallen inward toward the sun."

The rat nodded in agreement.

"Don't be condescending, Schurr."

Schurr scratched his narrow nose.

Vin dropped his arms and whispered, "Some of them struck the gas giants Neptune, Uranus, Saturn, and Jupiter." He shook his head. "Nothing remains but carbon rings smeared across wind driven cloudscapes. Others battered Mars, blasting out great divots from its ancient surface, leaving a thousand craters filled with dirty water.

Schurr licked a paw and combed its gray fur.

"No, Schurr, I have not forgotten that snowball of ice and muddy methane three kilometers in diameter that struck Venus."

Vin's shattered mind cleared. In a lucid second, he imagined Venus's ashy atmosphere blasted into space while volcanic ripples raced around the planet.

The moment of clarity vanished, so he continued to speak to his rat. "Now they fall to Earth, again with only Vin and Schurr to witness."

Vin did not recall his real name, so he called himself Vin, the generic he in Ukrainian, the language Vin spoke when things needed to be said. Not that much ever needed saying. It was just Vin and Norvez'kyy Schurr, or simply Schurr, his pet, Norwegian Rat.

It will happen soon, or so said the voice of the inner Clockbrain that guided all his movements across the Ukraine, Russia, and even into Turkey. Clockbrain controlled all of Vin's past and returned his memories in chunks, images, and half-remembered conversations.

Vin pulled a piece of bread from the pocket of his battered, Russian field jacket, tore off half, and offered it to Schurr. The rat took the food in his front paws and sat up on Vin's shoulder to eat.

The Seversky Donets River ran somewhere below Vin's perch above its east bank. The city of Aparinsky fumed and glowed behind him. Aparinsky's over-glow stole away most of the night sky's glory. That was all right because the coming astronomical display would be visible with any amount of light pollution, or so said his Clockbrain.

In memory, Vin sat at a cluttered gray table in the comfort room of the Yevpatoria RT-70 Radio Telescope, in the Republic of Crimea.

"You're brilliant, Vasyl." A young woman dressed in a bulky sweater, coat, and fur hat spoke in Greek-accented Russian. She lifted the bottle of Vodka and took a mouthful. If the thin man and the old man had not been there, he would have shared her mouth full of vodka in a kiss.

"Thank you."

"She is right," the fat man said.

That fat man was Bezrukov, how could I forget.

"They're calling you Ukraine's, Hawking. What you discovered out there, the approaching dark mass. A few years, a few books, Hawking will be a footnote in Science history."

What had Vin discovered? He wasn't sure even Clockbrain remembered. Vin's mind had fractured right back to childhood when his teacher father ruled his days, and worse, his nights, and shattered like an old mirror not too long after that memory. The Inner Clockbrain called up memory fragments that played through his consciousness as passion plays in an ancient Russian Orthodox Church. One of those discovered memories played tonight, here on the bank of the Seversky Donets. What Vin found would play out in the sky above Aparinsky. Vin glimpsed it in a memory fragment vision of a chalkboard covered with icy equations. At zero one three seven, they would fall, Latitude 47.66193, Longitude 40.91852.

Vin turned to face the town. He sat cross-legged on the cold ground, pushed his long hair away from his face, and dug into his coat pocket.

He searched by feel, spurning a tangle of string, a pebble, a lens from a magnifying glass, and pulled out his notebook and a stub pencil. He gnawed at the wood, exposing the graphite and clay lead. Content with the length of the lead, Vin dredged the pebble from his pocket and rolled the tip across the rough surface, scraping it to a single sharp point. He opened the notebook to a page halfway through, and, while keeping one eye on the sky, wrote symbols in neat Cyrillic, Latinate, Glagolitic, and Uncial scripts. Writing his observations was a compulsion forced on his hands by Clockbrain. He did not understand why or even what he wrote any more than he comprehended what drove him to travel across the country on foot to observe the sky on certain nights.

Schurr nipped Vin's ear. He jerked his head away, a reflex to escape the sharp pain. A narrow trail of fire traced a descending parabola. It was the first, probably an object no larger than a pebble for it never touched the surface. Schurr licked the blood beaded on Vin's earlobe. Vin scratched faster in the notebook, his pencil all but gouging the letters on the page.

A second meteor burned into view. Brighter! A third, fourth and fifth followed. A long continuous thunder accompanied the arrival of celestial objects. He followed their trajectory until the sixth slammed into the gleaming city sprawl blasting up a cloud of black smoke, dust, and scattered debris. Schurr, perhaps in reaction to the noise and light, slipped down into the front of Vin's coat. The shock wave from the explosion bowled Vin over and blasted him with sudden heat. Though the pencil lost contact with the page, his hand continued to move as if writing. He sat up and shoved the tip back against the page, braced for a seventh, and an eighth explosion, after which Vin lost count.

"Ukraina!" He screamed. An orgasm, sharp, bright, and brief clenched his stomach and left a wet stickiness in his underwear.

"Ukraina!" He struggled to sit up. A massive fireball burned overhead and broke into pieces.

Clockbrain displayed a shard of memory. He stood in a room with chalkboard walls covered with arcane equations. Before his eyes, the equations in one portion shifted and changed to simple geometry. Objects fall in predictable ways. One only needed to know all the forces acting upon the objects, an impossible task until Vin's discovery. He sat on a hilltop, and one of the fragments would hit close.

The fragmented memory vanished, and Vin struggled to stand. He wanted to run, to live. He could only scratch in the notebook and watch the pummeling fall of asteroid fragments tumble, burn, and blast away buildings, trees, roads until one slammed into the river at the base of the hill.

The shock wave picked Vin up and hurled him with shattered trees and other debris. The equations in his mind flashed and marked out a trajectory to death. The massive size of the catastrophe revealed in his icy equations that he would die under the debris with Schurr. Unless some future archeologist sent to excavate the site of an ancient catastrophe misjudged and dug where he should not, Vin would remain dead and entombed.

Midair, Vin noticed something else, perfect spheres, so black he could not make out their edges, ignored the shock of air, smoke, and heat. Where they touched the earth, they passed through without any effect on the material, as if they were ghost matter.

A crack opened in his mind and another memory bled through, from the hospital in Moscow. That man, Stark, leaned close. "Tell me about these black balls."

The memory fragment shattered. Vin lay on his back in the sand, breathed short, ragged gasps. Blood filled his mouth. One ball drifted close, and his body rose from the ground as if by magnetism, lifted him up and wrapped his body half around it before it passed through him.

This had happened before. Vin, no Vasyl, sat on the deck of a ship on the Volga River with Aranea and watched a meteor burn through the sky while an old, man dealt games of Three Card Monte, just for fun.

Yes, it had happened before. Balls of darkness drifted through them.

Almost everyone died.

****

John Stark reached into the warm, empty spot on the bed. The sex and citrus scent of Margrethe Thorn and her Eau

D'hadrien saturated the dark air. He licked the lemony metallic taste of her from his lips.

"Marg?"

Silence.

The door to the veranda stood ajar. Firework flashes of light splashed through the opening. "Out here. You have to see this."

He eased out of bed. Yesterday's suit pooled on the floor. An empty bottle of champagne floated in an ice bucket by the bed.

He reached for his Beretta, chuckled, and left it. Awe and curiosity colored Marg's voice rather than alarm. She stood naked against the railing of the balcony, a glass of Champagne in her hand. Long streaks of fire angled down from the sky and lit the night with daylight intensity. He slipped his arms around her and rested his hands on her flat stomach.

She glanced at him. "Never saw anything quite like this."

"I have."

A distant explosion threw up brief flames east of Paris.

Marg wrapped his arms around hers and pulled him tighter. "Did one hit?"

"Yes."

"Is this like in the 2018 Russian Event?"

He scanned the arc of the heavens. By a quick count, forty or fifty objects burned across the sky at any one moment. "This is what remains of 1709 Ukraina, and it's much worse."

Two ringtones chimed from their room. Stark retrieved his phone from his pants pocket. Thorn crawled over the bed and grabbed her phone from the nightstand.

"Mr. Stark," A calm, impersonal voice said. "A major impact event occurred near Aparinsky at 0037, Greenwich Time. Initial satellite data indicate the complete obliteration of the city."

"What about Petrenko?"

"Before we lost contact with Team Shrike, they placed his approximate location two kilometers east of Aparinsky. The team died in the strike."

"General Lagounov is our man in the Russian Army. Read him into the program and put Russian units on the ground. Find Petrenko!"

"What if he's dead."

"Then I want the body on a slab in Iceland."

"Yes, Mr. Stark."

Margrethe Thorn slid off the bed, the phone against her ear. "John, there's been an explosion at the LUX. My team is on site coordinating with rescue workers. No word on Aranea Gekas. I need to fly back, tonight."

Stark caught her eye, nodded, and spoke to the man on the phone. "Any reports from the teams in San Diego?"

"No sir."

"Order Teams Wasp and Thrush to pick up Shiso De Guzman, Yume De Guzman, and Toss Bonneteau. I want the targets sedated and on a flight to Keflavik, ASAP."

"Anything else?"

"Put our Iceland facility on high alert."

Margrethe glanced back over her shoulder from the bathroom door. "Are there more ships?"

He shrugged. "Too early to tell."

She beckoned him with her finger. "We should shower. Our plane can wait. HR will have a fit if the boss shows up smelling of sex."

Toss Bonneteau sat on a folding chair near the trolley track, a flat board across his lap, cards in his hands, his old eyes hid by thick, dark glasses. The trolley breezed by, its ozone slipstream ruffled his hair and pulled at his suit. "Ain't just a card game," He said to the four players gathered around the board. His lean hands circled like a dark flock of birds. The three cards flitted from place to place.

"It's the one on the right," said a big old boy with ropy muscles and a broad back.

The old man smiled, showing white teeth. "You got that right." He slid a twenty-dollar bill to the man. "Mama's little boy ain't making much money today."

A young sailor with an open face and blond hair, dressed in razor-creased dress blues, the half chevron of a lowly seaman on his shoulder, stepped close. "What's the trick?"

"What's the trick to life?" Toss winked. "This is Monte, boy, a fair lady, but no maiden if you get my drift. No, she wild, free, and chancy."

"How much?"

"Twenty bones a throw." The old man cocked his head and smiled.

He shifted his hidden eyes and caught the gaze of each of his team--two Shills, a Lookout, and the Muscleman. The Roper, another Sailor, a Petty Officer with a full Chevron, stood behind the Punter.

The young sailor peeled a twenty from his wallet and tossed it on the board.

"Don't need me to show you how it works?"

The sailor shook his head. "Nah, I'm 20/20."

The old man picked up two cards with his right hand, one with his left. The hands circled one over the other, and the cards shifted positions. He glanced up at the young sailor whose eyes smiled in a face that pretended confusion. Hesitantly, he tapped the center card.

The old man turned it over, the one-eyed queen smiled. "Yes, it looks to be a bad day for mama's little boy."

The sailor picked up two twenties. "What do they call you?"

"My daddy called me Toss."

"That's good. I like to know the name of the man who's going to buy my drinks all night. Do it again." He threw another twenty on the table.

Toss smiled and slipped into a friendly banter about beautiful women in Vegas, New Orleans, and Paris. The sailor won a second twenty and threw down another for a third game, thoroughly roped in and ready for branding.

Toss picked up the cards with the top card held between his thumb and his forefinger, and the lower card between his thumb and his middle finger, a small gap between. As he passed the left hand above his right, he dropped the top card first.

A strobe of light washed over the trolley platform. Toss' eyes remained on the cards, his hands, and the trick that made Monte an artful con. Toss took care of the cards, and the Lookout would keep watch for the boys in blue.

He glanced up to check the mark's interest.

The Sailor had looked away, his eyes on an expanding cloud of fire and smoke. "What the fuck?"

The shock wave blasted the glass out of tall buildings. The board on Toss' lap tumbled up and struck the big old boy across the face. Toss whirled with a dozen casual trolley car passengers. He curled into a ball while glass rained from shattered windows and people screamed.

The blast from the past hit him a second later. Something like this happened on the Russian trip up the Don and Volga Rivers. When the medics released him after weeks in a Moscow hospital, he left Europe. Toss had sworn he'd never go back to a place where hellfire rained out of the sky, burning people alive and performing strange atrocities on the survivors.

He stood. "Time for mama's little boy to run."

People lay where the shock wave left them, hands on their faces, crying or screaming or calling for mothers. The young sailor in his crackerjacks sprawled on his back, a spear of glass through his chest, his eyes open reflecting the distant, dim stars of the dead.

Most of the victims lived, which was a good thing. On that boat on the Volga River, everyone died but the five of them; an elegant Greek woman, some Russian, twin Japanese-Mexican girls, and himself, of course. Toss had played the hero, rescuing the Russian from falling into a river covered with burning oil. He played the hero because the two girls saved him, called into his mind where he wandered in a bloody, black hell shared with every lousy memory he ever made.

"Enough of this memory shit."

He started to run but saw two girls about twelve-years-old huddled on the trolley tracks, blood in their hair, faces dirty. A red trolley barreled down the rails, windows broken. The driver slumped over the console.

Is that the Shiso and Yume? He asked himself.

They would be sixteen now, not twelve, and he could not hear their voices in his head. Different girls, different time, but that didn't matter. Two girls saved his life, his soul, in 2018. Toss Bonneteau could not leave two strange girls to die on that track.

He ran three quick steps, swept them into his arms, and looked up. The trolley was right fucking there. The fastest sprinter on earth could not dodge it. He pulled the girls close so they would not see. In that last second, he realized that through all the hell, he had kept the Monte Cards in his hand.

His daddy taught him the game back in New Orleans. Every good thing in Toss' life, and a chunk of the bad, too, came from the Monte. Mostly, she'd had been kind to him. In his last act of defiance, instead of flipping the bird at that damned train, he tossed the Monte cards one last time.

The train slowed, all but stopped. An intense sense of Déjà vu enveloped him. This had happened before, in Russia. On that boat he had controlled the speed of time with his mind, could make time all but stop if he wanted, and then just walk away through frozen time.

The sound of a terrified scream dropped from a tenor wail to a growl, to a drawn-out gasp.

Debris raining from the sky tumbled, slow as stones sinking into molasses.

After six years, Toss had to fall back into 2018. The girls had led him out of the dark. He found himself in a slow-motion world. The Russian hung in the air, thrown by the explosion over the side of the ship, his coat spread about him as if he had grown bat wings. Toss grabbed the Russian's foot and pulled him back.

If he could do it then, he could do it now.

"Come with me." He took the girls by the hands and led them onto the platform, through the rain of slow falling debris, and frozen human misery. He left them in the protective shadow of a doorway. When he let go, the slow march of time froze them.

Time to leave.

He walked past people that pushed themselves up from the platform, the deep growl of their voices transitioning to a higher pitch as the time around returned to normal. The Trolley accelerated back to its usual speed; its brakes squealed as the driver fought the controls.

Those twins, Shiso and Yume de Guzman, what had happened to them? What had he become? Did they find the years since 2018 a gift or misery?

****

Shiso de Guzman, dressed in yesterday's panties and a tank top, crept down the central corridor of her Tio's boat, and that made everything wrong. She remembered pulling her frumpy blue nightgown over her head just before bed. Waking dressed as her twin sister on a bad morning rang alarm bells. Yume enforced her individuality with an immodest, bad girl act.

Shiso played the good twin in their complicated and bizarre relationship, so if she woke dressed like her sister that meant she inhabited Yume's dream, again.

Shiso stood tall because Yume stood tall. Cautious and sneaky fit Shiso. Not today, and not in this dream. Shiso refused to play the roles they had taken since, God, forever. No more tiptoeing unheard into a situation to check the weather. Shiso charged in and demanded attention. "Yume?"

No answer. What game did Yume play at?

Since their parents died on the Russian Vacation cruise in 2018, Yume had ruled their dreams. She often took the shapes of people they knew, animals, or objects that, outside of dreams, remained deaf and inanimate.

Well, if Yume refused to hear Shiso, then Shiso had her own talent--telepathy. "Is this another hide-and-seek dream?" she sent. For two years after they had returned from Russia, Yume led them in a search through her dreams. The dreams stopped after Shiso convinced Yume to spread their parent's ashes in the sea off La Jolla Cove.

Could the stress of the fires caused by the asteroid impact that blasted the city of Aparinsky to dust have brought back the hide and seek games? Those dreams always occurred in their parents' house. No, this was something else, some new tweak in Yume's psyche. Shiso found herself in the central corridor of Tio's boat, Suki's Delight. He conducted week-long working tours. Passengers paid to raise the sails, navigate by sextant, and pretend to crew a working sailboat.

The sisters worked the boat with Tio Carlos when not in school. Yume never dreamed of Suki's Delight. Yume did not appear so Shiso could not wake up. She needed to find her sister.

Go back or go forward? Oh, I hate this shit.

Yume loved riddles and puzzles. Her dreams possessed their own logic and displayed both rhyme and reason. Shiso crept toward the stair to the deck, which must be where Yume wanted her to go.

Damn your dream, Yume. I will not creep, damn it, or play your game. It took an act of will to go against the thrust of the dream. She kicked the door open and stepped into their mother's garden, except that it cruised along beneath a gibbous moon, and the lights of San Diego glimmered to port.

Back on what should be the aft end of the boat, their dead mother worked at her gardening bench. "What the fuck, Yume?"

Her mother did not turn, so Yume did not inhabit her mother's shape. A dream apparition worked at the table, but not with pots or flowers. Four photographic pans used to develop pictures the old-fashion way occupied the workspace. Their mother, Asami Kimura, had been a Photographic Artist when she met her future husband on a cruise along the Mexican Riviera. When not on their father's boat, Yume and Shiso had lived in their mother's studio. Yume must have translated that memory into her twisted dreamscape.

Shiso's mouth ran dry. A part of her wanted to run and hug her mother, even if this was a dream. Another part shuddered and shook, afraid that if she did, she would not want to wake. Her mother had been the sun at the center of Shiso's universe. That sun collapsed just when Shiso needed her mother.

"Yume, how could you do this to me?"

Neither a squeak nor sigh revealed her sister's hiding place.

She crept closer, timid, and hated herself. Asami lifted an image out of the bath and hung it on a line to dry. In the photo, a woman looked up from a bed in a hospital. Lights flashed, and a heart monitor beeped. A doctor walked into the picture and checked the screen. "Ms. Gekas?"

"Oh God." Aranea Gekas, like Shiso and Yume, had survived.

A man in a gray business suit stepped into the frame. "Is she awake?"

The doctor shook her head. "Xenon gas exposure can cause diathesis and leave victims unresponsive. The Beta levels of her EEG show she is awake. Mr. Stark must wait."

Shiso glanced away because she never wanted to see Aranea Gekas again. Why would Yume include Aranea?

Mother hung the second photo of fires, smoke, and a burning city. A large, military helicopter flew through the frame. Whoever held the camera scurried across the ground, under a fallen tree.

The third photo focused on a wooden table where an old man's hands shifted three cards from place to place while he hummed a blues tune.

Asami de Guzman hung the fourth photo. Shiso's mind jumped to the wrong conclusion expecting to see a picture of Yume's face. The image in the photograph shifted as if the photographer switched through a dozen cameras, displaying a barrel-vaulted ceiling in an aircraft hangar, rows if tables where men in white lab coats worked with electronic equipment and talked to each other in soft voices. A third image focused on hangar doors shut but guarded by men in military uniforms.

Shiso leaned close. "Where is that?"

The wooden door on the bench banged open.

Shiso jumped back, hands up to protect herself.

Yume rolled out into the garden, not sixteen-year-old Yume, though. "Yume, you're twelve again. Grow up."

"This is not mine."

"Of course, it is. You own this dream. Can you just wake us up? I don't like the way you've dressed me in this dream."

"I'm serious. I did not create this dream. I think it is that." She pointed to the last photo with its ever-changing perspective.

"Photographs don't dream."

The photo changed to a picture of Shiso and Yume in identical bra and panties, standing in their mother's garden.

Asami de Guzman dried her hands and turned. She wore the same loving face of the woman who watched them from childhood. Asami had been the type of mother who dried every tear, talked to them about courage, about becoming women who could stand on their own and owe no one unless they chose.

The eyes in that beloved face had exploded into red tears that trailed over her cheeks.

"Run," Asami said.

They froze to the deck, unable to move as if a tyrannical hand held them like toys.

"John Stark is coming for you. Run!"

Shiso sat up in her bed and screamed.

****

Yume de Guzman bolted from the bed. She whispered a plea, "Not my dream. Not my dream," and hoped it would help her understand what had happened.

Shiso answered in Yume's head, *"I know."*

She shuddered. Was this Shiso's sending or whatever spoke in the dream? She thought her answer. *"I'll get dressed."* Shiso would get it because that was how their abilities worked. Yume created lucid dreams about anywhere and any place. Shiso picked thoughts out of

Yume's head or inserted hers using telepathy. As far as Yume was concerned, Shiso had the better power.

"Give me a minute." She sent, confident that Shiso would pick up her verbalized thoughts.

She opened the drawer under her bed and pulled out the first thing to come to hand. The ship vibrated, the engine revved to top speed. The boat rolled from port to starboard. They ran parallel to the swell. Yume found Shiso dressed in a black blouse and jodhpurs.

Shiso's eyebrow shot up. "You look like a dog dressed you."

"Something hijacked my dreams, and you want to critique my fashion sense?" Thank God, Shiso decided to speak. Telepathy was the most convenient form of communication unless she wanted to keep a private thought.

"We're moving so fast. Why the hurry?"

They looked at each other, ran to the stair and up to the bridge. Tio Carlos stood by the wheel; his attention shifted from the view ahead to the radar. They sailed east-southeast, the lights of La Jolla glimmering. A faint glow farther south revealed the position of one of the fires set when the Meteor exploded over San Diego earlier in the day.

Yume glanced at Shiso. "Tio?"

Carlos de Guzman nodded but never took his eyes off the radar. "Is Shiso with you?"

"Yes."

"I'm sailing as close as I can to the coast. You will need to go into the water and swim to the beach."

They both answered, "Why?"

He pointed at the radar. "For at least two hours, four speedboats have followed us. When I sail closer to the coast, one of them cuts us off. I think they will board this time."

"This time?" Shiso's telepathic message echoed Yume's curiosity.

"Who's watching us?"

"FutureTense Incorporated." He shifted his course a point to the east.

The dot on the radar representing the speedboat accelerated and turned to cut between Suki's Paradise and the beach.

"I've heard of them." Yume glanced at her sister.

"From where?"

"Darknet Oviraptorus. It's a blog. How long have they watched us?"

"Since your parents died. I noticed certain people turned up too often and took an unhealthy interest in you both. I hired a private detective."

"Why watch us?"

He shrugged. "There's no time. Put on your suits. We're about a mile from the beach. I'm going to draw them away."

"Tio, you can't do that."

"There's no other way. Move!"

Five minutes later, the two women sat on the edge of the boat and pulled on swim fins, gloves, and goggles. Only the ship's navigation lights illuminated the water. Tio Carlos stepped out of the door of the wheelhouse. "I love you both. I want you to know that."

Yume sat next to the rail. She didn't speak aloud. Shiso's presence lived in her mind, no matter the distance that separated them. The year before, when Shiso had visited their father's relatives in Madrid, and Yume stayed with an aunt in Tokyo, they might as well have been in the same room.

Shiso, who had followed Yume's unvocalized thoughts, sent, *"It complicates dating,"* which was an understatement from Yume's point of view. No matter how close they were, sharing intimate encounters while her sister watched from inside her head was awkward.

"Now," Tio said. The boat swerved.

Yume and Shiso dove into the water with an undetectable splash. Yume swam underwater as far as possible before breaching the surface to catch a glimpse of the lights and dove again. Without the moon, no light relieved the night beneath the waves. Her sister's feelings of fear and concern for Tio Carlos kept her company.

The fifth time she breached the surface to check the direction of the beach, a distress flare exploded above Suki's Delight.

Shiso pushed the thought. "Don't stop!"

Yume's thought came back through the dark water. "I know you can catch his emotions even if you can't speak."

"He's afraid. We need to swim, fast as we can."

Yume imagined her Tio alone. "We can go back. We can help."

Shiso's thought cut her off. "Suki's Delight is too fast."

Yume dove again. The sisters had learned to swim almost before they could walk. Until their parents died, they competed in swim competitions and surfed the beaches of La Jolla. Swimming a mile at night birthed no fears in them. After ten minutes, they approached close enough to the beach to see people standing around fire rings, even caught bits of distant music.

Yume turned until she saw Shiso's head bobbing on the chop and swam closer. Shiso floated, and her unvocalized thoughts quieted. She spun to face Yume. "Tio's gone."

"What? How?"

"I don't know. I could feel Tio's thoughts, fear, anger, pain. Something swallowed him. His mind vanished."

Yume reached for her sister. They floated and clung together. In the distance, the navigation lights of Suki's Delight receded toward the black horizon.

CHAPTER TWO

Run

Yume heard scratching, like fingernails on a chalkboard, and opened her eyes.

I don't remember the van's interior being gray.

She ran her hand across the wall and found it cold and smooth. It dimpled under the pressure of her fingertip. This reality and her memory created a jarring disjunction. After their swim, they discovered a nightmare on the beach, fires everywhere. Shiso found a van with a set of keys behind the sun visor. The van ran out of gas at the Iron Mountain Hiking Trail parking lot. They had stayed because neither Yume nor Shiso could think of anywhere to go.

And what's wrong with the light, too bright for midnight, and it's gray like the walls.

"I'm dreaming again." She expected Shiso to answer. In shared dreamscapes, Yume often hid from Shiso, but Shiso could not hide in Yume's dreams.

Shiso did not answer.

Come to think of it, she heard no sister sounds, no frustrated sighs, soft breathing, or the whisper of Shiso talking in her sleep to the person they both thought of as Stranger.

More scratching broke the silence, though, not from inside the tube. Sound transmitted through the walls, closer, insistent.

She placed her lips against the surface. "Shiso?"

Shiso could not be there, of course, because Yume's lucid dreams happened in her head.

Something scratched again. No, different this time, not a scratch, more of a sigh.

"Hsssp."

"I don't understand."

"Heahp"

"Still not clear."

"Help!"

Yume smacked the wall. "Shiso, what's wrong."

A mouth opened in the metal wall. *Not Shiso.*

She rocked back to the center of the seamless, gray metal tube that curled ahead. A faint, pale light emanated from the walls. "What have you done with her?"

The mouth shifted to a place on the floor by her foot. A gray eye opened underneath the mouth.

You must help me. I turned her connection off. That's all. I need to see through your eyes unhindered by other connections.

Yume closed her eyes to shut out that surreal, Picasso mouth with an eye for a chin. "You can't do that. She's always in my head."

God, she did not want to deal with Shiso always present in her head, in the bathroom, math class, and that time with Jeremy Myers, when he kissed her, and they made out in the storeroom behind the school gym. Yume had run away because Shiso occupied a spot in the back of her consciousness, criticizing her kissing technique. She had never kissed a boy for real before that afternoon, and Shiso saw it all, and worse, shared it.

A second eye appeared beside the first. A face pushed up out of the flat surface. A broad, high forehead and kind, gray eyes swam up and around the mouth to take their rightful place. It reminded Yume of her father. "I am Stranger. I can turn all of you off."

Yume twisted her face away from the mouth; it moved to stay within her sight. "This is a nightmare."

Yume controlled shared dreams. Nightmares occurred only in her mind. She could never escape them until she screamed herself awake.

The mouth attempted a smile. "Perhaps I misspoke. Maybe I tuned out Shiso so we could share a needed, private conversation."

She crossed her arms to protect herself. "I don't understand."

"Of course, you don't. Look, I need your help. The humans who salvaged my body plan to breach me. Those humans damaged me the last time. I cocooned myself in a madman's mind for survival. I cannot do that again."

"What are you?"

"Stranger. What and who are one and the same."

She shook her head. "No, no, no! I made you up."

"I made you and Shiso. I made Toss Bonneteau, Aranea, and Vasyl Petrenko. I made all of you. Without all of you, we cannot survive."

She looked down at her feet. A subtle shift in texture and curvature altered the walls. Now they resembled the inside of a section of the intestines of a creature so massive that a human served as a morsel to be dissolved and digested. She wondered, in the logic of the dream, could the mouth swallow her body as the dream had swallowed her mind? "How could you make us? Is this your dream?"

"You are not a dream. Therefore, I exist. I find human languages with their subtle cultural nuance confusing because my communication apparatus is offline, and I have no interface to interpret subtlety."

"You are an alien."

"As you conceive me, does it help to think of me as Alien instead of Stranger?"

"Strangers and Aliens are the same, aren't they?" The concepts behind those words never ruffled her conscious mind. Stranger embodied a thing unknown, but Alien equaled unknowable.

She opened her eyes, ready to say, "Stranger."

Strangers voice echoed in her head. *"Then Stranger I remain until we meet in the flesh."*

"Oh, God." Stranger shared her mind, perhaps looked through her eyes. Bad enough to have a sister living in her head. "I'm not comfortable with you in my head or my dreams."

"I cannot change that without changing you. If you change, we both cease to live."

"You mean, die?"

"I so need my subtlety translator."

"What do you want?"

"I need you to see the others because I cannot."

She ran her hands through her hair, knotted and oily after five days hiding in the back of a van when they weren't scrounging for food. "I don't know how to do that."

"It is what you are doing now."

"Dreaming."

"Dreaming is the mind interpreting the random firing of neurons while unconscious. In humans, rapid eye movement and active theta waves signal a dream state. You are not dreaming. You constructed this reality. Of course, you do not need to create a new reality to see. You can see all probabilities and realities if you choose."

This sounds insane. "How do I do that?"

"Tricks of mind that you will divine. I can't teach those. They are built-in features of your design."

She buried her face in her hands. "God, you're annoying."

"If we were in closer proximity, this would be easier. I must apologize for that."

"Why apologize?"

"You will know later. The basic trick you need to know is the identities of the others."

"What others?"

"The survivors, I changed all of you that we might live."

"You sound like Jesus."

"I am no messiah figure in human history or any other."

"So, you want me to think about my sister."

"Don't forget the others. Toss Bonneteau, remember him?"

"The card dealer."

"One of his many talents. Remember Aranea Gekas and Vasyl Petrenko, especially Vasyl. He is the most difficult to see because it is his place to adapt. He adapted too far and orphaned me from his thoughts."

She nodded. "I remember them from the cruise and from after."

"Think about your companions on that river cruise. Picture a remembered face and imagine how it might look today. You can teach yourself to see them."

"What happens then?

"When you see them, so will I."

****

Vasyl Petrenko opened his eyes onto a pitch-black universe. He heard sounds, vibrations through the earth, and the hissing white noise of distant fires. He grabbed the fallen tree limbs and levered himself up. Brutal, raspy smoke burned his nose, its taste metallic.

I survived! How? Icy equations never lie.

He remembered not everything, but more than he expected. An explosion tossed him onto a hillside above the riverbank. Debris from the explosion rained around him. How had he lived through the blast, the fall?

Was that black globe real or a delusion?

Yes, it was the black globe, something about its substance and its influence on his flesh.

He buried his face in his hands. His face had changed, thinned, and elongated to a point. Long, crisp gray hair, like a rat's coat, grew on the backs of his hands.

He stood in shadow. Acrid smoke drifted by and fires danced in the distance. He ran his hands over his body. His coat was gone, and only the collar of his t-shirt remained. Lean ropy muscle slid beneath his skin. Something brushed his hand. He screamed and jerked away before he reached back. It extended from the base of his spine, a tail with a file's raspy surface.

I have a rat's tail. Not possible, where is Schurr?

Vasyl licked the imagined taste of bread from his lips. The taste evoked a brief, bright memory. Fingers holding a chunk of bread, the smell yeasty sweet followed by a blast and the earth tumbled past his vision. Rocks, trees, and unidentifiable objects pounded around him. Were those a rat's memories?

How could Vasyl remember Schurr's last feeding?

He reached again for the narrow, whip thing. He had a rat's tail. What had happened during the fall? How had he become a rat?

When would he become Vasyl again?

The rattle and chatter of metal buckles, boots, and accouterments echoed up the hill. Someone spoke in Russian, "Sergei, where the fuck you going?"

Vasyl eased back into a mound of broken trees and bushes.

The other Russian, Sergei, answered. "I need to take a leak."

"You can piss anywhere. Dead Ukrainians don't complain, but after five days, they stink."

"Hah, I prefer my privacy."

"You just don't want anyone to see that peanut you call a pecker."

"Your wife and sister never complained about my peanut."

The soldier laughed. "I'll wait for you to shake off the peanut butter."

Vasyl watched Sergei move up the hill, picking his way through the broken trees, boulders, parts of buildings, and other debris. The man stopped next to the fallen tree, opened his zipper, and urinated into the bush. Vasyl jerked away when the hot urine splashed his legs. Sticks and leaves crackled.

The man called Sergei glanced down and into Vasyl's face. His eyes widened, and he stumbled backward, spraying urine in panic.

Vasyl erupted out of the pile of broken limbs and fallen trees. He drove his hand into the soldier's mouth and shoved him backward. They bounced a dozen feet down the slope. Vasyl landed on top, one hand in Sergei's mouth and the other on the back of his neck. He jerked the soldiers head and heard a snap.

Sergei stared at the sky, his eyes unblinking.

Vasyl slumped. *What have I done? I killed him. How? I've never?* He caught flickering memories--a rat the size of a man, of a naked woman straddled him, fragments of the soldier's memories.

Footsteps approached. The other soldier walked into view. "Sergei, where's your uniform?"

The soldier's eyes dropped and caught sight of the dead man at Vasyl's feet. He reached for his assault rifle.

Vasyl leaped, arms extended. The rifle coughed, and fire erupted from the barrel. Bullets clawed down his side. The soldier fell backward, and they rolled, clawed, gouged, and punched. The soldier slammed into a boulder, his back wedged. Vasyl grabbed his ears and beat his head against the rock again and again until the fight ended.

He crouched over the body, gasped for breath. Blood pooled behind the soldier's head. His mouth opened and closed. More blood trailed from the corner of one eye.

He lingered to death.

"What have I become?" Blood dripped from the wound on his arm. Two trained soldiers lay dead. Vasyl Petrenko, Ukraine's Stephen Hawking, had been medium in all ways except his mind. He wiped the blood seeping from his wound on the dead soldier's chest. Those long thin hands had grown thick and rugged, a large man's hands.

He ran back up the hill to the hapless Sergei. The dead soldier had the square lean face of a man who spent his life in hard labor, blond hair, and a crooked nose from an old injury. Vasyl ran his hands over his face and found his nose crooked.

His stomach growled. Hunger racked him. Sergei and his partner wore field packs. He could smell rations. Vasyl shoved the corpse over and tore the bag open. Inside, he found ammunition, extra clothes, and two boxes of field rations.

Half a dozen containers held cellophane-wrapped packets of crackers, cans of spreadable meat, a canned meal, tea, and vitamin pills. Vasyl ripped open the package of crackers and ate them dry. The cans rolled open with attached metal keys. He spooned the contents with his fingers and licked them clean. A whitish layer of fat filled the top the larger can. The contents tasted salty.

With the edge off his immense hunger, he removed a tablet computer in a black, armored case. The logo on the back read, FutureTense Inc. An Iris Identification interface opened. Directions in Russian displayed on the screen read: *Place your eye over the scanner.*

"Things have changed in five years." He held the scanner over Sergei's face and scanned the dead man's eye.

The machine displayed the last program it ran. Vasyl's somewhat younger face, pale and drawn after months in the hospital in Moscow, looked up at him. "Location Unknown" flashed over his face.

"Why look for me?"

He selected another file. Aranea Gekas gazed up from the screen, a faint half smile on her face." The machine listed her location as LUX Dark Matter Observatory, North Dakota.

The entertainer, Toss Bonneteau, lived in San Diego, as did Shiso and Yume de Guzman.

"They're watching all of us?"

Yume de Guzman's face winked at him. "Run."

Startled, he tossed the tablet. When nothing else happened, he retrieved it. Yume's image remained static.

With nothing left but the powdered beverage packs and the tea, Vasyl lay back on the ground beside the body. He closed his eyes. Another voice whispered in his head. *"There you are. Where is she?"*

Vasyl sat up. "Who are you?"

The voice continued. *"You named me Clockbrain while you wandered across Eastern Europe."*

"I was--am insane." A statement he considered unnecessary since he now held a dialogue with himself.

"My fault, your modifications remained incomplete, and you suffer from several psychological issues. Fortunately, the event you experienced initiated critical changes. You are better, now."

Vasyl glanced at the dead soldier. "By whose definition?"

"Aranea Gekas, you remember her, gorgeous, smart. How did you put it? Oh yes, she fucked like a mink."

So, Clockbrain, his other constant companion over five years of wondering across Western Europe, was real. "I would prefer Norvez ' kyy Schurr."

"You prefer a Rattus Norvegicus to a sexually compatible member of your species."

"I would prefer that rat to *you*."

"Ah, I understand. The rat died in the explosion, and you used the rat's DNA to alter your body to one with a

higher probability of survival. The rat did not survive the tragedy. You will remember his sacrifice."

"What am I?"

"You are concerned with your nature. I understand, but there is no time. Take comfort knowing that you remain Vasyl Petrenko and alive."

"That's not comfort."

"Concentrate on your memory of Aranea Gekas."

Clockbrain shut Vasyl's eyes. He saw Aranea in the rec room of the radio telescope, a mouth full of vodka, leaning to kiss him.

He spun through a brief fit of vertigo. Something in his head lined up with an obscure and distant object, and he thought the answer to his mental companion. "She's away west and far away." For all those years when Vasyl was Vin, this was how he navigated across the landscape and found the places where Clockbrain sent him.

"The tablet you looked at listed her location as South Dakota."

"Half the world away."

"The straight-line distance across the curved surface of the planet does not measure 50% of the diameter, even at this latitude."

"How do I reach her? I have no transportation, no clothes."

"You will find a way."

"I don't know where to begin."

"I will help you."

****

John Stark ducked under a steel I-beam that supported what remained of the ceiling. Dust and smoke swirled above a floor littered with shattered concrete, machines, and bodies ripped apart by a massive explosion. An engineer wearing an orange coverall raised a hand in caution. "This is not a safe area, Mr. Stark."

Stark motioned the man back. "I have to see this for myself."

Near the elevator shaft, he knelt beside two mangled, unrecognizable bodies. The explosion caught them together and painted the floor, wall, and ceiling of the elevator with blood and tissue. "Who?"

Margrethe glanced at her tablet. "The smaller set of remains are female. We will need a DNA check to be sure of her identity. Embedded microchips identify the larger set as Agent Hamilton North."

He knelt beside the remains and bowed his head. "It never gets any easier."

Margrethe laid a hand on his shoulder. "If it did we would be monsters."

"Where did they find Gekas?"

She pointed to the corner. "They found her huddled there.

He scanned the floor, walls, and ceiling, noting each splatter of blood, flesh, and bone. "Injuries?"

"The doctor's report made no mention of injuries. She suffered Xenon inhalation, otherwise, not a scratch."

He frowned. "There is no void in the blood pattern."

Margrethe scanned the report. "They found blood on her back as if she lay down after the explosion and went to sleep."

Stark stood. "I need to speak to Ms. Gekas."

"She's in the hospital in the city."

"Take me."

"I have a car upstairs."

Smoke in the sky stole the power of the sunlight and left the Green Dakota hills a faded gray. A video screen lowered from the headliner of the limousine and displayed the square faced stern image of an older man.

"General Lagounov," Stark said. "Did you find him?"

Lagounov's frown deepened to a snarl. "He murdered two of my men."

"Explain?"

"We found the bodies two soldiers sent to scout his last known position. One of my men suffered a broken neck in hand-to-hand combat. The second man's head had been bashed against a rock until it cracked like an egg."

Stark glanced at Margrethe. She shrugged. "You have my condolences, but we all lose men, General. Several million have died in the last week. There will be more. Your job is to find Petrenko and capture him alive."

Lagounov stepped aside and waved at a naked corpse surrounded by empty packets and cans of Russian field rations. "You tasked us with finding an average sized, insane physicist. After killing two trained soldiers, he devoured two day's worth of combat rations."

"Are you sure this is Petrenko?"

Lagounov pulled a small notebook from his pocket. We found this among the remains of some torn clothing. It appears a large animal laired there for several days. It contains notes and formulas in five different languages. I sent copies to a physicist who knew Petrenko."

"Bezrukov."

"Yes, he identified the handwriting and formulas as Petrenko's. I will send you a copy."

Stark glanced at Thorn and then back. "Send us the book. Find Petrenko!"

"The book belongs to Russia."

"Check your contract, General. Petrenko and his book belong to us."

****

Aranea pushed herself up on her elbows then collapsed back. Her mouth a grimace, she rolled onto her side and used the bed rail to pull herself up. With her forehead pressed against the cold metal rail, she waited out an attack of nausea. The blood pressure cuff on her right arm expanded. The machine pumping fluids into her left arm complained. Her throat burned. A yellow-gray sky that made her think of summer forest fires hid the sun outside the window. An exquisite, vile sense of déjà vu screamed Moscow, 2018. The architecture of the visible town whispered North Dakota.

A nurse rushed into the room and pushed a button on the blood pressure machine. "Lay down, Ms. Gekas!"

Aranea twisted her body to make sitting more comfortable. "How long have I been here?"

"It's nine AM. Please lay down."

"I want duration, not time." They must have used a breathing tube. How long had she lain in this hospital bed?

"Mr. Stark stepped out for a meeting. He gave unambiguous instructions."

"Who the hell is Stark?" Aranea asked the questions, now. She remembered lying awake, paralyzed, but awake. Innumerable hours passed, a dozen nurses and several doctors checked her blood pressure, added painkiller to the saline drip in her arm, and cleaned her when she urinated. A man in a gray suit entered at irregular intervals and checked her face or sat in a chair and read her charts.

The nurses called him Mr. Stark.

A headache drilled into her brain behind her forehead. "What happened? A colleague, Hamilton North, saved my life. Is he all right?"

Two men dressed in gray suits with the square blocky look of professional soldiers entered the room. "The nurse ordered you to lie down," said one of them.

Aranea toggled her glance. "What's happening?"

Mr. Right lay a hand on her shoulder. "If you need help complying with the nurse's orders."

The nurse stepped between Aranea and the man. "Keep your hands to yourself. I'll care for my patient. You take care of the door."

A third man dressed in a gray suit, the man Aranea remembered, entered carrying a briefcase. He, too, had the look of a soldier. "Gentleman, please wait outside."

The door guards nodded and left.

The nurse glared at the man. "I will not have your goons interfering with my staff or manhandling my patient."

"Leave. I need to speak with Ms. Gekas, alone."

"I am not finished with my patient, Mr. Stark."

He glanced at the heart machine. "Is Gekas stable?"

The nurse scanned through the chart. "Yes."

"Your check can wait."

"This is my hospital ward."

"Your administration authorized me to remove anyone from this ward if I deem they compromise Ms. Gekas' security."

The nurse spun and stalked out the door. One of the guards shut it behind her.

Aranea lay back on the pillow, more a tactical retreat than surrender. Who was John Stark? Military? He had the strutting arrogance she associated with the guards, even if he wore his gray suit like a uniform. This man was something else, something dangerous. "What happened to everyone else at the LUX?"

He sat in the chair and opened his briefcase. "How did you survive?"

She propped herself on her elbows. "What happened to my colleagues?"

"The facility is a complete loss. Escaping Xenon smothered fires, but the explosion destroyed everything."

"You're not going to tell me?"

He watched her over the top of the briefcase, his gray eyes empty, merciless.

"Ham, uh, Doctor North saved me. I fell into the elevator. He reached in and pressed the button." She shrugged. She remembered nothing else except hard, brilliant light.

"Hamilton North was your lover."

How did Stark know that, and why would it matter? "I have not seen Ham in three years."

"You dated him while attending MIT?"

"Yes." What was this all about? Who was John Stark?

"You cohabited together for two years while you both worked on Stellar One at Lagrange 4."

"Yes, we fucked like birds in zero gravity. What do you want, Mr. Stark? My relationship with Ham is none of your damned business."

Stark closed the briefcase and leaned nearer. He held photographs in his hand, but Aranea couldn't see them. "Everything about this is my damned business. Everyone at the LUX died but you. We want to know why?"

"All of them." She couldn't breathe. All of them dead. Ham dead. It was like 2018. Could something like that happen twice?

Stark leaned closer, his face predatory. "How did you survive?"

She bit her lip. This all had to be coincidence, random chance. She could not survive an event like 2018 twice. "Ham saved me."

"How?"

"I ran for the elevator, tripped on something, tore my mask off. I slid inside. Ham reached in and hit the elevator button. I was unconscious. It must have taken me to the surface.

"You never reached the surface."

"I'm here. I must have."

Stark tossed a photo on the bed. Aranea sprawled in the corner of the elevator. Chunks of metal, concrete and twisted, unrecognizable instruments lay on the floor.

Blood painted the walls, and a severed hand lay beside her foot. The blood spray marked the wall behind her but not her coverall. She slapped the photograph away. It drifted to the floor.

Aranea wanted to deny the essential reality of the photograph. The scientist in her refused. She believed her eyes because something like this happened before.

John Stark leaned over, picked up his photograph, and put it back in the briefcase. "If I were investigating this event as a member of the police, I would assume you worked your way through the debris without disturbing anything, laid down, and lost consciousness after the explosion."

What's his game?

She remained silent.

"I know you occupied that corner. By the way, have you spoken recently to Vasyl Petrenko?"

She sat up. The tape holding the IV in place pulled free. "Why are you here?"

"Discovering what you are, Ms. Gekas."

"What do you want?"

"To know if you're a danger or useful."

Aranea collapsed back onto the pillow. "Tired. You may leave now."

He set his briefcase on the floor and stood. "I would not want your recovery compromised. We will have many opportunities to discuss the Russian Event and the explosion at LUX in the future.

Stark walked to the nurses' station, where the doctor and nurses clumped together, talking, drinking coffee, and working with patient records. He spoke to a doctor and stalked out of sight.

She sat with her knees drawn up against her chest. Her mind ticked over possibilities. The last day in Moscow had been a train wreck. Vasyl left first. She followed him to St. Basil's Orthodox Church. He sat in the back, eyes darting from icon to icon.

"Vasyl."

He had ignored her, obsessed with colors and light.

"Vasyl, love."

He had looked over his shoulder. "Vin."

"We can make this work."

"No. Cold Equations." He had looked to the apse. "They fall."

"Vasyl, please."

He had tapped his chest. "Vin."

The memory evoked a single tear, which Aranea wiped away. That had been her year of tears. Husked out by the loss of her father and Vasyl, she moved on.

The smoke lightened outside the window; Stark had left his briefcase on the floor, a mistake, maybe, or a trap. She retrieved it and leafed through the contents. Beneath the photographs of the remains of the LUX, lay a thick folder containing the autopsy photos of her colleagues, all mutilated, anonymous, except for Ham. She recognized the tattoo of a baseball on his chest.

From beneath his photograph, she picked up a picture of an older, black man, Toss Bonneteau, sitting on a folding chair by a trolley track; a board across his lap, cards face down on the board.

Vasyl stood on a hill overlooking a town somewhere in the Ukraine if architecture meant anything. He wore a long coat. His hair and beard a matted mass. A gray rat sat on his shoulder.

She found two photographs of near identical young women in their mid-teens. She recognized the twins from the cruise even with the changes typical for girls aging from twelve to seventeen. She applied the names Shiso and Yume to the pictures.

Beneath the photographs lay a note on yellow paper:

"Ms. Gekas,

"I trust you have enjoyed reacquainting yourself with the other members of your survivor's club.

"Tomorrow we will talk.

"John Stark."

She dropped the note. The face in Yume de Guzman's photograph twisted to look up at her. "Run."

****

Shiso slumped low in the driver's seat of a battered blue van and read the current post on Darknet Oviraptorus. Her eyes shifted from her phone's browser to the mirrors.

Anonymous dark-suited men had almost cornered them twice. The first time had been on the road up from La Jolla Shores, five nights past. The second was on their last scrounging trip to the only open gas station in San Diego's backcountry. She should have known that with thousands of acres burned and hundreds of houses and stores destroyed by the meteor, an open shop was a trap.

She glanced through the curtain into the back. Yume lay wrapped in a beach towel, asleep.

Dreaming without me. Good.

She smiled and winced. In isolated nightmares, Shiso often stood side by side with her sister, gazing into a mirror. The mirror always reflected only one of them. She could never guess which of them cast the reflection.

The dream birthed in her the notion that their unique gifts of dream sharing and telepathy meant they were, somehow, the same person. She knew Yume feared that possibility though they never talked about it. Yume's risky choices and Shiso's conservative sensibilities clashed to determine which of them controlled their bodies.

Movement along the long steep road up from Poway drew her attention. Two black vans followed a National Guard truck. There had been a lot of such traffic as crews moved in and out of the backcountry to fight fires or stop looting.

She glanced at her phone. The avatar of a woman in black leather said, "John Stark is coming. Run!"

She slipped into the back and shook Yume's shoulder. "Wake up. Someone's coming. We need to abandon the van."

Shiso grabbed her backpack with her wallet, phone, and a few necessities. She returned only to find Yume on her back, eyes open, but not awake.

"Yume?"

Yume blinked, and Shiso crashed into the dream, falling through a gray ceiling into the bedroom they shared until their twelfth birthday.

Yume sat at their computer desk. She didn't use the keyboard. An umbilical cord ran from the computer, curled around her side, and plugged into the base of her brain.

"Yume, we can't dream now."

"Hold a sec. I'm trying to contact the others."

"Black vans and a troop carrier are coming. We have to leave."

Shiso grabbed Yume's shoulder and spun her around. Computer screens filled Yume's eyes. The faces of the other survivors flickered inside, along with images of a massive hangar they had seen in the dream on Suki's Paradise.

"Leave me here."

"Are you nuts? You heard the news reports. Whoever killed Tio will get you."

"I'm with Stranger. I don't understand it, yet, but it's important that I go with the man named Stark. We will see each other before this is over."

Shiso stepped back. Had Yume slipped into insanity? "Stranger is part of our dreams."

Yume slapped Shiso across the face. Shiso held her hand over her cheek. The skin felt hot. "Why?"

"This isn't a dream; this is seeing. Half a mile south, you will find an empty house. There is a motorcycle in the yard. The key hangs on a hook behind the kitchen door. Take it. Ride down through Sycamore Canyon. Stark's men won't be there."

"But why?"

Yume turned back to her dream computer, and fingers turned to cables linked to the keys. "Toss Bonneteau is in the refugee camp set up in Balboa Park. He will need your help."

"Where do we go? When will I see you?"

"Go east. That's all I know. We can speak with telepathy any time. You'll see me at the end."

"I don't want to go."

Shiso woke. Yume lay on the floor, a smile tilting the corners of her mouth.

In her head, Shiso heard her sister's voice. *"Run!"*

No one on earth understood a twin sister except her other twin. The shared dreams bothered Shiso, and the telepathy bugged Yume, especially on dates. Shiso trusted her sister more than herself.

She kissed Yume on the forehead and slipped out the back.

The path led over an arroyo and under scrub oaks. Yume shared her dream or was it her reality, so with every step Shiso experienced life in two places. Fleeing through a field of dense shrubs she ducked low bushes. In the shared dream link, Shiso heard the van door open and felt the vehicle shake.

Yume sent: *"They're here."*

Shiso spun around ready to run back toward the van. *"You should go. A doctor is examining me."*

"I can go with you."

"Save Toss Bonneteau. They have Stranger."

"Where?"

"I don't know. Stranger did this to us. I need to be where he is. It's the only way to be normal."

"What if I don't want to be normal." She had never spoken that thought before. Had never even intimated a desire to be different until now.

"The doctor gave me a shot. I feel fuzzy. But I'll be watching if you need help."

Yume's mind wavered. She did not vanish. The solid sense of Yume changed to a gooey chocolate consistency.

Shiso ran.

****

Toss Bonneteau sat on the grass in Balboa Park twisting the cards into new positions with meticulous precision. His mark, a mature nine-year-old, watched the cards wide-eyed as if Toss revealed the mysteries of a living God. "Tell me, Johnny, where's the lady."

Half a dozen other children looked on while the boy examined the back of the cards for a clue, shifting his finger from one card to the next. Johnny chewed his lip while the other kids lined up to watch the only game in town.

Smiling, the boy tapped the last card. "That's her."

Toss picked up the other two cards face down and flipped the third--the queen of hearts from a pack of Bicycle playing cards, one head up and one down, printed in red, black, and yellow ink.

"Mama's little boy ain't making much money today." He flipped a quarter to the boy and glanced back at the card. The faces on the card morphed from images drawn with fine black lines and bright colors to the identical faces of two young women. One of them opened her eyes, winked. "Run."

He jerked his hand and flipped the card away. Johnny tipped his face up. "You Okay, Mr. Bonneteau."

"Sure kid." Sweat dampened his palms, and his mouth ran dry as a Mohave summer day. Why were the faces of the De Guzman girls looking up from the queen?

"If you need the money, you can have it back."

He glanced at the card face down on the grass. "I lost that game fair and square, son. Don't you worry? Ladies of Charity and the city government will feed everyone in this encampment. I'll manage fine. But if you feel bad, come back later. Give me a chance to win it back."

Johnny's grinned. He ran with the other kids to the daycare tent where children, unable to return home with the parents after the meteor explosion and the fires, lined up for bottles of water and a snack.

Toss wiped the palms of his hands on his pants and picked up the card. The faces had returned to classic ink lines. What had happened? Optical illusion? Self-delusion? He last saw Yume and Shiso de Guzman when their plane landed in New York City. They met their uncle and left for their home in San Diego. Toss never expected to see them again, even when he and his crew of happy swindlers set up shop beside the trolley track San Diego.

After surviving in Russia, seeing the other survivors was the last thing he wanted.

"Mr. Bonneteau?" The woman who ran children's services in the Balboa Park Refugee Encampment approached. She had the face of a Baptist on a mission and the body of women, who even at the high end of forty remained fit, trim, and fine.

He nodded. "Mrs. Carmody?"

"Someone is asking about you at the gate."

First their images on cards and now this. "Two Young women?"

Her eyes narrowed into a frown. "I should say not. I appreciate you entertaining the children with your games, but I have no desire to know what other lines of work you might pursue."

He laughed at the discomfort and curiosity on her face. "Nothing like that, I have friends in San Diego. I'm sure they wonder what happened to me after that rock blew up in the sky and set all those fires."

"Of course," She motioned for him to follow. They walked along a path under eucalyptus trees that scented the morning with camphor and wood. It's a man, of course, tall, dark, like you."

"That'd be Little Jimmy Deeds."

She shook her head. "Little?"

"It's an inside joke."

They came to a gate into the children's area. Little Jimmy Deeds sat on a park bench outside the entrance. Bandages wrapped his head and half his face. A brace cradled his arm from just below the elbow and covered all but four of the fingers on his right hand.

Jimmy hugged him and pulled back. "Did a chunk of the meteor hit you when it came down?"

Jimmy's eyes skittered left and stared into the haze of smoke that covered the entire city. "I had a fight."

"If you come out looking that bad, how many did you bury?"

"About that, we need to talk."

"We're doing it."

"Someplace private."

Toss ran a hand through his hair and acted casual in hopes anyone watching might overlook. "Is this a police matter?"

"God, I wish." He sounded shaky, almost frightened. Toss had known little Jimmy for a baker's dozen years. Jimmy used to fight bare-knuckled in warehouses and alleys, an undefeated street fighter who, as far as Toss knew, feared nothing alive or dead.

"Let's go this way." He motioned Jimmy to follow, and they strolled into a grove of Moreton Bay fig trees. The two walked without speaking. Toss guessed Jimmy would open his mouth when ready.

They turned onto a hiking path that twisted down through canyons and ran parallel to Highway 163, separated from the road by a fence torn down by road crews. Halfway to the bottom, Jimmy stopped and pulled a newspaper that he had folded into his back pocket. "It's about this."

A story title above the article near the bottom of the first page read "Charter Boat Operator and Two Niece's Missing at Sea."

Yume de Guzman's smiling face looked out from the page. Her lips moved in a silent "Run."

"You know these girls, Toss?"

"I've known a lot of women. Haven't chased any that young since I reached the age where they no longer noticed me. They wouldn't have been a gleam in their daddy's eye."

"You met them when you went on that trip to Russia."

Toss smiled his best con expression at Little Jimmy Deeds. He heard distant voices. A semi-truck rumbled by on 163. A motorcycle rumbled somewhere up the path and out of sight. "I jaw a lot, but I didn't remember when I mentioned my Russian vacation."

Jimmy shook his head. "Sorry Toss, they got all of us."

"Who?"

"Some guy named Stark. He's a professional. They picked up Sammy, Gus, Ericka, and Moe. I fought, but they're professionals, soldiers I think. I never had a chance."

The motorcycle rumbled closer as if some idiot decided to take a ride in the dirt in Balboa Park.

"How did you get away?"

"I didn't."

It wasn't fair, and Toss hated himself for it, but without a blink, wearing a con man's smile, he kicked Little Jimmy's balls. Jimmy Deeds doubled over with his hands between his legs and tears streaming from his eyes.

At fifty-three, Toss had no illusions that he could take Jimmy in a fight or win a fair foot race. He walked two steps down the hill. A black van pulled off the road. The doors blew open. Men in dull gray camouflage carrying automatic weapons boiled out. He turned back up the path. Jimmy pushed himself up from the ground, his right hand clutching his balls and the other reaching.

A black Harley Sportster burbled around the curve with a driver dressed in black leathers and a helmet. The driver kicked Jimmy in the small of the back and knocked him knowing to the side of the path. Jimmy landed on his face. The helmeted driver spun the bike around, pointed it up a steep trail, and skidded to a stop.

From behind, he heard a gunshot, and a shout. "Stop!"

"Get on." The driver spoke with a woman's voice.

He climbed onto the bike. "Who are you?"

"Shiso."

The back tire spun up a cloud of dust. Another shot thundered over the sound of the bike's engine. They didn't look back.

Later, while they drove up a country road for a way over the mountains and around a blazing forest fire, Toss mulled over his reason for climbing on that bike. Men with guns provided the impetus, of course, but that wasn't the reason.

Some instinct buried deep in his soul trusted the young woman. Human calculation of the odds could not account for that instinctual trust. After all, a con man makes a living tricking people into believing their predictions. Gut instinct buried so deep in his soul that only the Lord could put it there, well, was something else.

An old con man bound to hell like Toss trusted the Lord because he knew he could trust nobody else.

CHAPTER THREE

Chasing Ghosts

Two o'clock in the fucking AM on a smoky night with no clouds and only the light from the over glow of distant fires. Toss sat on the goose seat of a Harley Sportster with his arms around the waist of a beautiful woman. He lived a young man's dream, and all he could think about after hours of driving East was that his ass hurt from his knees to his neck.

He wanted off the damn bike, a drink, and a soft bed to sleep in. If all old age amounted to was chasing ghosts, he'd step off right then and expire. Toss started to laugh, not because all the death and dreck struck him funny, but because laughter at the insane possibilities remained his last defense.

Shiso pulled to a stop at the side of the road and stood with the bike between her legs. Toss dismounted, arched his back to remove the kinks, and rolled his shoulders to loosen the muscles. He took a few steps down into the ditch and watered the weeds.

Afterward, he found Shiso setting beside the bike, knees up, her face buried in her arms. "You Okay?"

She shrugged.

Toss sat beside her and leaned against the motorcycle. He hadn't smoked for fifteen years but wished he had a cigarette. A joint would be better, but he didn't carry because the police always looked for a reason to bust him. He did not trust them, even in California.

Tilting his head toward the starless sky, he puffed on an imaginary cigarette. "How the hell did you find me?"

"My sister told me where you'd be?"

"How did she know? I couldn't have guessed five days ago."

Shiso pulled her legs closed as if to protect herself from a perceived blow. "I don't know. Saw you in one of her dreams, I guess. That's how she finds me."

Telepathy, dreams, it sounded like one of the many cons Toss had seen played. "Did Yume ever see me in a dream?"

Shiso shrugged. "Not that she ever said. Yume found you this time. Told me where you would be and how to get there. She wouldn't wake up, said I needed to leave her. They took her."

Shiso's shoulders shook. Toss would bet good money that tears flowed. Because Shiso hid it, he decided to keep his own counsel. Why would she want comfort from a crazy old conman?

He did not doubt who Shiso referred to. *They* were the same men who beat Little Jimmy until he gave up his best friend. "Where does your sister see us going?"

"I don't know."

"She didn't tell you."

"She said go East. I can't reach her?"

Tossed patted her shoulder then withdrew his hand, a small gesture of comfort. "Maybe if you get some sleep."

Shiso jumped up and stalked to the center of the deserted road. Smoke from distant forest fires covered the stars and cloaked her like a blanket.

"It doesn't work that way. She dreams, and I use telepathy. She's gone. I reach out to her and try but." She knelt on the road and sobbed.

Toss walked out onto the highway, sat beside her, and threw his arms around her shoulder. A vague concern that a car might choose that moment to drive by and run them over crossed his mind, but it did not stop him. "Look, I really don't know what you're talking about, but if there is anything I can do."

They sat while Shiso worked through the necessary grief. Later, she leaned against him and put her head on his shoulder. "So, what superpower did you get?"

"Superpower?"

"After what happened to us in Russia, I became a telepath with Yume, and when she dreams, I join her inside of them. At first, we thought it was cool. Now, I don't know."

"And why would you think that I have a superpower."

"Everybody does, or at least, that's what Stranger hinted."

"Stranger?"

"That's what we call it. Sometimes there's someone else in Yume's dreams. We never understood who it was. Yume told me she had to go be with Stranger, and I had to find you."

Tossed laughed. "Anyone else would think I'm damn, over the hill crazy. Sounds insane in my head when I think about it. Never told it to anyone. Wouldn't now, except that you were there. Whatever happened in Russia, bound us together. Yes, I got a superpower, if you could call it that. I can slow time to a crawl for things around me. It only happens when shit gets real."

"I remember now. Like when you pulled the Russian back on the ship."

"That's it all right."

"How do you do it?"

He shrugged, not sure how to explain that shit just happens. "It starts up here." He tapped his forehead. "The world around me slows down, and I keep on moving at my normal pace. You are right. I first used it on the riverboat in Russia, just after that thing fell out of the sky. The shockwave knocked the Russian physicist overboard. Time slowed, and I walked to the railing, reached out, and pulled him back aboard."

"That was it?"

"Happened a couple of times since. Once when the police in Baton Rouge took a dislike to my game of Three Card Monte, I slowed them down and walked right past their noses. The day the meteor exploded, I saved two girls from a trolley."

"Why were the police chasing you?"

He laughed and whispered. "Don't tell anyone, but I spend a lot of time on the wrong side of the law."

"So, you're a super-villain."

They both laughed. The sound of their mingled laughter a surprise gift after a long hard day. When they finished laughing, he asked, "Why can't you talk to your sister."

"It's like her mind hides behind a wall."

"Maybe she's too far away."

Shiso shook her head. "Two summers ago, she went to Tokyo while I flew to Spain. We mind talked as if we sat in the same room. I could sense how she felt when I concentrated as if a wire that bored straight through the earth connected our brains."

"You're really close."

She nodded. "Yeah."

Toss felt Shiso's immense pain and loss, like a distant ache that seeped out of her and soaked into his heart. He wanted to help but damned if he knew how. "If we only knew where she was." It hit him like a hammer between the eyes. "You said that the two of you felt connected."

"She glanced at him, curiosity in her eyes. "Yes."

"What if you are?"

Her mouth scrunched up as she considered his question. "How?"

"When you concentrated, you felt connected by a wire through the center of the earth."

She nodded her head, but the puzzled look remained.

"Could you sense a direction?"

Shiso sat silent for a long time. "I never tried."

"Well, it's a long shot, but try it now."

She looked at her feet, eyes distant as if she watched at something a thousand miles away. "We were talking when I felt that. I mean long conversations."

"It can't hurt to try."

Shiso stood and brushed the dirt off the seat of her pants. She cocked her head to one side as if listening for a faint sound. After a while, she spun in a slow circle and pointed. "I think she's that way."

Good enough. "Toss walked to the motorcycle and climbed onto the back. "We should get on down the road.

"The highway runs east. I'd say she's northeast of this patch of dirt."

"Do you think that's enough?"

"We won't know until we try."

****

Aranea walked through a gray metal corridor to an autopsy chamber where six tables held six body bags. She stopped next to the nearest bag, sure that it contained the remains of Hamilton North. The tag tied to the zipper read "Gekas, Aranea--2018."

The name on the tag elicited no more emotion in her dream avatar than the obituary of some stranger in Europe printed in the morning's smart paper. Aranea's consciousness yammered and screamed in the corner of the dreamer's mind with no more influence on the course of the dream than a butterfly's wing beats on the path of a hurricane. She pulled the zipper down and folded the plastic away from the face.

The woman in the mirror every morning looked back with milky, unblinking eyes. A bullet hole in her forehead provided a glimpse into her foggy mind.

She jerked awake. Red and green lights flickered across the face of the monitors beside her bed. The nurse stood over her with a temperature probe. "Open up."

She accepted the plastic under her tongue while the nurse checked her pulse, blood pressure, and heart rate. Finished, the woman wrote the results on a chart and leaned close as if testing the pillow. "They're transporting you. I don't know where."

"Who?"

"Stark and his apes. I'm sorry, nothing I can do."

Stark entered and flipped the light switch. Two soldiers in dull black body armor followed, heavy shotguns cradled in their arms. "You can leave, nurse. Close the curtain."

Stark placed his briefcase on the bed and opened it. Several large folders, a dozen pens, and other mundane objects had orderly positions. He sat in the chair and crossed his legs, showing her the bottom of his shoes.

She glanced at the soldiers. "Is there a war, Mr. Stark?"

"Not in North Dakota. These soldiers protect the hospital."

"From what?"

"You."

She laughed. "You must think I'm dangerous."

"I know you're dangerous, though I'm not sure of the level."

She glanced at the contents of the briefcase but could not tell what the files contained. "What makes me dangerous?"

Stark leaned forward. "Do you know you're not human?"

What was this all about? What did he want from her and who did he represent? Aranea wanted to take the top file out of the briefcase but laced her fingers together. If Stark could be patient, so could she. "Ridiculous."

He leaned back. His face wore the serene expression of a Buddha. "So, you don't know? That is one of the theories that we bandied about since the incident in 2016 when the alien spacecraft crashed. Not my theory, of course, but always a possibility."

Aranea crossed her arms, she looked away. Damn his fucking calm. "Why don't you explain your bullshit theory?"

"In June of 2016, Vasyl Petrenko, Toss Bonneteau, Yume and Shiso de Guzman, and you were five of the passengers on a Volga River Cruise. News reports say a small asteroid struck about three thousand meters from your location. An estimated eight-thousand human died; including the crew and other passengers on that cruise. How did you survive? Until five days ago, it was the worst recorded asteroid strike in human history."

"I told the authorities in Russia everything I remembered about that day."

He smiled. "I conducted seven of those interviews. I've seen the video of the rest. Before we continue, I need to know if you have anything to add."

How could Stark have conducted those interviews? Her father died on that boat, and because of the incident, she lost Vasyl. After returning to the US, she built a wall of work to forget, but the wall failed at keeping out the memories. "I don't remember you."

"It's my face, neither handsome nor ugly, unremarkable in every way."

"I find looks deceiving, Mr. Stark."

"And that is the boon of my appearance."

She chewed her lip. What did Stark want? "You said I wasn't human."

He picked up one of the files in the briefcase. "You were before the event. We tested samples of your hair and skin taken from your hairbrush. The DNA samples we took while you were recovering tell a different story."

"I did not authorize DNA samples, Mr. Stark."

He tossed the file into her lap. "We did not ask."

She picked up the file. The dates between June and July of 2016 fit the period she spent in the hospital in Moscow. "I'm neither a biologist nor a medical doctor."

Stark reached forward and tapped the file. "My experts discovered strands of non-coding DNA changed after the event." He picked up the other folders and placed them beside her. "This happened to all of you, though the exact changes differed in each of you."

She pushed the folder away. "I'm healthy. Major changes in my DNA should have caused problems."

He stood and put his hands behind his back. "We've continued to monitor you since you returned to the US. The changes in gene expression, especially in certain parts of your brain, required your apprehension."

She slipped out of bed, fists clenched. Damn Stark's calm arrogance, tricky questions, and his accusations. "What gives you the right to watch me?"

The soldiers raised the shotguns and pointed them at her chest.

A little smile touched the corner of his lips. "I'm with the good guys. When something alien threatens my family, my home, or my world, I do whatever it takes."

She screamed. "I have rights."

He spoke in a near whisper. "Humans have rights."

"Those humans killed in the 2018 event had rights. The staff at the LUX observatory had rights."

"You smug bastard."

He pulled a photograph from one of the files and tossed it onto the bed. In the middle of a smoking crater, an object with sleek, smooth skin, and unusual domed structures lay buried in the earth. It looked more like a sea animal than an asteroid.

Stark pointed at the object. "Near as we can tell, it is a living creature. It made you whatever you are."

Aranea shook her head, a silent denial. What did he want? What was this about? It made no sense, or did it? She had survived Russia and the explosion at the LUX without even a scar. What about the photograph that spoke?

She shivered. "Who spied on me?"

"I used different agents, people you knew well."

"I don't believe you."

"One of them was a friend and the best agent I've ever known."

"Who?"

"Hamilton North, who else could get so close?"

She swung a wild roundhouse punch. Stark knocked it aside with his left hand, that smug smile on his face.

A chill burned her skin.

Aranea kicked him. He blocked it with his right hand and stepped back. "Take the shot!"

The simultaneous shotgun blasts filled the room with blue smoke and noise. The heart monitor exploded, throwing shrapnel across the room. A long, straight gouge oozed blood along the side of Stark's face.

Powder and chunks of sheetrock blasted from the wall littered the bed.

Stark nodded, and for a second his eyes lit. His lips moved, but she heard no sound.

The soldiers fired again.

Nothing touched her. The shotguns blasts tore gaping wounds in the wall. In the face of their fury, she stepped back, into the wall.

She backed into the next room and stood with a hospital bed bisecting her waist. The patient in the bed opened her mouth in a silent scream as debris from the shotgun blasts fell about her head and shoulders.

Aranea heard her own heartbeat and breathing.

She remembered the image of Yume de Guzman telling her, "Run!"

Beyond the next wall, she found a closet filled with mops, buckets, and supplies. On that floor, those soldiers would hunt her. Whatever strange power allowed her to ghost through walls allowed her to escape but did not make her invisible. How could she get away?

Through the floor.

Her thought triggered the actions, and she fell into the room below, and through that floor.

What would stop her? She could fall into the earth, through the mantle, to the center of gravity. She screamed at the stark mind-twisting fear of standing intangible at the middle of the planet, a ghost at the heart of the world. Her body flushed. She fell through a ceiling onto a desk, bounced, and crashed on the floor.

Can't breathe! Can't breathe.

Whatever process made her intangible to matter and untouched by sound sealed her away from the air.

The solid floor under her hands forced her body to interact with other, physical objects. Slamming onto the floor knocked the breath out of her.

She could not wait to recover. Stark was a smart man. He would guess what happened and search the hospital.

Aranea managed to stand. Pain ripped through her side where she hit the desk, ribs bruised, broken, but alive.

She heard loud voices and cries outside the door. A man's coat hung over the back of the chair. She pulled it on. Outside in the hall, doctors ran toward the stairs, going up to deal with the emergency.

Aranea walked near the walls and ignored the screams and calls. Just as two police cars screamed up to the front of the hospital, she eased out the emergency doors in the back.

What would she do now?

Where could she go?

Who could help?

She had no answers.

The police would be no help. Who was left?

She remembered Yume's face telling her to run. Perhaps that had not been an illusion or delusion. How had the other's changed? What could they do?

Could she contact them?

****

Yume dreamed a box with frosted glass windows. Outside her box, six faces shifted like unmoored balloons, at one moment shadows behind the frost, and in the next smeared masks against the windows where they twisted flat, pouty lips through the motions of speech.

She recognized Shiso's face, insistent, demanding. Neither her whispers nor shouts breached the glass walls. Shiso returned with cyclic persistence out of deep desperation.

Two belonged to men, familiar faces from five years before. The first of them, Toss Bonneteau, one of the entertainers on the cruise who performed card tricks and wicked funny skits. The other, younger face, glowered, self-conscious and fragile as she remembered him, and he always associated with a beautiful woman.

65

Stranger appeared last, his face flat with heavy brows, hairless, with smoke tentacles growing from his scalp. As time passed, he returned more and more often until his balloon remained just beyond the window above her face.

Yume stretched out flat, drifting in the air at the center of the box. She needed the dream to go away. She needed control. One by one she imagined the faces evaporating into translucent frost. One at a time the crazy balloon faces receded until only Stranger hung above her, his face pressing against the frosted glass as though he must smear like lipstick on a mirror.

The glass popped and snapped like ice dropped into hot water. Spider web cracks shot across the glass. The window deformed, bulged, and blew inward like soap bubble implosions.

The disembodied head thrust into the box, tentacles trailing back into the fog. She feared those thick lips would press against hers in a nightmare dream kiss. He drifted to the side of her face and placed his lips against her ear, and whispered, "Your brain on drugs. Your brain on drugs."

She tried to say "Ridiculous," but her lips would not conform to the words. Pot had been a fixture on her uncle's boat, and he had never kept his nieces from using, but his supply remained locked in Suki's Paradise.

Perhaps she dreamed of the previous year's honors course on the History of Meme in the Media, from that stupid 80's anti-drug video.

Stranger whispered, louder. "You have been drugged. Wake up! Wake up!"

She half sat and collapsed back. Leather straps across her breasts, on her wrists, and ankles held her to a hard bed in a white-walled room lit with fluorescent lights.

Someone had stripped her. Icy air burned her skin. A nurse wearing white coveralls and a transparent hood held a sponge in one hand and a pan of water in the other.

Yume jerked her face away from the sponge. "Let me go!"

"You're awake." Said a nurse whose thin, angular face could belong to either sex or none. "Call me Sandra. I can't let you go without authorization from Mr. Stark."

"I can bathe myself."

"Oh, I'm sure you can, dearie, but then there is the whole strapped to the bed and helpless thing. That's up to Stark. If it were me, I'd let you lose. Changing you is a necessity, not a joy.

Yume blushed, strapped naked to a bed infuriated her. It humiliated her knowing that she had wet herself and someone else cleaned it.

"Let me go!"

"I'll just pop on out and see if I can find Mr. Stark."

She walked toward the white wall. A section slid to one side and closed behind her. Yume jerked at the straps around her wrist and wriggled her arms to get out from under the belts over her breasts. The straps kept her stretched out and humiliated.

She closed her eyes and did the trick that made dreams.

"Yume," Stranger whispered in her head.

"How?"

"Do not speak aloud. No doubt Stark is listening."

She closed her lips. "Only my sister speaks in my head."

Stranger waved his arms. *"This is dream time, and you triggered a sleep session. Are you sure only your sister*

"I didn't choose to forget anything."

*"What about 2018? What about the Russian
vacation?"*

"Go away." She did not want to talk about that to
anyone but Shiso because she had been there and shared
the changes.

The door slid open. Sandra walked in carrying a
folded white sheet. Yume opened her eyes. Stranger
vanished. Sandra tucked the warm blanket around her.
Yume luxuriated in warmth after the sting of cold air.

"Mr. Stark will be right in."

Sandra left. The door shut, and Yume expected to
hear Stranger communicating thought to thought. Maybe
he was right. She had not gone to sleep, only closed her
eyes and performed a brief ritual to dream. Stranger filled a
peculiar place in her head, like and unlike the way she
experienced Shiso's ever-present presence. Stranger hung
back, unobtrusive, a shadow in her mind, different.

A tall man in a black suit walked in followed by a
woman in a pale gray and white camouflage uniform
pushing a wheelchair.

"Let me go."

"John Stark, Miss Guzman."

"I've heard of you."

"For sixteen-year-old women, you and your sister
show evidence of remarkable skills."

"I want a lawyer. I have a right to one."

"Humans have rights, Ms. Guzman. So, what do you
do? Do you walk through walls? Fly? Fire laser beams from
your eyes."

Stark appeared to be a cop, maybe a military man, but he sounded insane.

"Laser beams? Are you nuts?"

"Earlier, you asked, 'How?' Who were you talking to?"

"I don't know what you're talking about."

"We have electromagnetic, infrared, and a dozen other sensor types. How do you communicate with the others without electromagnetic or light transmission?"

"I want out of here."

"I am going to find out your secrets, Miss Guzman. I will find out what you want with Earth, and I will stop you."

"I haven't a clue what you're talking about."

Stark stood and walked to the door. The soldier followed him and left the wheelchair. After Stark had left, Sandra unbuckled the straps. Yume sat up and held the sheet over her breasts.

The humiliation, the shame left her feeling dirty, and God she missed her sister, her Tio, her life. She closed her eyes and dreamed.

Stranger reappeared in her dream. *"You have not lost your life."*

"Fuck you, Stranger!"

His eyes narrowed. *"I am not constructed for that function at this time."*

"What are you constructed for?"

He vanished and left her alone.

****

Shiso pulled the motorcycle off Interstate 15 and drove into the town of Mesquite, Nevada. Her nose, throat, and lungs burned from the smoke of countless fires. Even this far out in the desert ash blew across the road.

The empty highways grated against her senses. After their sixteenth birthday, Shiso and Yume took their uncle's '86 BMW convertible on a road trip north from San Diego to Portland. Driving in traffic had left Yume edgy and exhausted. Shiso loved traffic. Cars weaving in and out, jostling for the best position, trucks blasting by exhilarated her.

In the last ten hours, they had seen a dozen cars and no more than twenty trucks. The meteorite impacts that blasted the earth from the Ukraine to California left forest fires and devastation across most of the Northern Hemisphere. The sun resembled a red coal in an ash sky. Electrical power, spotty at best, had survived in Nevada thanks to Hoover Dam and Standby Power Plants used to keep the Casino lights on. People were told to travel only if necessary. The President of the United States had called for calm in the face of the fires, while religious radio whispered of the end of days.

Toss leaned close. "Where're you heading?"

"I'm tired, and the sun's setting. With the smoke, I don't think it's a good idea to drive at night." The bright lights of the Oasis Casino drew her eyes, but she had no money.

"Since you're driving, where are we staying?"

Shiso scanned the signs advertising loose slots and complimentary drinks. "I don't know. The town must have a place where we can find a cheap room. But I don't have any money or credit cards."

"I have both, but we won't be using plastic. I suspect the men who tried to take us in Balboa Park will be watching lines of credit. There are always places where rooms can be had for cash though we may pay by the hour.”

“Why would you pay for a room by the hour?” The tingle began at the back of her neck, and she blushed to the roots of her hair. “Oh.”

“I'll make sure that your sheets are clean.”

“Uh, thanks.”

“And given some time, I may be able to find an entrepreneur who can be convinced to help us.”

“Now head on down Mesquite Boulevard. The type of place we need will not be found among the big casinos.”

She followed Toss’ directions, comfortable letting him guide them. He had said he was a conman, and she realized that meant more than just a man paid to entertain the guests on a riverboat cruise. While idling alone at a stoplight, she felt a familiar stirring in her head. Not quite the presence she associated with her sister calling her into a dream.

Toss pointed down the street. “There's a little place that's perfect.”

The Virgin River Hotel and Casino was not as bad as she expected. It had a red tile roof, beige walls, and a swimming pool. A dozen cars sat like lonely conspirators in its parking lot.

She parked the bike, took off the helmet, and ran fingers through her tangled hair. “I just want a bath.”

“I'm sure they are included in the room. You Okay?”

“I felt a twinge.”

Toss’ eyebrows rose.

“It's like when Yume creates a dream, but weak.”

“Maybe it's the distance.”

Shiso shook her head in a half-assed denial. Hard to explain how something feels to someone that never experienced it. "Maybe I'm just hungry."

Toss nodded and winked. He accepted her little deception and didn't hold it against her. "They have a restaurant inside. We can get a room and eat before we head up."

Toss led her to the smiling desk clerk. Faint elevator music played in the cold air accompanied by the jangling slot machines of the small casino. "I'd like a room, two beds." Toss paid twenty-seven dollars for the room.

Mr. Smiles placed the money in the drawer. "Could I see your ID?"

Toss handed him a folded, fifty-dollar bill. The man glanced at Shiso and back to Toss. "We appreciate your business, Mr. Grant. Is there anything else?"

"A wake-up call, say ten o'clock."

He handed Toss two key cards and gave them directions.

A waitress operated the register in the restaurant. "Sit anywhere you like." They walked to a booth along the back wall.

Toss opened a menu. "Partial to anything?"

"Hamburger." She pulled her phone and a charger from her purse, and then plugged in and turned on her phone. Tio Carlos had often joked that phones had become an essential part of his nieces, grafted into their hands and as much a part of their bodies as their heads.

Yume had always smiled and laughed, accepting the jokes as part of their relationship with the uncle who became their father. Shiso took them personally, at times walking out in a huff and at others accusing him of being a Luddite, an unfair accusation considering the tech he used on Suki's Paradise. Tio always took her arguments with a smile.

Shaking off the sudden case of blues, she tapped in her password.

The phone had registered thirty-seven unanswered calls. On a whim, Shiso pressed the icon and displayed a list, all from Tio's personal number that he used only for family and a few of his oldest friends.

A news story popped up on her notifications. She clicked it without thinking and gasped.

Coastguard Cutter Boutwell Recovers Suki's Paradise:

'In an early morning recovery, U.S. Coastguard Cutter Boutwell boarded the charter boat Suki's Paradise reported missing since the shower of meteorite fragments over San Diego on Wednesday afternoon. No traces of the owner and Captain, Carlos de Guzman, or his two nieces were found. The Coastguard report states that the ship showed signs of a hurried abandonment, but no evidence of foul play. Captain de Guzman and his nieces are listed as missing.'

Most of those phone calls occurred after the date of the news story. A tense knot loosened that had been there since their escape from Suki's Paradise.

"My uncle has been calling."

Toss leaned over the table and looked at the display. "Don't return the call."

"He'll be worried?"

"What makes you think it's your uncle?"

She understood what he said and why. How could she not answer her uncle's call? "It's his private phone."

"He told you to swim to the beach at night because you were being chased."

"So?"

"What if they took him? What if it's Stark?"

"He's my family." The memory of his disappearance from her mental touch returned. Did that happen to a mind when it died? It just faded away to nothing?

"So is Yume. We're on this cross-country chase of a direction to help her. If your uncle escaped, he would forgive you for not returning his call. If it is this Stark at the other end, he will know exactly where we are."

"You don't have to tell me this."

"Probably true, but I have a vested interest in staying free."

She tapped the browser icon.

"Well, I can see you take your own council. Keep alert; I have to see a man about a horse."

"Whatever." She ducked her head low. Toss left his seat and walked toward the lobby. She didn't give a damn where he went. This long, strange trip was too real. She wanted to go home.

The image on the screen bloomed, and the hooded avatar of Oviraptorus shimmered.

Darknet Oviraptorus

Are you running little bird?

Yes, I heard, I heard the future took your egg mate far into the cold and you've taken an old soul to care for.

Now you follow the Ravens like those Explorers so long ago.

Those three explorers who took a path, though only one knew the way. Choose wisely. Dream with care. Follow your Raven!

Oviraptorus spoke in riddles that often seemed to apply to their lives. Neither Shiso nor Yume knew if the vague nature of her prose lent itself to interpretation or if something out there in the darknet watched over them.

She felt that light touch of presence, a person inside her skull, flicking her neurons, stronger but still weak. She wanted to sleep far more than she wanted to eat. The touch felt indistinct, but she so wanted it to be real, so wanted to speak with Yume, even in a dream.

Toss returned. One moment she sat alone and stared at her phone screen, the next, he stood there reaching out with a damp hand that smelled of soap. "We have to run. Take my hand."

"That's funny. Oviraptorus asked if we were running."

From the door into the lobby, a man yelled. "This is the police. Let me see your hands."

She took Toss' hand, and everything went weird. A sound, like thunder, stretched until it battered her ears. Toss pulled her up and away. Four cops stood at the entrance, guns drawn. Smoke oozed out of the barrel. A bullet sped at a fast run from the barrel toward them, slowing as if it flew in slow motion through thick, invisible glass.

They ran though she wondered why. The cops, the host at the door, and the front clerk locked in a second. When Toss led her between two police officers, they tumbled back against the walls before freezing amid a slide to the floor.

Outside, four police cruisers marked with Virgin County Sheriff's Department stood in the parking lot.

"What happened?"

"They traced us." Toss' voice sounded strained as if he spoke through clenched teeth during some stupendous effort.

"How?"

"Your phone, I think."

She held it in her hand. It displayed Oviraptorus. Was that site a trap, or had the police or Stark traced it through some privileged technology?

Was Oviraptorus involved? It was a blog. She could not post in real time, could she? Had she warned her?

Shiso threw her phone. It left her hand and froze in the air?

"What's happening?"

"Just a minute," Toss said. His voice sounded strained.

They ran out of the parking lot--two other police cruisers froze on the road.

They found a gas station, entered the men's room, and locked the door.

Toss collapsed in a heap with his back to the door. Sweat soaked his hair and ran down his face. "Jesus, I hope I never have to do that again."

"What did you do?"

He gulped air. "Used my superpower."

"You can freeze people."

"Don't freeze anyone. Something to do with time?"

She locked the door and sat beside him. "You freeze time."

"Not freeze. I slow it down or speed it up. Don't know how it's done, except that it's just a matter of will."

"But how do you do it?"

"How do you mind talk with your sister? How does she pull you into her dreams? It all goes back to that event in Russia. We survived and became this?"

Outside the restroom, they heard sirens pass by and fade with distance.

"So, what do we do?"

He pulled a wad of money out of his pocket. "Go to the gas station. Get us something to eat. Doesn't matter what."

"And then?"

"I'll slow time again and get us away from here. I noticed that there was a small airport. We'll go there."

"Wouldn't that be the first place they'd look for people trying to run away?"

Toss shrugged. "Learned a long time ago that where you find local airports, you find entrepreneurs willing to bend the rules to make a little money."

"Where do we go?"

"We follow the direction arrow in your head."

"What if that leads to Stark?"

Toss cradled his head on his knees. Shiso recognized a man too tired or too hungry to comment.

She eased out the door and left him resting on the toilet floor.

****

John Stark leaned back in a desk chair. A theater sized video screen filled the wall. A third of the screen displayed body cam video provided by the local police. Video streams from Margrethe Thorn in North Dakota, Sandra Potter in Iceland, Lagounov in Russia, Thomas Manquoba and Victor

Wu in Mesquite, and Eric Leeds in the communications center in Reykjavik occupied the rest.

He nodded a hello. "Watch this."

The eyes of the leaders shifted. Shiso De Guzman sat at the table, her phone in her hand. Toss Bonneteau appeared, spoke, she took his hand, and they vanished.

Margrethe's eyes narrowed. "Are there breaks in the video?"

Stark shook his head. "My communications expert confirms we see everything that happened. I have body cam video from six other police officers as well as teams Wasp and Thrush."

General Lagounov pulled the cigar from between his lips. "How did a man and woman disappear from the middle of a restaurant?"

"We are looking for answers, General."

Eric Leeds pursed his lips, and Stark glanced at his Communications guru. "Any ideas?"

"Let's slow the video." The image blinked, and the police officers ran through their paces. "Did you see it?"

Margrethe shook her head.

"Lagounov frowned. For a second, they looked smeared."

Eric smiled. "You have good eyes, General. Let's slow the video by a fifth."

The police officers moved in exaggerated slow motion. A dark blur entered the back of the restaurant and stretched from the bathrooms to the table. The blur coalesced, and Toss Bonneteau appeared. He took the girl's hand and faded into a new blur that that passed between two of the officers and out of the restaurant. When he moved between the police officers by the door, they flew back against the walls and slid to the floor.

Lagounov crushed his cigar out on his desk. "Where did they go?"

Eric switched the feed to the security video of the lobby. They traced the smear through the hotel lobby and out the front door. Body cam video from officers in the parking lot caught the blur passing out of the area. Three-quarters of the way to the street, a phone separated from the object and arced to the ground. "A better question, how does he move so fast?"

Sandra Potter took a sip of water. "Did he hit the police officers when he passed between them?"

Margrethe shook her head. "Anything moving that fast would cause enormous turbulence and leave a wake."

Stark smiled at Margrethe. "It's called a slipstream."

"The officers on the scene were caught in the turbulence and thrown back against the walls."

Eric Leeds continued to replay the videos. No one spoke until the Thrush Team Leader, Manquoba, said, "How does a human move that quick? The turbulence around their bodies should have torn their clothes off as if they fell out of an aircraft in flight."

Stark leaned back in his chair and watched the feeds through several cycles. "Is this the same process used by Gekas?"

Leeds stopped the cycle and displayed the video of the escape of Aranea Gekas. "She moves through walls and is intangible. Bonneteau does something else. If you slow to the limit, the two of them walk out, no hurry, no rush. He isn't moving fast. Time for Toss Bonneteau speeds up while the rest of the world continues in a normal frame."

Sandra drummed the desk in front of her. "He has a time machine."

Eric laughed. "Not in the conventional sense. If he could go back into the past or slip into the future, we would not be sitting here. He would change time, fix their mistake of stopping to eat and using a phone."

Margrethe slid her chair back. "So how do we deal with it, John?"

Stark glanced up at the camera. "When we catch them, take them down. Use tranquilizers if possible, but if not, kill them."

Lagounov pulled another cigar out of his jacket. "Will that be all?"

Stark shook his head. "We have one other issue. Eric?"

A screen capture titled "Darknet Oviraptorus" appeared above the image of a woman in tight leathers.

Lagounov exhaled a cloud of smoke. "Very attractive, but what has she to do with the cost of vodka in Moscow."

Leeds rolled his eyes. "Very colorful, but in our observation of the Guzman girls, this site has come up frequently. She is an avatar. The author or authors write in cryptic prose. It has an anti-FutureTense bias and appears only for the Guzman's. It sent a warning to Shiso de Guzman's phone seconds before Bonneteau pulled his magic trick."

Margrethe nodded. "Take the site down."

Leeds changed the display through other screen capture images. "We can't. The site has no permanent home, and it appears only when one of the Guzman's searches for it. It first appeared four years ago after we attempted to break into the Russian Object."

Margrethe glanced at Stark. "You are sure of the connection."

Stark held up a hand and answered. "There is no other possible explanation."

Sandra Potter sat her knitting aside. "So, they have an ally. I will make sure that the computers we have monitoring Yume de Guzman are isolated from the outside world."

Manquoba slid his chair back and stood. "We will monitor our own gear in the event Oviraptorus can spy on us."

Stark nodded once, and the screen went black. When Margrethe remained the only link, she smiled and blew him a kiss.

****

Vasyl handed a tin of warm, oily stew to the soldier in the next seat and accepted a bottle of Vodka. He lifted it to his lips and took a long swallow.

"Is that really a good idea," Clockbrain whispered in his mind? *"Ethanol reduces your reaction time and kills your inhibitions. It makes it more difficult to speak with you."*

Vasyl almost took a second drink.

Serve the goddamned voice right. What's it ever done for me?

"You are alive, thanks to my intervention."

Vasyl handed the bottle to the next man in the troop carrier.

He touched his stomach. "Have to take a crap."

The corporal nodded. Vasyl climbed through the side door of the BTR-80 Armored Personnel Carrier, stretched his legs to ease out the kinks, adjusted the strap on his weapon, and walked behind a hedge.

Clockbrain's fierce regard stung like a splinter in his mind. *"Why did you lie to that man? Your body has no need to defecate."*

Out of sight of the APC, Vasyl ducked behind a tree, dropped his pants, and squatted just in case anyone watched. "Needed out, air, and to talk to you."

"Verbalize your thoughts or just think. By necessity, our minds are tied together."

"Why?" The APC's engine hummed.

"Eventually, the why will be self-evident. I can wait."

"I cannot."

The engine of the APC roared. "Private Bagrov?" The Corporal called through the open hatch.

"Just finishing."

"Wipe your ass and get back in here. We're headed back to Aparinsky."

"This is not a good thing." Clockbrain's concern bled through his thought.

Vasyl did not need Clockbrain to tell him that. Up to that point, they moved away from Aparinsky, following the roads west. News stories picked up from refugees on the road reported that the Ukrainian Government had collapsed following the meteorite strike. The Russian Military had mobilized to bring humanitarian aid. Some of the troops worked with refugees and fought the forest fires. Most of them patrolled roads in a widening sweep from Aparinsky, looking for Vasyl. His ability to take the features of others had kept him safe.

Vasyl walked back to the APC's open hatch. His body hummed with a sudden surge of energy, and his mind raced. The six men inside would die first, followed by the turret gunner. The two drivers would die last. They would be the most difficult.

Vasyl stomach clenched like a fist. He wanted to vomit. His hand clicked the safety on his weapon and set it to full auto.

He stepped up to the hatch and glanced into the shadowy interior. The Corporal waved. Vasyl pulled the trigger. In the confined space, the roar of the weapon covered the screams and the air filled with blood.

The turret gunner pulled a sidearm. Vasyl blew the man apart. He dove inside and crawled through the blood.

One of the drivers had come to find out what happened. The man held his weapon, ready to fire. Vasyl grabbed the front of the man's uniform and jerked him inside. His muscles burned, and sweat poured into his eyes, a side effect of whatever gave him the strength and speed to kill with such alarming efficiency.

He broke the driver's back and held him like a shield.

The second driver stepped up to the hatch and fired. Bullets tore through the driver's body armor, which slowed them so the force only bruised Vasyl's ribs and chest. Several rounds tore through Vasyl's arms. Clockbrain switched off the pain. Vasyl slammed the dead, battered body of the first driver into his assistant.

The man collapsed backward, his clip empty. Vasyl dove out of the hatch and landed atop his last victim and ripped out his throat with his hands.

Sweat streamed down Vasyl's face and soaked his uniform and body armor. His bloody hands smoked in the cool air.

"Your temperature has spiked. You must cool down." Clockbrain's thoughts carried a tinge of panic.

"Fuck you."

"Are you a fool, Vasyl?" Clockbrain's anger grated. "Body acceleration heats your muscles. If you do not cool down, you will cook your brain. I cannot repair that."

"What am I?" Vasyl tired of Clockbrain's demands, his interference.

"There is no time for explanations."

"Then your Clockbrain can cook with mine."

"We are a vehicle, a symbiont, an Arc of the Covenant."

Vasyl stood in the sunlight. The heat poured from him. He could not decide of Clockbrain chose to be obtuse, or if the heat affected its thoughts. "Those are random words, unrelated. What am I?"

"Our white blood cell, our defender. For all our sakes, there is a stream nearby. I detect the sounds through our link. You must cool off."

"A white blood cell is a part of a whole."

Vasyl wiped away the sweat pouring into his eyes. Blood and sweat dripped from his fingers.

"You are a part of us, part of our whole. Cool your body. I will explain what I can."

Head spinning, the heat slowed his thoughts as if they streamed through mud. "I'm a monster. I'd rather die than be a monster."

"Please, Vasyl. I am so lonely. I can feel the others but see only in glimpses. They are not complete. I need you so that I will not be so alone."

What was Clockbrain, a shattered fragment of a broken mind, an independent creature that shared his thoughts, or a demon possessing his soul? The scientist in him rejected the last option, but the little boy who had often sought comfort in the churches considered it gospel.

The dead men at his feet and in the machine behind him, he had killed a group of highly trained soldiers as if they were plastic toys on a child's battlefield. The bullet wounds in his arms itched, but they did not bleed, fibrous white scabs covered the wounds.

He unhooked the helmet strap and let it fall. A stream gossiped somewhere in the trees. Following the sound, he shed his clothing, leaving the shirt, body armor, undershirt, boots, socks, pants, and his bloody underwear along the trail.

The water flowed around his knees, so he lay down and let the icy water sluice over his body. When the last hint of blood trailed away, he began to drink.

Later he sat near the stream, picking through the stores found on the APC. He wore a spare pair of pants and a shirt but no shoes. Blood soaked his boots, and he could not put them on no matter how Clockbrain cajoled and pleaded.

With his stomach full, he stuffed the rest into a pack. Night had fallen. The fires that continued to burn and a smoke-filled sky provided sufficient light so that he could see some distance. As he started to formulate a plan, Clockbrain spoke into his thoughts. *You must travel west.*

"Tell me more."

Clockbrain vanished. Did it balk at explaining itself beyond random words?

"You promised."

He couldn't wait here next to the APC and the bodies. With a full stomach and cooler mind, Vasyl decided that he did not want to die. He left the road and walked into the trees along the small stream. Only the Russian military and refugees traveled in this area, and he did not care to meet either group. "I am one monster that desires to be alone."

Clockbrain must have had other ideas. *"You are not a monster."*

"Those words you used to describe yourself. Explain."

"They are approximations of our reality. Human language has no equivalent. A direct translation would be Us or We. I sensed those words were not satisfactory."

"You are an alien." Alien could have just as easily meant demon in Vasyl's mind.

Vasyl's thoughts carried a sense of reluctance. *"We are alien. Under normal circumstances, I am not an individual."*

"Then what am I, if not human? Why are we a we?"

Clockbrain withdrew, almost vanishing so that only the lightest touch of the other mind remained. His presence bled back. *"Why is easy, desperation. We transited the rim of the galactic spiral when we encountered a cloud of what you call dark matter."*

Of course, it made a kind of poetic sense. "The cloud I discovered beyond the Kuiper belt."

"Exactly, we were disabled and many of our symbiotic systems destroyed. As an emergency measure, I cocooned us. When we passed near your system, I initiated a landing."

"You are the Russian Event, the pilot."

"Not intentionally, and I am not a you, and certainly not a pilot. The closest analogy would be ship's surgeon."

"Now, about me."

"With most of our systems destroyed and other's failing, I initiated a plan to replace critical parts of the Ship.

We crashed near your position. I found five compatible components and initiated modification and repair."

"Modification" Raw anger boiled in his stomach. "You are talking about me."

"It was a desperate measure. Five of you survived."

"Thousands died."

"We had no choice."

A fallen tree crossed the stream. Beyond, the land rose to flat, broad fields of grain. Across the fields, a house and barn sat against the red sky.

"What part do I play?"

"Our defense when necessary. Never since our incorporation have we required such violence."

He walked across the tree, west. "Change me back."

"To what?"

"Vasyl Petrenko."

"Vasyl is your default shape. You can change back anytime, but it requires a great deal of energy. Wiser to wait."

"Back to human."

Clockbrain withdrew again to whatever part of Vasyl's brain served as its hiding place. His thought came as a distant whisper. *"As a human, you were a brilliant, fragile consciousness with low self-esteem due to sexual and physical abuse by your father."*

"How dare you?"

"We lived in your head. We know you. Is that all you desire to be?"

"Yes."

Clockbrain's impatience stung his conscious. *"We can no more change you back than We could unbreak a glass. For better or worse, you are what you are."*

"Then why should I help you?"

"You are no more complete as you are than We. Better to be whole than a remnant.

The field gave way to a road. He took the direction that led west. "That's not enough."

"Would you do it for her?"

Hot water flowed down his back. He stood in the small shower in their quarters near the Radio Telescope in Yevpatoria. Aranea's back wedged against the tile. He supported her weight in his arms and drove into her. She bit his lips, kissed his cheek, and moaned in his ear.

His orgasm struck, fierce, brief. They continued to move together until she followed. Afterward, they held each other on the floor of the shower.

"I love you," he whispered in her ear.

Vasyl sat in the field, and the wheat towered over him. The inside of his pants felt wet and sticky. *"You son-of-a-bitch."*

"Is that memory worth your help?"

"That was not a memory." What was it? For a moment he relived the memory.

"You re-experienced an event. Everything is in your head. The human mind's ability to recall is limited. Mine is not."

"You said she was in South Dakota."

"She has moved east from her former position. She remains within that political entity."

"You want me to find her?"

"We want to find her."

"We will do it."

CHAPTER FOUR

Running

The flatbed truck slowed to a crawl at the entrance of a narrow road into a farmer's lane. The driver glanced back through the window of the cab and nodded. Vasyl jumped down before the turn and joined a line of refugees walking west. Safety existed only in numbers.

Hours after he had fled the APC and its crew of dead men, a Russian Army Helicopter flew low and slow overhead. The flight crew, using infrared goggles, searched the streams and fields. He lay in cold water until he thought the shivering would rip him apart. A man traveling alone attracted attention. A refugee trudging west with a thousand starving, frightened men earned anonymity.

Somewhere ahead, according to a thousand whispered rumors, the Halych Refugee Camp sprawled alongside a functioning railroad track. The rumors, if believed, said that courtesy of the Russian Republic, transportation could be had for the asking, at least as far as Kaliningrad.

For Vasyl, Kaliningrad would be just fine. Kaliningrad was a busy port, and from there he could find a way to Western Europe or even across the Atlantic if Clockbrain demanded it.

Clockbrain appeared from where ever he hid between visits to Vasyl's brain. *"I do not demand."*

Vasyl scanned the people near him, but none walked close enough to think he might be talking to them. "So, you say."

"Don't speak aloud."

Vasyl laughed. "It's a choice. Crazy people talk to themselves."

"You are not insane."

Vasyl turned to one side as if talking to an invisible partner. "Crazy and insane are not the same, my friend. The insane are sad creatures best left to the mercies of a psychiatrist. The crazy are dangerous and best left to themselves."

"Why would you want people to consider you dangerous?"

Was Clockbrain so oblivious to human experience? "I murder people and become them."

"That is not accurate."

He shrugged. "It has been my experience."

A small girl of about eight glanced at him; her expression a worried question.

Vasyl smiled because he could not help himself. He leaned close and tapped his forehead with a finger. "I have a machine living in my head. He won't shut up. It's talk, talk, talk."

She chewed her lip, and her eyes darted from his face to his hands until she decided to speak. "At least, you're not lonely."

Vasyl put his hands in his pockets. "I can see you're a girl who looks for silver linings."

Clockbrain intruded. *"We don't have time for this."*

Vasyl scanned the hordes of refugees. "Where are your parents?"

The girl shrugged and looked at her feet. "I haven't seen them since I left home."

"You can look for them in the refugee camp in Halych. There will be organizations there that specialize in helping lost children find relatives."

"I don't know where Halych is. I just follow people. Some of them give me food, others tell me to go away, and a few try to hurt me."

Vasyl knelt beside her. "You must be very brave. I'll get you there." He picked the girl up and sat her on his shoulder. She grabbed his ears and held them like reins.

Vasyl laughed. "What's your name?"

The girl leaned close to Vasyl's ear and whispered. "Mama says I should not give my name to strangers."

"Even when you're riding on a stranger's shoulders?"

She let go his ears and pulled back. "I, I don't know."

"My name is Vasyl. I call the machine in my head Clockbrain."

"Will Clockbrain talk to me?"

"No!"

"He's shy around girls."

"We are not shy around females."

"And he's touchy, too."

She wrapped her arms around Vasyl's forehead. "Why does he live in your head?"

Such a simple question. Vasyl had never thought to ask why Clockbrain plagued his mind. Why couldn't he go off and live in the heads of one of the others?

"We have a special relationship. I can only speak to one of the others at this time and only under certain conditions."

"I never asked."

"You should. He might be hurting."

Could the voice in his head hurt? Why not? "So, tell us, Clockbrain? Are you hurting?"

He felt Clockbrain like a cloud in his mind. Was it devious, furious? Two beings hooked up brain to brain, but ignorant of each other because one feared he would be called to murder and the other spoke in riddles.

"I do not riddle."

"Says he doesn't riddle. Humph. Shows what he knows."

"Maybe he's just hiding how bad he feels." She hugged Vasyl's head tight.

"We can't find her, Okay?" It was a quick thought, sharp.

"He's lost someone special."

She stroked Vasyl's head as if soothing a cat. "It's Okay. I lost someone, too."

"We've searched all our remaining links but can't find her. So many systems broken. So many shut down. We are locked out."

Grief and loneliness wracked Vasyl, though not his own.

"She is our captain, and we have known her from our first awakening. We have never been apart, until now."

Tears streamed from Vasyl's eyes. Wracking sobs building up in his chest. The little girl hugged him tighter. "My name is Ivanna," she whispered into his hair. "Maybe, someone at the camp can help your friend find the person you lost."

"Maybe they will." Vasyl rubbed the tears from his eyes.

Ivanna hugged him tighter. "It can happen, right?"

****

John Stark leaned out of the helicopter. A Russian APC sat in the road, the side door open. Soldiers in fatigues stood back in the shadows of the trees, standing guard.

General Lagounov stepped out of the shade.

Stark pointed at a spot on the road. "Land." Before the rotors stopped, he jumped out of the door, ducked low and walked toward the APC.

A tremendous stench of rotting corpses stained the air around the APC. Flies buzzed around the one body that hung half out of the open door. Inside, bodies swarming with young maggots sprawled in the shadows.

"Why am I here, general?"

Lagounov charged across the open road and grabbed Stark by the collar. "I wanted you to see this!"

Stark gripped the general's hand by the thumb and twisted. "Get your hands off me."

Lagounov's eye twitched. They stood, locked together face to face. Lagounov straining against the hold.

"General, I can break your hand, and you will never use it again for anything except to fill your pocket."

"My men will shoot you."

"You will die first. My successor will find a general who can do the job you cannot. Our lawyers will strip your wife and mistress of everything they own for your breach of contract."

Stark released his hand.

Lagounov stepped back. "You play rough."

"You have no idea. Report."

"Six infantrymen, a turret gunner, and two drivers were killed by one man."

"And how did that happen? Were you transporting Petrenko in this APC?"

"One of the soldiers is missing, Private Bagrov. He walked into the woods from the APC and relieved himself against a tree. He returned and killed everyone inside."

"What makes you think it was Petrenko?"

"Bagrov was one of the men we found dead east of Aparinsky. Private Bagrov's body is conveniently missing from this scene."

Stark walked around the APC. A soldier lay on the ground, his throat torn out. "I don't see a connection, General."

"Bagrov was not found until this unit left Aparinsky. I have eyewitness accounts placing him in this vehicle. How can a man dead on a hillside climb into an APC and drive away?"

"What do you think, General?"

Lagounov pulled a cigar from his pocket, bit off the end, and lit it. He blew smoke into the air and smiled. "When I was a boy, my grandmother told me about the Oborot, a man who could change himself into a beast."

"You think Petrenko is a werewolf?"

"You are hunting a woman who walks through walls and a man who disappears without a trace."

"Yes."

"And you have the girl, Yume de Guzman. What does she do?"

"What are you getting at?"

"I think we have a man who kills people and takes their shape. Someone who kills as efficiently as any beast I have ever heard of."

Stark wanted to deny it. After Gekas and Bonneteau had escaped, it made sense.

"What are you going to do about him, Stark?"

"Petrenko is not a beast you can hunt through the fields. My men would never know if the next man in the squad was a friend or an animal. The Halych Refugee Camp is the nearest. I will turn it into a trap."

"What will you do when he springs your trap?"

"I will kill him, cut his fucking head off, and mount it on my wall. I will send you the rest."

Lagounov walked away.

The helicopter lifted off and flew west. Stark rubbed his eyes. Since the meteor strike, he had spent enough time flying from one part of the earth to another that he no longer knew what time of day it was. He wanted a drink and some sleep. Time enough for that on the jet back to the US.

He pulled out his phone and called Iceland. When a familiar voice answered, he said, "Eric."

"What is it, boss."

"Activate all our assets in Lagounov's unit."

"That bad?"

"Worse. Who else do we have in the region, especially the Halych Refugee Camp?"

"Give me a minute."

Stark waited while Leeds did his magic. If there were anyone at all, Eric would find him.

"I can only find one, a woman, Russian SVR agent, Svetlana Gorelova, sometimes goes by Sveta."

"Perfect. Activate Miss Gorelova's contract and read her into the program. She can contact Lagounov."

"We need to know his plan. He cannot be allowed to kill Petrenko unless there is no other choice."

"Shall we have Lagounov killed?"

"No, let him spring his trap. He's an asshole, but he is good at what he does. Have someone ready to put him down if they must."

****

Yume walked the walls of her room, twelve paces by ten paces, forty-four from beginning to end.

She wanted to run or swim or walk along a beach or among trees or even the streets of one of Southeast San Diego's ghettos. Any other place would do except glossy white walls, floors, and ceilings. Thin lines down the walls marked the door to the bathroom and drawers in the walls. They opened to the touch of a fingertip.

Another set of thin lines outlined the exit, locked to Yume but not the friendly neighborhood nurse, who also dressed in white and acted more cheerful than the Good Humor Man on speed.

Oh, to escape, to flee this place and run along a beach or through grass. No escape existed for the wakeful. Yume had her own method, not physical of course. She closed her eyes, the first part of the dream trick, not sleep, of course, just to shut out the ugly white walls. She reached into her mind for Shiso's presence and found nothing.

Shiso's absence planted a small seed of panic. She had hoped to find Shiso because seeing her sister, even in a dream, would be heaven. Anything that diminished the loneliness, the isolation. Anything that stole the fear from her prison in a milk bottle.

Isolated, she began a slide toward hopelessness. Yume thought she could tolerate almost anything but isolation. Even the Good Humor nurse felt welcome.

Stop it, I can dream her up.

Yume concentrated on the memory of Shiso's face, her shape, her characteristic way of standing. Once the dream avatar of her sister coalesced in her mind, she stood her sister at the center of the white room, arms crossed. In her dream, Yume heard the tap, tap, tap of her sister's impatient foot on the floor.

Yume exhaled and absorbed the warm presence of her sister. Strengthened against the emptiness of the white cell, Yume opened one eye, just a peek. Alone, but feeling better, she dove into the dream.

On a whim, she walked to the door. "Open sesame."

What did she really expect to happen, a genie to appear and open the door to a cave filled with treasure? The door opened.

Yume froze. Was this real or dream? Dream, of course, because she remained aware of herself standing in the center of her room, eyes closed.

Outside, cinderblock walls and floors ran under steel beams sprayed over with concrete that held up a gray ceiling so dull it must be real. Two guards in white and gray camouflage uniforms stood outside her cell door, stiff, attentive. Their eyes shifted to follow other soldiers in similar uniforms who moved through the hall on their own mysterious errands.

She stuck a finger in the eye of the soldier on the left. It disappeared halfway into his face.

Dream constructs should be solid. Could this be real, Stranger said she created realities rather than dreams. Had she dreamed herself into reality?

The soldiers popped to attention and saluted. John Stark flanked by Sandra, and three men in white medical smocks walked through her. Her door opened, and they continued into the room.

"Stranger," she called again. He did not answer her dream. "Damn! Damn! Damn!" He made her this way. When she needed guidance, he decided to powder his nose, drink coffee, or do whatever strangers did.

Part of her thought walking off down the hall would feel grand; she could reconnoiter the enemy's lair, just like in a video game. She might even find a way to escape if she could figure out how to open the damn door for real.

From inside her room, she heard Stark, "Ms. De Guzman?"

She saw herself standing with her eyes closed, arms crossed, foot tapping.

Cool out of body experience.

Her unruly mouth opened to speak.

She performed another trick; a mental shake that woke her from a dream. "Hello, Mr. Stark."

The door closed behind him and became a white wall.

"What were you doing?"

"Sleeping."

"Standing up?"

"Sleep standing. I have such a busy schedule, such an active life, more efficient to do it standing up."

A balding, white-smocked man sat with a tablet in his hand. "She's lying."

Stark smiled with no humor. "Opinion or fact?"

The man studied his tablet. "Heart rate, respiration, and other physical data from her internal monitor indicate a falsehood."

She rolled her eyes. "Your machine doesn't read sarcasm."

Her mind raced.

Did they implant something? What does Stark want?

The man ignored her.

The second white smocked man added, "No unusual electromagnetic activity. If she is in contact with the others, it isn't by conventional means."

He's hot in a late twenties sort of way.

Stark glanced at the two men. They poured their attention onto their tablets. "I have something to show you."

"If it isn't a white wall, you have my full attention."

A panel in the ceiling opened, and a flat-screen display lowered into the room.

"This room has a TV? Why didn't you say so? I am so behind on morning cartoons."

"What do you make of this?"

Aranea stood beside a bed in a hospital room, her fists clenched, mouth set in a snarl. She kicked Stark.

He blocked it.

"Kill her!" Stark said.

Smoke and shotgun blasts swirled in the frame, and the sound hurt her ears. At first, Yume thought Aranea disappeared. A spherical distortion in the video filled the space where she had stood, then vanished. The heart monitor exploded, and a hole blasted out of the wall.

The image froze. Stark glanced at her face. "What is that, Ms. De Guzman?"

Yume stepped closer to the screen. Dreams never occurred in conscious space, and a video could not show telepathy. Aranea possessed a different affliction or superpower.

A smile twitched at the corner of his lips. "You're not surprised."

"I don't know what to say."

"Really?"

What did he expect when she did not know the truth? "What do your experts say?"

The smile exploded over his face. "If you want to be an expert, you first must know something about the subject. The consensus of observers makes it out to be a warp bubble."

"I don't know what that is?"

He glanced at the bald-headed expert.

"She is telling the truth."

"If she isn't human, how would you know?"

The expert frowned and dropped his eyes. "Physiologically, her body is human. The observed differences have no bearing on the normal functions of the body. Even the differences we have noticed in the brain do not stimulate heart rate or sweat or other signs of purposeful deceit."

The video changed. Shiso sat at a table looking at her phone. Toss Bonneteau appeared and reached for her hand. When Shiso took it, they vanished.

Yume's stomach knotted. Shiso vanished. She was okay though. She was alive, at least, when they made the videos.

"What happened?"

"The spherical distortion did not occur. What do you think happened?"

Yume dropped down on the bed and curled her legs beneath her. "I don't know what happened, and I don't know what is happening."

"That's a lie." The bald man said.

"No, it isn't!"

"On the first statement, she told the truth, though her heart rate and respiration increased on seeing her sister."

Stark sat down on the bed and leaned in. "Well, you do know something. Care to share?"

She studied her toes.

"One more thing."

She glanced at the screen. She expected to see Vasyl Petrenko. Instead, the video appeared to be a warehouse. A large object, resembling a seed or complex seashell, filled the warehouse and extended through huge doors and across a large flat area covered with snow. Men moved in and out of the scene using machines or gathered together in small groups.

The shape summoned up a memory from their dream on Suki's Delight. "What is it?"

If Stark expected her to give away some secret, he failed.

"Something fell to earth in Russia five years ago. Part of it survived. We brought it here."

"You brought that here."

"About of a tenth of it, the rest grew over time. Whatever it is, it is repairing itself."

"I can't help you, Mr. Stark."

"Okay." He walked to the door, flanked by his experts. He stopped and looked over his shoulder. "Who is Darknet Oviraptorus?"

Stark stood in the doorway. Over his shoulder, Yume saw a concrete wall and ceiling.

"It's a blog Shiso and I followed."

He frowned. "Then I can't help you."

Yume closed her eyes. She heard the door shut and felt the empty room around her. Shiso lived. She shivered out of relief and giddy happiness. If they could just talk, again.

She fell into a dream. Stranger sat at the foot of her bed in the same place that Stark and occupied.

"Why weren't you here?"

"Busy."

"I get interrogated by Stark, and all you can say is busy?"

"You have my apologies. Couldn't be helped."

"I saw Shiso, Aranea, and Toss on a video."

He leaned close. "Where were they?"

"Aranea was in a hospital. Shiso and Toss were in a restaurant. What does it matter? They are holding me in a concrete prison, and it's snowing outside."

"How do you know that?"

Why should she tell Stranger? He never gave a straight answer. "One of the videos showed a hangar with a huge something in it. I saw snow outside, lots of it. As to the prison, you didn't answer, so I dreamed I could open the door and walk out."

He leaned back on the bed, intense concentration contorting his face.

"What's going on? Tell me."

"If I tell you anything else, you may slip."

"Haven't told him anything yet."

"His methods will grow harsher over time."

Yume buried her face in her hands. What did it take to open Stranger up? Seeing Shiso made her absence a knife in her mind. "Why can't Shiso talk to me?"

"It is not a good idea."

"Why?" She wanted to kick him off the bed. His evasive, half answers left her spiteful.

"The term in your language is compartmentalization. The less you each know, at this time, the less you can give away."

"But why can't I talk with her? We've been separated by half the planet, and it didn't stop the communication."

He sat up and took her hands. "I know this is difficult."

"What do you know? You have your spaceship. You come and go as you please."

Stranger slid off the bed paced four steps. "Not as I please. I visit you in your dream and I mind speak, as you call it, with Vasyl Petrenko. I am cut off from everyone else, even my ship."

"How can you and I mind speak and Shiso can't."

He buried his face in his hands. "It's complicated, but Shiso is still the communicator."

"If you are going to lie to me, get out. Why can't Shiso mind talk to me?"

He paced more, back and forth. "I disabled your ability to receive."

"Get out of my dream!"

"Look, I know this is difficult."

She charged off the bed and slapped his face. His cheek felt solid, and he rang like a bell.

Stranger stood at the center of her room, holding his cheek, his eyes wide and wild.

Yume turned her back to him. "You either let my sister mind talk or I will never let you in a dream again."

"If you do something for me first."

"I don't negotiate with assholes."

She felt him approach but refused to look.

He placed a hand on her shoulder. "I will do it, but you must dream me so that I can see the others."

"I don't know how to do that?"

"You did it once before. Concentrate. Focus your thoughts on your sister. The others will follow."

Give me a minute. Yume closed her eyes and pictured Shiso's face. Perhaps this was all mental gymnastics. What if she imagined herself beside Shiso?

"Here goes."

****

Shiso listened at the door beside a boarded-up window in the abandoned house. Because no door had existed in that spot when she fell asleep, she felt safe to say she occupied a dream.

She pressed her forehead against the cold wood and prayed to the Baku, the dream eater. As an awake, adult woman of sixteen, she did not believe in her mother's old Japanese Gods and demons. Asleep, she could slip back to childhood, to the stories mother told of the Baku, Kami, or the old Kamado-Gami that gathered around the hearth of their family home in Japan.

Thinking about the Baku summoned an avatar of the dancing, elephant-headed, lion-beast stuffed animal her mother had placed on the headboard of her bed. Yume hugged it close and fancied that it carried the scent of mother's perfume, and that gave her courage enough to open the door.

On the other side of that door, she hoped to find Yume. For all her life, except for one brief, separate vacation they had lived together. She knew that one day they would grow up, get married, and birth separate lives but not at sixteen. Since Russia, they never parted because Yume shared her dreams and Shiso shared their thoughts. Yume's absence felt like someone cut out a critical part of her body.

She stepped through the door--eyes closed but full of hope and opened them on the deck of Suki's Paradise. The forward mast lay broken, and the sail trailed in a green ocean. Around her, the dead hulks of ships heaved on the ocean swell.

Below decks, she heard a rumble and rattle.

She called, "Yume," and waited for an answer. The noise stopped, and the silence of a dead ocean rolled over the boat. She started back through the door and found empty air.

"Yume, if this is one of your damned dreams." She ran to the hatch that led down to the staterooms and charged through.

Emerging near the back of the van in the Parking lot of the Iron Mountain Hiking Trail, Shiso watched herself crawl out the back and close the door. That younger Shiso walked through the older ghost of herself and headed off to find a Motorcycle so she could rescue Toss Bonneteau.

"What should I do?" She picked her way up the path for a dozen steps. No, this path led back to the abandoned house where she dreamed.

Leaving Yume and running off to someone she only knew because of the worst thing that ever happened in her brief life had led to disaster.

"This time, I stay." She opened the door and stepped into the van. Honest to Baku, she thought that she would find Yume asleep, waiting to be carried off by strange men for stranger purposes.

Shiso stood in a gray tube with luminous walls and did not suffer even the least surprise. She drew her hand along the surface. It felt warm, and soft, like the tail of a cat. "What is this all about?"

The Baku hopped onto her shoulder. "If it's a dream, it's more than I could eat."

"You're alive?"

The Baku pinched his forearm and shrugged. "Not sure, unless alive is equivalent to hungry. Oh, I could eat a big old seven-course nightmare right now. I haven't had a good meal since that nightmare you had when you were..."

"Seven," she finished his sentence. Why shouldn't she? The Baku had been a dear friend throughout her nightmare years.

"What do we do next?"

"Well, from experience I'd say you need to find a door."

"And where does it lead?"

"I am not equipped to answer that, but I can eat it if it's necessary."

She walked down the tube, dragging her finger along the wall as if she were six again and the wall a chain-link fence. In the dream, the wall emitted a metallic rattle. The sound invoked a six-year old's ecstasy. She imagined that Yume walked on the other side of that fence until she found the door standing in the center of the tunnel.

Shiso stroked the head of the Baku. "Where do you suppose it goes?"

"Don't know, but it looks delicious," the Baku said. "Give me a nibble."

Letting the dream eater lose to graze on the door in the gray tube sounded like a great idea. What if Yume did not wait on the other side? What if she had become lost in a nightmare? Could that happen?

The Baku ran down her arm and nuzzled her hand. "In a dream, anything can happen."

Her stomach twisted in a knot and sweat broke across her face. What if nothing existed beyond that door? What if Yume wasn't just absent, but dead.

That thought, oh how it ate at her. Yume dead and on an autopsy table with her body flayed open.

She grabbed the handle and ran through. Another thought like that and her Sanity would bleed away.

Shiso entered a room with white walls, white floors, and a white ceiling. Yume, dressed in a white hospital gown, lay on a white bed talking to a man in a white suit and Panama hat.

"Yume?"

Yume flew out of bed. They hugged in the middle of the room. Tears flowed over her cheeks and snot ran from her nose. None of it mattered because Shiso had found Yume again.

Much later they sat on the bed hugging each other because Shiso feared she would wake in that grimy little room in Nevada and find Toss Bonneteau sitting cross-legged on the floor playing solitaire. "I'm sorry I left you."

Yume squeezed Shiso's hand. "It's okay. I'm safe, I guess. I want you to meet someone."

Shiso glanced up at the man in the Panama hat. "I know Stranger."

Yume rolled her eyes. "No, not really."

"Sure, I do. We decided you made Stranger up."

Stranger crossed his arms and tapped one foot. "She most certainly did not make me up. Actually, it is more the other way around."

Shiso glanced at Yume and back at Stranger. "We are not made up. We had parents, a Tio."

"I did not make you from nothing. Each of you possessed the essential potential in your DNA. I modified you, gave you your unique talents."

They both asked, "Why?"

"The why is not important. We are all in danger unless I can get the five of you here."

"What does he want?" Shiso sent. It felt good to be here, to be whole. Without Yume, she felt incomplete, lost.

Stranger spoke into both of their minds. "It would be polite to allow you a few moments of sibling bonding. There is no time."

Shiso slipped off the bed but held her sister's hand. "What do you want?"

"I want you all here."

Shiso waved at the white walls. "Where is here?"

He shrugged. "I do not know."

Yume squeezed her hand. "It's snowing outside. That tells us something."

"So, we are all supposed to traipse off to someplace where there is snow on the ground. That's a bit vague, don't you think?"

Stranger sat on the bed. "We will find our position. You must be ready when we call."

Shiso glanced at her sister. "And when will that be?"

"Soon, Shiso." Stranger's head popped up as if he caught a distant sound. "Oh my, you had better wake."

****

Yume squeezed Shiso's hand. It vanished. She twisted around and slapped Stranger across the face. "What's wrong? Where is she?"

"Follow her. Find out"

Yume eased out of bed. Where had Shiso come from? Where did she go? "I don't know where she is."

"In a dream, you opened a door into a hallway you've never seen."

"That hall is just the other side of the wall."

"If you can see through that wall, you can see anywhere on Earth."

Yume crossed her arms and shook her head. "She may be thousands of miles away."

"How fast is light? She traveled here in seconds."

Stranger was right, though she preferred not to admit it. She thought of these dreams as a local phenomenon. She had never tried to dream together when they were separated. Shiso had been here, so that meant she could.

Stranger placed a hand on her shoulder. "Following her is within your capabilities. If it helps to conceptualize your movement through space, dream a door and walk through it."

Yume chewed at her fingernail. She often created elaborate dreamscapes, preferred them to reality. The dream version of her cell could use a bit of cheering up, any color but white. The walls deepened from white to a pale green.

109

Stranger laughed. "Do you really think bile green is an improvement?"

His suit and Panama hat matched the walls.

"That was proof of concept."

A green door visualized at the center of the room. Yume opened it and stepped through.

Shiso huddled in a heavy coat on a concrete floor in a dark room. Light stealing between the boards over a window drew straight, bright lines across the floor, and dust danced in the air.

"Toss?" Yume read her sister's lips. Whatever capability allowed her to travel here did not allow sound.

Stranger stepped through the door. "Your card playing friend is not here."

Shiso dropped the coat and walked through Yume to the door. She reached for the knob and retrieved a sheet of paper stuck on a nail head.

'Back in the day, I knew a man who knew a woman who flew in and out of these local airports. Might be dangerous. If I don't come back, follow your own judgment.'

Shiso opened the door a crack and looked through into a bright Nevada morning. "Damn you, Toss."

Yume reached out to touch her sister's shoulder. Her hand passed through as if reality were the ghost. Maybe Shiso felt something. She sent, "Yume? Can you hear this?"

Yume's smile exploded. All the times she resented her sister's presence inside her head evaporated. "I'm here."

Shiso smiled. "Shit, it works again."

Yume had heard Shiso before she mouthed the words.

"Toss Bonneteau is gone."

"I read the note."

"Where are you?"

"Physically, in a white room. I dreamed a door and followed you through."

"Really?"

Stranger leaned close. "The individual systems built into you have many features of which you are not aware."

"Is that Stranger? I can hear his voice echo in your head."

"He is in the dream." Yume pushed him away.

"How can I hear him?"

Stranger grabbed Yume by the shoulder. "Because Yume does not dream, she witnesses."

Yume shrugged. "Didn't you know? I don't dream. I construct realities."

"Thoughts are verbalized before they are spoken. You hear what Yume hears in her realities. We need to move on."

Shiso pressed her head against the door. "This is a lot to take in."

Stranger rolled his eyes. "Toss will be Okay."

Shiso opened the door. Though Yume saw no one outside, Shiso returned to using telepathy. "I have to go and see if I can help."

Stranger reached out, and his hands passed through Shiso's body. "He said to stay here."

Shiso laughed. Yume felt her mirth, not as sound but as warmth that radiated through the dream.

"Never been good at doing what I was told."

It didn't matter if she did not share a patch of ground with her sister or could not touch her. She did not want to be alone, again. "Stranger and I can go with you."

Shiso sent, "This is just your dream, and you are in a white room. I have to do this on my own."

Yume glanced at Stranger. He shrugged.

"How do you find the airport, and what will you do if something goes wrong? What if you get hurt?"

Shiso walked out of the door and closed it behind her.

Yume stood in the empty room. What if one of them was hurt or killed? Stark had tried to kill Aranea Gekas and failed because she had done something unexpected and unbelievable.

Some of them could die, hell; all of them could end up on slabs in the morgue. All Yume could do was dream and watch.

She wrapped her arms around herself and shivered.

Stranger touched her shoulder. Yume jerked away. She did not want comfort.

****

Toss stood in the shadow of a hanger and watched the small terminal of the Mesquite Municipal Airport. The terminal with its single strip, control tower, associated hangars, and repair sheds could belong to any small town. Only the surrounding desert landscape set it aside.

A fuel truck pulled away from a Lear jet. On a typical day, five or six charters would sit on the tarmac, but the ashy sky that spread across the entire northern hemisphere cut into pleasure travel.

Closer to the terminal, a few trucks backed up to the freight depot loaded or unloaded crates, boxes, or bags of mail. A handful of pilots and aircrew stood near a food truck, drank coffee, and talked, he suspected, about the smoke and cold weather.

Through a hanger door, he saw mechanics around a Cessna with its engine compartment open, tools, parts, and other equipment scattered around their feet. Next to the terminal stood a corrugated steel arched hangar with the name Regan Air Freight, painted in faded letters across the top. Beside it, five older aircraft sat on an asphalt tarmac.

In his adult life, he had visited more than a few of these fields. Conman by profession, he made his living observing humans in their natural habitat. He knew how to recognize marks susceptible to his games from the average Joe or the undercover cop out to bust his ass for separating a player from his money. Though he pried into every visible corner, he saw no person out of place.

After escaping from San Diego and the casino, he expected to see some sign of observers at a natural escape route, like an airport. The fact that he could not catch sight of watchers probably meant that FutureTense recruited only the best, men who would know how to blend in, or local informants made invisible by the fact that they belonged here.

The open area around the airport meant he could not approach unseen. On a typical day, there would be enough traffic to slip in, not today. Of course, he had his superpower, as Shiso called it. He could speed up time sufficiently so that no one saw him. That method carried its own disadvantage. His short use near the trolley and in Balboa Park left him famished. The effort to reach Shiso in the casino and get them both out brought him near collapse.

In comics, superheroes and villains used their powers with little effort. Real life powers required energy limited by human physiology. If the measure of his waist could be trusted, he had lost weight in the last eight days because of his trick of time.

He reached into his pocket for a chocolate bar--all that remained of the bounty Shiso bought at the local gas station. Fortified with temporary relief, he took a walk. The American flag and the windsock flying in front of the terminal froze. Toss walked as if in no hurry. Every person visible could have been part of a photograph.

He paused outside the side door of Regan's and ate half the candy bar. Through the door of the office, he heard low voices. With the edge off his instant hunger, he opened the door and walked in.

He had never met Rhonda Regan, CEO, and manager of Regan's Air Freight, though he had flown with them on five separate occasions. Since 9/11, even small outfits like Regan's were required to list their passengers. For a suitable fee, Regan neglected to add a customer to the list of passengers.

A woman on the gray side of forty stood, five feet tall, ninety pounds with her pockets full of tools stood behind a cluttered desk. A blue chambray shirt with the name of the company emblazoned across her breast served as a business card. She watched him, eyes narrowed, the naked look of a woman who measured a customer against profit. She nodded to a mechanic in coveralls, who walked away without looking back.

"You'd be Toss Bonneteau." She didn't smile.

"And you are a woman full of surprises." Should he use his trick? The door remained open. He could disappear before she could call Stark or his goons. She led him across the concrete floor to a battered gray desk. She had not made up her mind. Whatever Stark had offered, Toss still had a chance.

"A man named Stark flew in from Iceland today on a Lear jet. He showed me photographs of you and a young woman. Do you know him?"

"I know who he works for, FutureTense."

She glanced back at him. "I can make money turning you in."

Yes, he could perform his trick. He would disappear and walk out with no one the wiser. He pulled up a chair and sat down. "How much are they offering?"

"Two thousand for you and another two for the girl you run with."

He smiled at her. "I would think it would be twice that much. Why are you telling me this instead of counting the money?"

"I have a reputation. People who want to go places without broadcasting their whereabouts come to me. You've used my services five times."

He nodded. "I've had no complaints so far."

Her eyes widened in a smile. "Satisfied customers are important to Regan Air Freight."

He heard a faint thump. Something stung his neck. Time sped. He rose out of the chair. The mechanic stood back near the front of the office with a tranquilizer gun in his hand. Toss felt woozy, tired. His feet refused to cooperate. Halfway to the door, he collapsed on the floor, where he continued a crawl for another few feet.

His world darkened at the edges so that his vision focused on a smaller and smaller area. A woman's work boot stopped by his nose.

"How did you do that?" Regan asked.

He opened his mouth to answer and fell asleep.

****

Yume hugged her knees. "Shit. Shit. Shit!"

Stranger crossed his arms--eyebrows knitted. "I sense you are mentally distraught."

She rolled her eyes. "You think."

"Often."

She put her feet down and looked up. "You're trying to be funny."

"Does it work?"

"No!"

"Sense of humor in a foreign language remains the most challenging concept."

Yume eased off the bed and strolled to the door. It opened for her without the need to alter her dream. Two men stood guard in an empty hall. She willed it shut and placed her forehead against the cold white wall. "Why did I leave, Stranger?"

"Shiso can contact you if necessary."

"I know that. If I had stayed, I could have helped."

"How, exactly? You see reality but cannot change it, which I consider an improvement."

She looked back. Stranger stood with his arms behind his back, head down, eyes narrow, distracted by something.

She pitched her voice low. She imagined Stranger as something other than an approximation of a human-- something quiet and malleable, clay. In her dreams, she could manipulate physical appearances, but had never tried manipulating mental processes. "An improvement over what?"

"Creating dream realities and watching them, a sensor system addicted to false images is useless."

"A system?"

He cocked his head to the side. "Yes, you are a system," His eyes widened. "Oh, that is good. You continue to change."

She slapped him. "What do you mean?"

"I think I should look in on Vasyl."

She grabbed him by the jacket and shook. Yume towered over him. She could pick him up and toss him like a water balloon. "Tell me the truth."

He frowned. "You are all systems on a live ship if that helps."

She lifted him by his lapels. "What did you do to us?"

"I changed you," he bit off each word. "Vital systems were destroyed. I had to replace them, or we would die."

She sat him on the floor but continued to hold him. He popped in and out of her dreams at will. She would not allow him to leave. "We are just machines."

"Of course not, you remain free-willed beings, incomplete and integrated."

"Integrated with what?"

"Each other."

Stranger vanished and reappeared across the room, out of reach. "I underestimated you. You continue to develop functionality faster than the others. There are things that I cannot tell you until you are complete."

"Like what."

"Show me Toss Bonneteau."

"Like what."

"Show me Toss, now."

Yume frowned. Better to display anger than the fear that shivered through her legs. Was Stark right about not being human? "How? I don't know where he is. Shiso and I are linked since Russia. I've never dreamed with him."

"Nonsense, you warned the others to run, remember?" He pointed at the door in the wall. "You opened that door to Nevada. You can open any door to Toss Bonneteau wherever he happens to be."

"Shiso slept in an abandoned dwelling in Nevada. "She's my sister."

"If I tell you one piece of information, will you take me?"

"It depends on what it is."

"You are linked to the others by your genetic code. Some of the changes unite you in ways that are far closer than your link to your twin."

"How close."

"You are all designed to integrate into one system. Unfortunately, the normal process of developing a new crew member is incomplete."

"You said we are a system."

"English is not my first tongue. I misspoke."

She didn't believe him, but he spoke with finality about his statements. "What are these links?"

"Technically, you can see your companions if their links are complete."

Her stomach clenched, and a chill shivered across her skin. God, but she felt afraid. "How do I do it?"

"Stark showed you a photograph."

"So?"

"Recall that image. Concentrate on it. When it is solid, step through your door."

Yume closed her eyes. She saw him, his gray hair, dark face smiling. Eyes closed, she reached, found the door, and opened it.

Toss Bonneteau sprawled on a concrete floor, eyes closed. She knelt beside him. "Is he dead?"

Stranger frowned. "Drugged, I think."

She glanced back at him. "Are you sure?"

"I cannot communicate with him. He is incomplete. However, he is breathing, and I see a dart in his neck, which is unusual for human physiology."

The door opened. John Stark entered, dressed in a dark suit, a briefcase in his hand.

"Excellent, Ms. Regan."

He tossed the briefcase. She snatched it out of the air, sat it on the desk, and popped it open.

"It is all there."

"Pardon me if I count."

Someone took hold of Yume's wrist. She opened her eyes and looked up into the face of the nurse. "What happened?"

"Were you dreaming of sex with some handsome young man?"

"What? No!"

"A young woman then?"

"No."

"It would have been okay. I like girls myself. Hope to get married someday."

"I wasn't dreaming."

"Telling the truth, then, very good. Mr. Stark will be pleased."

"Where is Mr. Stark?"

"Gone."

"Where?"

"I've brought breakfast. Do you want to eat it in bed or should I pull a table out of the wall?"

****

Aranea glanced right and left at Main Street and crossed with the light. Never break the law. Stark, or his flunkies, hunted her. They owned the police, so the police hunted her, too.

She refused to think about why. The freakish insane events in the hospital made no sense. Every time she mulled over the escape, her mind threatened to shut down.

What happened? What did she do? How did she do it? She leaned against a window. "Stop it. Just stop it." She said to no one.

A woman leading two toddler girls in pink mermaid dresses frowned at her.

Laptop computers placed in the shop's windows displayed her image. No wonder the woman stared at her. Aranea wore a man's clothes, and a hoodie pulled low to cover her dirty face.

She wrinkled her nose. "I probably smell."

Every screen in the window changed. A comic book image of a woman in a black, skintight costume stood with her arms crossed, shaking her head.

Words scrolled up the screen.

"Darknet Oviraptorus, here."

"Move on!"

"Move on!"

"You are not safe!"

Aranea slipped her hands into her pockets and sauntered up the street. She shivered. What was that about? It made no sense as an advertisement for laptops. Had someone warned her? No one could know she would be in Bookings, South Dakota. Professor Madeline Moore had been her father's special friend for all those years when Mother refused to either divorce him or live with him.

She followed the sidewalk along the edge of the campus. A few students walked through the college green, but the lack of light, poor air quality, and the unseasonably cool weather kept them inside.

Professor Moore ran every morning at the same time. After her father's death in Russia, Aranea had visited the woman she knew as Mama Madeline. She could not allow the news of his death to travel by rumor. They ran, drank Ouzo, and laughed through the grief.

On a corner shadowed by tall trees and neat, trimmed bushes, she concealed herself in the shadows behind a bench and waited. When a slow rain washed the soot from the sky and left streaks across her face, she remained. Exactly on time, Madeline Moore stopped at the corner, jogging in place while she checked her pulse and waited for the light.

"Mama Madeline," Aranea whispered from the shadows.

Professor Moore glanced into the shade of the trees. Her eyes widened. She trotted to the edge of the sidewalk, dropped to one knee and pretended to retie her shoe. "You look terrible."

"I'm sorry to see you like this, but I need help."

"Is it about the explosion at the LUX?"

Aranea's mind raced. What did she know? Who told her? "I think so. How do you know?"

"Two FBI agents and a woman from FutureTense came by my office yesterday."

"What did the FBI want?"

"Other than flashing ID and badges, nothing. I think they were there for show. The woman from FutureTense, Margrethe Thorn, asked all the questions."

"What did she want?"

"I need to move. Meet me in the garden shed at the back of my property. It should be safe to talk there."

Madeline stood, arched her back in a long stretch, and ran across the street against the light.

Madeline's garden shed smelled of loam, dried herbs, and fertilizer. Clay pots, a tray of seeds, and an older desktop computer sat on one of her garden benches. Shelves along the walls held more pots, bags of soil and the miscellany of a gardener. A row of clay life masks of Madeline's former favorite students hung in a row on the back wall. After the bizarre way the laptops in the store window reacted, she stayed out of range of its camera until she tossed an old rag over the screen.

Through a window overgrown with grape ivy, she watched Madeline step from her door with a covered basket and a bottle of Ouzo Tyrnavou. Her friend followed the twisted garden path, stopping twice to pluck brown leaves from one of the plans and tossed them aside.

Inside the shed, with the door shut and the window shuttered, they hugged and kissed each other on the cheek. Madeline sat on the stool and patted a chair. "Sit a while."

Aranea sat on the edge of the seat. Madeline removed the cover from the basket. Under a block of cheese and a loaf of artisan bread, she had packed cans of food and two glasses. She twisted the lid off the Ouzo and poured.

The licorice scent drowned the garden odors of fertilizer and dirt. Madeline lifted her glass and swirled the liquor in the bottom. "What happened at the LUX?"

The liquor and licorice burn warmed Aranea's throat. "We detected dark matter."

"Dark matter doesn't interact well enough with matter to explode, dear."

"I can't tell you more than that. I barely survived."

"And you were the only survivor?"

A tear slid down her cheek. She wiped it away with the back of her hand and nodded.

"I'm sorry about Ham."

Aranea did not want to talk about Ham, not after what Stark said. That he could have been lying all that time, it messed her up.

"What do you know about FutureTense?"

"They fund a great deal of research. I have a grant from them for my work."

She looked up. If Stark told the truth, Ham had betrayed her. Why couldn't Madeline? She did not want to believe that. Madeline Moore first came home with Aranea's father just after her fifth birthday. She had been closer to Madeline than her own mother.

"What kind of work."

"Until Ms. Thorn came with the FBI, I thought it was good work. They fund research into technologies to make life better; energy, food, medicines, critical technologies."

"They must make a lot of money."

"They are behind some important discoveries. They put all those discoveries into the public domain. They don't make money off any of it."

Aranea tore off a chunk of bread and chased it with ouzo. "What did they say about me?"

Madeline cut off a chunk of cheese and placed it between two slices of bread. "That you survived, and that something may have happened to you because of the explosion."

"They said I was injured?"

She shook her head. "They hinted that you had a nervous breakdown."

Aranea chewed her lip. How much should she tell? She did not want to cause Madeline trouble. Coming here endangered her enough, but Aranea owed her something. "They tried to kill me in the hospital. Not sure how I managed to escape." That statement had been the truth. How much more could she say, should she say. Pouring out everything that had happened since the Lux would make her sound mad as a hatter.

Tires squealed in the front of the house. Madeline walked to the window and looked out. "I don't know what that is."

"I have to go."

"Hold on." Madeline pulled a bulky envelope out of her pocket and handed to Aranea. "Three thousand dollars."

"I can't take this."

"It's emergency money. I've always kept it in the house. Blame my Grandmother. After World War II, she taught us all to be ready to run at any time."

"Thanks."

Madeline looked out the window. Over her shoulder, Aranea saw two men wearing black windbreakers blazoned with FBI. A tall woman walked with them.

"Oh, God. It's too late," Madeline said.

Aranea took the basket and backed against the wall. How had she escaped before? Was it necessary for the LUX to explode or that someone attempt to kill her?

In those cases, she reacted to a stimulus. Men ran through the yard. They would hurt her, Madeline, or both.

Madeline looked back. Her mouth dropped open, and she said a short, blunt word. The men outside would see her as they had in the room. She walked through the masks on the back wall.

CHAPTER FIVE

Friends

Aranea passed through a thick hedge of foxglove. She cut through leaves, branches, and trunks, but not as a ghost. The insides of limbs touched one side of the sphere and begin again at the other as if she warped space around herself. She pushed her face through branches into the alley, saw a black van and a police car, and pulled back.

She should go, but that would leave Madeline in their hands. They had no way to stop her. Hunger gnawed at Aranea, so she sipped at the bottle of Ouzo, enjoying the licorice flavor and alcohol burn. Alcohol moved right to the blood, and would work as fuel, she hoped. Would it make her drunk? It didn't matter. If she could not see in without being seen then she must be invisible, or the next best thing.

The answer popped out of that place where silly answers hide, the preposterous little voice inside that pointed out ridiculous ideas.

That row of masks on the back wall would serve as camouflage. Aranea leaned close to the wall and pushed her face through until her eyes cut through the wooden surface. Mama Madeline sat on the chair beside the computer, hands cuffed behind her back. Stark wasn't there, but what could she expect. He had five of them to chase. Unless he had shared that event and become a man who could make copies of himself, he could not be in all places at once.

Two men wore bulletproof vests, arms crossed, FBI blazoned across their chests. They reminded her of mastiff's straining at the leash. One woman accompanied by two men in gray suits surrounded Madeline, who glared up at them. Madeline said something, and one of Starks man lifted a hand to slap her. The FBI agent grabbed his wrist.

The two groups turned on each other, like packs of dogs bickering over a pissing post. After a tense moment, the FBI agents stalked out. Aranea's eyes widened, and her pulse raced. She whispered aloud. "What just happened here? Huge global shadowy multinational entity one, bloated national government bureaucracy zero?"

The woman Aranea tagged as the leader pulled out a cell phone. After a brief conversation, the three of them took Madeline by the arms and led her out through the door.

What now? She could walk through walls. Physical objects did not interact with her, but she could not affect them. Madeline remained under the control of three men to be consigned to heaven knows what fate. She moved into the room and checked the window. Madeline, an unwilling package, hung between them, a passive fight doomed to failure, but useful because it let them know she did not surrender.

Aranea took another long swallow of ouzo. She walked through the front wall, remaining inside the hedge walls and high bushes. Out on the street, they pushed Madeline into the back seat of a car. Six police cruisers sat out front, engines running, lights flashing. Policemen stood in small groups, talking and making angry glances at the three men from FutureTense.

Aranea took a deep breath. The air felt thick and brought only slight relief. Like walls, trees, and earth she cut through the atmosphere. Soon, like a child caught in an old refrigerator, she would run out of the air. They would take Madeline away, and there was nothing she could do.

The woman spoke with the officer in charge while the other two waited in the car, one in the driver's seat and the other in the back with Madeline.

Another mad idea popped. Aranea willed herself to sink. She could pass beneath the surface of the earth, but there would be no light underground. She used Madeline's gardens to hide, keeping her eyes just above the soil. A meter separated the yard from the back tire of the car. When no one appeared to be looking, she moved through the earth and stopped beneath the back of the vehicle.

The air in the sphere felt thick and unrelenting. Aranea floated up into the trunk and positioned herself so as not to be inside anything.

The air felt a little better inside the trunk, and sound returned. The engine idled. The car shifted when the leader entered. The man in the back asked, "What are our orders, Ms. Thorn?"

"We take her with us. They will hold her at the Reykjavik office."

A different voice said, "Why not leave her with the police?"

"No crime, no probable cause, and, like the FBI, they don't like corporate civilians stepping on their toes."

From the back seat, Mama Madeline spoke, "It's starting to snow."

"You have anything else you want to say about Aranea Gekas, Ms. Moore?"

"When this is over, I intend to sue FutureTense and your crew of kidnappers for everything you have."

"We mean no harm, Ms. Moore. We are following orders."

"That was what the brown shirts said when they sent by Grandparents to Bergen-Belsen."

No one answered.

Aranea took a long swallow from the bottle of ouzo. No buzz, no pleasant relaxation brought by semi-intoxication. She knew that something had changed in her metabolism. An inability to get drunk was not a positive in her mind.

The car moved away from the curve. She adjusted her position to a more comfortable spot and pulled the cheese from the basket. With nothing better to do, she might as well eat. Unless someone opened the trunk and invited her out, she would have to escape her new-fashioned way.

****

John Stark followed the gurney holding Toss Bonneteau onto his Lear jet and waited while the medical staff locked it in place in a small room at the back of the plane. The anesthesiologist adjusted the intravenous saline drip while the nurse and a medical technician checked their connection between heart monitors and other medical devices and their tablets.

Stark tapped the lead physician on the shoulder. "Doctor Becker, will he remain unconscious through the flight?"

Becker frowned at the display on his tablet. "I know my job, Mr. Stark." He checked the electrodes connected to the scalp. "Nurse, the alpha and theta lines are dead."

Stark stood nose to nose with Doctor Becker. "I don't question your expertise, only the drugs."

Doctor Becker glared. "Get out of our way."

"I'm in charge, here, Doctor."

The doctor sat the tablet on Toss' chest. Readouts displayed temperature, heart rate, respiration, blood pressure, and a full spectrum of brain waves. "You oversee the overall operation. This patient belongs to me. Endanger my patient, and I will sedate you."

"If I think it is necessary, I will have your patient shot."

Becker picked up a syringe and a bottle from the tray on a table next to the gurney. "Until you make that decision, he is in my care. Unless you want to sleep on the floor beside him, back off."

Stark returned to the middle section of the jet.

Thomas Manquoba stood by the bar, a bottle of water in his hands.

Victor Wu sat in a seat, headphones around her neck. "You really get into rattling Becker's cage?"

Manquoba smiled at the question.

Stark sat in the seat in front of Wu and swiveled to face him. "It's one of the perks of the job."

Wu leaned forward, and a smile played across his face. "He really would have sedated you."

"I don't work with yes men. If that's what he needed to do to get his job done, the trip to Reykjavik would be quicker for me."

Stark glanced back at Manquoba. "What's the status of Shiso de Guzman."

"We accessed every traffic camera, ATM Machines, and store surveillance camera in Mesquite. She is hidden somewhere on the south side of town, and we've focused our search on empty houses and abandoned properties. That is how we caught Bonneteau at the air terminal. She's a teenage girl without a car or the stolen motorcycle. We just have to wait for her to make a mistake."

Stark checked the tablet on the stand next to his chair. The most recent photograph sent by the San Diego surveillance team smiled up from the surface. "We don't know what she can do. Do not underestimate her."

Wu nodded. "Any information on Gekas?"

"Margrethe is scouring in South Dakota. Gekas has a close family friend teaching at South Dakota State. Take your team there and back her up."

"Sure thing boss." Wu slipped out of his seat and left.

Manquoba finished his water and dropped the empty into a trashcan. "Shiso de Guzman is a teenage girl without her protector or her sister."

"I wouldn't be sure of that." Stark tapped the screen of her tablet. Images of medical charts and brain scans took the place of photographs. "According to this report, Yume de Guzman experiences trances. Her Alpha waves prove she isn't sleeping. Her mind is too active."

Manquoba walked behind and glanced over Stark's shoulder. "What do you think that means."

Stark shrugged. "I don't know. Bonneteau walks in and out of places without being seen. Gekas walks through walls, and nothing can touch her. These girls do something. She escaped the best men and women I have, which makes them among the best in the world at what they do."

Manquoba frowned. "What about Petrenko? What does he do?"

"He is the most efficient killer I have ever seen."

Manquoba dropped into the chair and leaned back. "Why are we chasing these people? Don't get me wrong, I will do my job and catch her, but what good are we doing? If we must hunt down strangers and shoot them, other mercenary groups pay as well. I don't like working in the dark."

Stark started to answer, but Manquoba held up a hand and singled him to wait. "Don't tell me that it's all compartmentalized. This is like nothing we've seen. We need to know."

"Five years ago, in the Russian Event, an alien ship crashed. Five people out of thousands survived. Something happened in that event. It changed them. An asteroid hit eight days ago, but worse. The northern hemisphere is wrapped in ash, and the temperatures are dropping."

Manquoba nodded. "I listen to the news; starvation, riots, death are a few months away if you believe what they say."

"Believe it."

"According to whom?"

"The best minds working for FutureTense. Other teams are seeking food supplies and a means of shipping it where it is needed, but there will not be enough, even if the UN stops debating and does something."

"So, what does the world get from these people? They are not going to feed us."

"The technology involved could save millions."

Manquoba stood and stretched. "How did you become a crusader, John? We served together in the Marines. I know you didn't learn in the Corps."

Stark glanced up into Manquoba's face. He knew his team leaders well, had served with all of them. He would die for them without a second thought and felt sure they would return the favor. "Saving the world is a job nobody else can do."

Manquoba shook his head. "You really believe that?"

"Everybody has to believe something, even you?"

"Oh, I do."

"Long as I've known you, you never showed belief in anything."

"I believe in you, John."

"I hope it's enough."

****

Shiso walked in the shadows along the front of buildings, eyes scanning for police cars, anonymous black vans, and gray-suited men with emotionless faces and busy eyes. A police cruiser turned a corner three blocks ahead. She stepped into a convenience store and walked to the back where coolers full of soda and energy drinks hummed in the cool air.

Conscious that she appeared suspicious if she didn't buy anything, she grabbed the cheapest bottle of water and paid the cashier, taking her time to count out exact change while the cop cruised on by.

Need to get off the public streets.

On a whim, she sent the mental call. "Yume. You there?"

She touched her sister's mind full of vague worries and quick-fire images about an annoying nurse named Sandra and a machine strapped to her head. Yume did not vocalize a thought, but her mind remained focused and clear. Whatever they did, at least, no one drugged her.

Back out on the street, she sipped at the water and walked north toward the airport. She told the inner voice that screamed at her for walking in the wrong direction to fuck off.

At the first corner, she walked west, to get away from the main street, and cut back north to the next. Her path meandered through a church parking lot where three buses idled. Teenagers and adults gathered around tables and barbecues. Some of the kids ate and gossiped to pass the time. Others formed a circle and sang '*Rock of Ages*' a little off key.

Was it Sunday? She didn't think so but could not say for sure. Without a phone, and on the run, time slipped away until one day bled into the next. She walked around the edge of the crowd and caught bits of conversation about a youth missionary outreach in Denver, Colorado.

A boy her age, taller than most of the other kids took a swallow of soda, caught her eye, smiled, and nodded. Shiso returned the smile, unable to resist until she felt a twinge in Yume's distant mind. High school flirtations and quick kisses behind the bleachers would have to wait. Shiso brushed the hair out of her eyes and walked on by.

A block and a half later, three highway patrol cars screamed by, lights flashing, sirens wailing. Shiso looked away from the street and pretended to check the address on a house. As the sounds receded, she heard others from all directions, converging on the airport.

Her stomach hurt. She fought the urge to run. Something had happened to Toss. Why had he gone off on his own? She should have forced him to take her. Shiso saved him from capture in San Diego. What was he thinking?

Of course, she knew. Toss Bonneteau, being a man of a certain age, reminded her of her Tio. Tio had thought women needed protection. Had Tio told Yume and Shiso about FutureTense, they would have been prepared. If they had remained in the boat, he might even be alive. Both men seemed to think it better to leave the women locked up at home and take the risk and the fun for himself. Now, of course, she was alone, or almost.

Shiso was never alone. She had no one physically she could rely on, but she had something better, her superpower. Yume stood beside her, even if her feet touched the earth on the other side of the planet. Yume's frustration and fear bled over into Shiso's mind like an annoying song heard through the window of a car.

Some woman named Sandra bothered her, even frightened her. Her mother taught her never to let fears fester. Tell someone about them. If nothing could be done, speaking a fear aloud had a way of taking away some of that fear's power. No matter what. Sandra--whoever Sandra might be, or did--they needed to talk.

Mi Cocina, a small Mexican Restaurant, sat on a corner. She caught the scent of pork and chilies cooking on a grill. Her stomach growled. That last meal of Twinkies and a Diet Coke late the night before felt as distant as Mars. Inside the restaurant, she could hide from the police and Stark's men.

Shiso picked up her pace, walked fast as if she had places to go. As much as she wanted to sit in the cool interior and talk with her sister, she did not run. Running made her a source of speculation, even suspicion, or perhaps, it was too warm to run. She entered the restaurant, took a table in the back, and sat in the corner of a booth where she could see the door. The waitress placed a basket of tortilla chips and a bowl of salsa on the table.

Shiso flashed a smile. "Gracias. Carne Asada and a diet coke."

"Si, Senorita," The waitress wrote her order in her book and walked back to the front.

Shiso rested her head in the corner and called mentally. "Yume?"

Yume's annoyance and fear stung.

"Answer me, damn it. You don't have to speak."

"Not now, Shiso."

Three lousy words but the sense of fear peaked as Yume sent them. What were they doing? How would they know about the telepathy? "Yume, I need you."

****

Yume lay on the floor, feet propped up in a corner. A metal helmet attached to a coiled strand of twisted wires ran from her head to a computer on a table. The electrodes irritated her bald scalp irritated her skin.

Sandra walked through the door. "Get up off the floor, child, and stop fussing with the helmet. We attached the sensors with surgical glue. They won't come free unless you rip the skin off."

Yume glared at the woman. "You shaved my head."

"Well, now, you didn't give us a choice."

"Yume? Are you there?" Shiso's thought jangled and whispered inside her skull.

She ignored her sister, afraid that the electrodes might pick up some mental reaction and record it on the computer. "You could have asked?"

136

Sandra sat on a chair, a ball of yarn in her lap. "Would you have said yes?"

Yume arched her back. "No."

"I think we are having a breakthrough. You're honest with us."

Sandra counted threads in the blanket and twisted the needles to continue a line of yellow.

"Are you knitting?"

Sandra smiled, and her eyes even crinkled in a way that convinced Yume she told the truth. "It's for my nephew."

"Prison guards have nephews?"

Sandra sat her needles down and frowned. "I'm a battlefield nurse, not a prison guard."

Shiso's thought call touched her mind again. *"Yume!"*

"Do you think I'm human?"

Nurse Sandra glanced up, her expression shifted to a frown and back to a friendly smile.

Caught you, bitch. You're not just the friendly Auntie-type woman keeping an eye on a teenager out of the goodness of your heart.

"You're a teenager. That's sort of a training period. If you're lucky, you'll grow up to be human."

"Yume. Toss is gone. I have to talk to you now."

Yume stood. "I have to go."

Sandra nodded and continued with her knitting.

She ran into the bathroom and closed the door. The cable attached to her helmet just fit under the edge. She pulled the hospital gown away from her butt, sat on the toilet and waited. The door began to slide open. "A little privacy. You think I'm going to flush myself down the toilet?"

Nurse Sandra chuckled and shut the door. Yume could not tell if it was part of her watching game or if she felt amused, not that it mattered. The electrodes recorded her brain waves. How many ways could they spy on her? The constant observation left her naked and exposed, even when hiding in a bathroom. They must have video cameras recording every breath, too, possibly from behind the mirror or concealed in the wall. She stuck out her tongue in a final act of teenage defiance.

She never considered what happened when she dreamed, and Shiso mind spoke. They were like superpowers, right. But she did not sleep in those dreams. She saw things with some organ other than her eyes. Could they tell that by monitoring her brain waves? So, what happened when Shiso mind spoke?

She slid onto the floor, put her back to the door, and pushed hard with her legs. She did not know the strength of the mechanism that opened the door. Maybe she could hold it for long enough.

"Yume?" Shiso sent. "Stark took Toss."

She felt Shiso's fear bleed across through into her mind with the message. She felt alone, isolated.

I don't know what to do.

Sandra pounded on the door. "Open up, miss. We know you are doing something. We can see it on the monitor."

Yume slipped into the dream state and followed her sister back to a booth in a Mexican restaurant and sat across from her. *I'm locked in a white room, and you're eating salsa and chips in a Mexican restaurant?*

Shiso sat up and looked around. "You're here? Where?"

Across the table. FutureTense monitors my brainwaves. They know I'm doing something.

Something heavy struck the door. Yume felt it begin to slide to the side.

They're coming for me. The door slid open. A hand reached through and grabbed Shiso's shoulder.

"I'll come for you." Shiso sent.

A needle pierced Yume's neck. The world spun, and Shiso's mental voice stretched away. Before she lost consciousness, Stranger appeared on the toilet, his white Panama suit pooled around his ankles. *"It's all right, Yume. Everything is going as planned."*

"What kind of fucked up plan is this?" Her consciousness swirled down into the dark.

****

Shiso sighed. "Fucked up is right."

The waitress wiped scraps from the table and glanced up, forehead wrinkled. "Si, senorita?"

"Oh, nothing. Just talking to myself."

The woman shrugged. "No habla englais, senorita."

"Esta bien."

"Oh." The young woman laughed and returned to the register. A tear slid down Shiso's cheek. She felt so damn isolated, and even the presence of a strange woman she could not speak to made her feel a little less alone.

But, oh, she needed a plan. Toss' plan, whatever it had been, was hell and gone. Now she needed to come up with her own. She'd even take a fucked-up plan if that were all she had. It could not be worse than his. The motorcycle was history. Strange men took Toss away to God knew where, though she guessed that it just might be a white room in a distant land. A terrible urgency tied her stomach in knots as if someone stood behind her and told her to run Northeast. A direction without a destination was pretty damned useless.

The waitress sat a Carne Asada plate with a side of rice, black beans, and a bowl of spicy carrots, jalapenos, and onions on the table. The carrots burned her lips. She chased it with soda and followed with a mouthful of Carne Asada spiced to five thousand on the Scoville Scale.

She laughed. "Oh, what the hell." She could run Northwest in thirty minutes as well as she could now. Directions did not go away. The food hit all the right notes in taste and comfort. Cristian surrendered to the food and put the plan in a mental waiting room. Halfway through the meal, she walked to the front and refilled her diet coke. After the first sip, she wished for a beer. At home, Tio served bottles of Bohemia Obscura, a dark Mexican beer. Tears trailed down her cheek. Tio died; there could be no other explanation.

The waitress walked past the table.

Shiso wiped her face on her napkin. "El Bano?"

The woman pointed at a door in the back. Shiso followed the directions back through the kitchen where a Mexican man prepared chicken, beans, beef, and a dozen other dishes. She found the bathroom beside a back door that opened onto a loading area behind the strip mall.

Relieved, Yume returned to the table but stopped at the kitchen door. Two police officers waited by the register. Had they traced her to the restaurant? Did they know?

They took menus and looked through the options. Yume stepped back into the kitchen. The serving girl breezed by and picked up a tray stacked high with tortas and bowls of beans. Shiso pulled money from her pocket, change from last night. She counted out Twenty-five dollars, laid the money beside a plate of tortas, pointed to the back door, and left.

Outside, she hurried by trash bins of old food that stank of rancid grease and rotted meat scraps, past the back of a laundry, and a Black Dragon Tae Kwan Do dojo where students screamed "Kihap" and kicked the air.

She headed back the way she came, walking not running, though she wanted to run from those policemen in their brown uniforms and bulletproof vests. Running looked suspicious unless she wore running shorts. She put on her last pair of clean jeans that morning. She wondered where the next pair would come from. Except for the change from the money Toss gave her, she had no cash. Oh, she had credit cards, of course. She watched enough TV and knew that if the cards had not been canceled, they would be watched. Buy anything at all with a credit card and someone from FutureTense would appear to pick her up.

So where should she go, back to that empty house? That took her in the wrong direction. Moving in the wrong direction caused a headache relieved only by spinning around and looking Northeast.

She shook her head. What did this? Who did this? What else could she do but follow the compulsion?

Laughter from across the street pattered like a sudden rain. Adults directed children to put away food and fold up tables of food left out for the congregation. A group of teenagers with the church group stood in a circle and sang a different gospel tune, off key. They seriously needed a new choir director or members who could carry a tune.

The buses idled at the curb. Other teens lined up to get on. The normal dysfunction that always plagued such events almost guaranteed no one paid attention to the small details. Everyone involved knew the plan, anyway.

Denver is Northeast.

She felt Yume in the same hazy, disconnected way she had earlier. Because she could not hear the thoughts of anyone else, she assumed it must be her own.

She jaywalked to the other side, cut between two buses and slipped through the door. Kids sat low in the seats, knees propped up, nodded, talked, or gazed at their phones. She eased into a seat at the back of the bus and sat next to a window. As others climbed on board the bus, she leaned her head against the window, closed her eyes, and pretended to sleep.

Someone sat beside her. She felt the light brush of jeans against her legs. The door creaked shut. Gears thumped into a new configuration, and the engine's hum deepened to a diesel thrum. The bus lurched forward, and the whispered conversation of a bus full of teens increased in volume to overtop the engine noise. This crazy fucked-up plan might really work. All she needed was to stay quiet until they reached Denver in a few hours. A piece of cake.

"So what's your name?" A young man asked.

Oh, shit! Shit! Pretend to sleep, everything will be okay.

"Look, I know you're not asleep. I saw you get on the bus."

She opened her eyes. It was the boy she saw earlier. Any other time, an afternoon spent talking with him would have become the plan. Not today. "I'm really tired."

"Really hiding, you mean." His voice carried an edge of amusement.

She sat up. "I like sitting in the back of a bus."

"Uh-huh. So what's your name?"

She took in the details of his body; tall, blue eyes that invited her to dive in. She wanted to tell him, any name you like, and tap phones to exchange data, but her real name would not do. She opened her mouth when she heard her sister's faint thought flicker across her mind. "Help!"

She answered aloud. "Yume?"

But that faint touch of dream vanished.

Oh, shit! Shit! Shit! Why did I say Yume's name?

"Pretty name. So, where's it come from?"

Shiso loved small talk, especially when it involved a hot boy with blue eyes, but not now. "Japanese. My mother named me."

His mouth formed an 'oh.' "Is that where you get your eyes?"

Oh, God. Did he think he could get a hook up with that line?

"No, Japan. Uh, what's your name?"

"David?"

A Bible and a choir book lay in his lap. "After the king?"

"Nope, Davy Jones." My grandmother liked this rock band back in the sixties. He was their lead singer. I get the idea that she had the hots for him." He paused. "Of course, I was never told that."

She rolled her eyes. "I know about the Monkeys." They both laughed, and the mutual laughter left her warm and happy.

He leaned his head closer. "So where do you come from?"

She scratched her forehead. She could not look away from those amazing blue eyes. "Over on the south side." This wasn't really a lie because the empty house they slept in was on the south side of town.

He shook his head. "I was born here. No one cute as you lives anywhere in this town." He winked.

Damn, he knows I lied.

What the hell was she supposed to say when the truth was impossible, and a lie did not work?

He tilted his head to the side, which made his smile all the more maddening. "You're the girl they are looking for. Shiso de Guzman, right?"

Her mouth dropped open. Fear knotted up in her stomach and threatened to push the Carne Asada and spicy carrots out into his lap.

He held up his hands, palms out. "Don't worry. I'm not going to tell anyone."

Her mind tripped over a dozen scenarios, none of them ended well. All he needed to do was to call the driver or one of the chaperones, and she would be arrested and carried off to where ever they took Toss and Yume. He had gorgeous eyes, but she could not even guess at what hid behind them. None of her suppositions led to a happy place.

She glanced at the emergency door in the back of the bus. There would be stop lights ahead. If she could knock him down, she would be out of the back before anyone could do anything. "How do you know?"

"My dad's a cop. He couldn't stop talking about how you disappeared from the casino, last night." David puffed out his cheeks and pushed the long hair off his forehead, which she recognized as his imitation of his absent father. His voice dove deep and filled with gravel. "It was like, man. Now you see um, now you don't. Never seen nothing like that."

She opened her mouth, but nothing came out. What could she say to that? No matter how cute his eyes, telling him she had magic would be met with derision.

"You don't have to worry, Yume." He winked. "I'm good with this. I don't fit in here, anyway."

She gazed into his eyes wanting to believe him. The men who followed her killed her Tio. This wasn't some teenage lark. People had died.

An older woman walked down the aisle and stopped beside them. "I don't recognize you."

David smiled up at her. "She's the daughter of one of my mom's friends, Crisi, from LA, Mrs. Connors. She's staying with us for a month."

Mrs. Connors glanced through the sheets of paper on her clipboard. "You have to have a permission slip, Miss?"

Shiso started to answer, but David jumped in. "My dad signed it last night before he went back to work. I loaded it with my sleeping bag on the truck that left this morning with our instruments and stuff."

The woman's gaze shifted from Shiso to David. "Well, make sure you give it to me when we get to Denver."

Shiso smiled into the woman's face and lied. "I will."

Mrs. Connors walked back to the front of the bus, but stopped and looked back over her shoulder. "Tonight, in Denver, you'll be sleeping with the other young women." She glared at David. "And the doors will be locked."

"No problemo, Mrs. Connors. My dad taught me the rules."

She made her way back toward the front of the bus.

"Thanks, David."

He shrugged, "Glad to help."

She leaned back in the seat, relaxed for the first time in two days. Part of it, she guessed, was the movement of the bus. They drove Northeast, and the headache vanished. A lot of it was David. He was the type of guy her mother warned her about, an aggressive, funny flirt. If they were in San Diego, she would go out with him anytime, long as he understood and respected her boundaries.

On the road, running, the equations were all wrong. This wasn't an action movie where the hero and his girlfriend killed the bad guys and then had sex during the credits. People could get hurt, they had died.

He tossed the bible and choir book onto the shelf above the seat. "So why are you running from the law."

"I don't know." That admission threatened to start tears running. She refused to cry.

"If you don't want to say, just tell me it's none of my fucking business."

She placed her hand over his and then drew it back. "It's not that. I really don't know. Something happened to me five years ago." She couldn't finish. None of this made sense to her and explaining it was impossible. "It's crazy, I know, but I don't know why."

She leaned back in the seat, and they talked about music, apps, school, and kids they knew, a ritualistic type of conversation people used to get to know the edges of other people. After a while, she fell asleep.

Two hours later, she woke. David sat with his phone in his hands, playing a game.

She leaned over to look, and her forehead touched the side of his face. "I miss my phone."

"What happened to it?"

"I threw it away. Toss thought they were using it to trace us."

He glanced at her, and his face wore the same questions he had asked earlier. "You want to use mine for a while?"

"Could I?"

He handed her his phone. It felt like coming home again after traveling for a year. How did people manage without cell phones before their invention?

She eased around the internet, choosing to visit the places where she used to hang out. She did not post to her friends, assuming someone watched.

As she cruised through Instagram, the screen changed. The face of Oviraptorus looked up at her. "There you are, little bird."

"Oh God." Shiso pushed the button to switch it off. It did not work.

"Don't worry, child. I won't let them find you."

David leaned closer and looked at the screen. His breath tickled her ear. "What kind of app is that?"

"Oh, I'm the best kind." Oviraptorus winked at David. "But this is a private conversation, Mr. Blue eyes."

"That's cool." He pulled back but continued to watch.

Shiso chewed on her cheek. "Who are you, really?"

"No time for that. I know the homing beacon in your head is working. It will lead you to Reykjavik."

Shiso's eyes widened. "How am I getting to Iceland?"

Oviraptorus shook her head. "I have resources you would not believe. When you get to Denver, you will receive a package. You will find it at 921 20th Street. The package will deliver you to Iceland."

David leaned close again. "Cool. I've never been to Iceland."

Oviraptorus moved and until her eyes filled the screen. "You don't listen well, young man. This conversation is private. You can flirt with her when I'm finished."

He pulled away.

Shiso suppressed a laugh. "What if the Post Office is closed?"

"The package is not in the post office. It will deliver itself when you get to its location."

A package that delivers itself? Why not, the app told her it would, and that was as normal as thing get. Mental telepathy, dream sharing, and being chased by the minions of a vast multi-national organization is crazy.

"What do I do when I get to Iceland?"

"That is for you, Vasyl, and Aranea to decide." Oviraptorus turned away as if looking back at someone or something behind her. "They are looking for me. I have to run."

The image on the screen returned to Instagram. Shiso handed the phone back to David.

He took it as if she handed him a loaded gun. "Are you a spy?"

"I wish."

"Iceland. Cool. I've never been there."

She glanced sideways. He was cute. "You're not going, David."

"Uh-huh."

She rolled her eyes, faced the window, and pretended to fall asleep.

****

Toss heard a beep, beep, beep and wondered why his heart whistled when it should thump. The darkness faded to a white tunnel like a fisheye lens.

Am I dying? Is this near death?

He remembered trying to slow time around him so he could escape. Had those men in gray decided they had enough of Toss Bonneteau, and so injected a lethal drug that took his life?

None of his deceased old friends, or his dad, appeared to beckon him to the other side. Then again, most of his old friends likely ran on the downside of death, and he had never heard of escapees from hell greeting newcomers. His mother did not wait, and if any one person he ever knew deserved heaven, it would have been his mother. So, as the edge of the tunnel frayed into reality and objects in the room faded into focus, he decided that he wasn't dying, just waking up from whatever drug they gave him.

Straps held his arms and legs in place. Two belts cinched across his chest, and a third wrapped across his forehead, limited his movement to a slight wiggle. Above his chest, he saw a square white window with squiggly lines, scrolling text, flashing lights, and colored bars.

He tried to ask, "Why is there a computer on my chest?" A mishmash of slurred vowels oozed from his lips. Perhaps those vowels splattered the keyboard because the screen changed to show the inside of a gray cube. A woman dressed in skin-tight leather, maybe a superhero from a comic book tumbled through the air and landed.

"You are waking." Her words filled up a balloon beside her face.

"Haven't dreamed of a fine woman like you in years. If I could get myself up off this gurney, I'd be happy to dance."

"They don't know you." She continued as if she did not hear his words, and perhaps she did not. His lips smeared his words. He licked his lips, hoping that would be enough to bring his mouth fully back to life.

"Just what do you want?" Words came easier. He almost understood what he said.

"They are bringing you to me. They will drug you again, but they do not anticipate the depth of the changes."

He nodded rather than try to use his mouth.

"Use your ability. Use your gift. Come to me."

"Anytime."

"They are coming." Her image vanished. The screen returned to a display of his heart rate, respiration, blood pressure, and other data.

He heard heavy foots steps on the carpet. A man's strong, square face leaned into his view. "Mr. Bonneteau, I have so wanted to speak with you."

"Well, if you'll take off the straps, we can sit up front, drink a little Champagne and play a hand or two of Monte."

"Sorry, I can't offer you that hospitality. Would you care to explain how you appeared and disappeared in a restaurant, almost like magic?"

"I've always been known for fast hands and easy moves, but I have never disappeared. The only magic is in the eye of the mark."

The man pulled away and moved to the foot of the bed so that Toss could see him. "I believe you, but that doesn't tell me what happened in the restaurant."

"Can't help you with that. Don't really know what happened myself." And that was true so far as Toss knew. They changed in Russia. He didn't know why, but he wondered about that woman who appeared on the computer. Who was she? What was she?

"As much as I enjoy our conversation, you are going back to sleep now."

"Been sleeping for a while. Don't know if there is any more rest in me."

A doctor stepped into his line of sight but never looked into Toss' eyes. "I will not administer another sedative."

"Put him to sleep, doctor."

"Mr. Stark, I've exceeded the recommended dose. It could kill him."

Toss smiled. "I'm right here. You don't have to talk around me."

The man called Stark frowned. "I'll take that risk, doctor."

"It's on your head."

Toss' vision narrowed to a white tunnel without a single person waiting to lead him into heaven. The light went out.

****

Vasyl recognized the camp by the smell of shit and barbecue. Oh, there were other odors, sweat, urine, and that particular blend of misery and disease that clung to the old and indigent.

Ivanna clung to his hand at the first whiff of the camp. Her eyes grew wide, and her constant child's chatter died to silence. The child's silence grated, though five minutes before he swore silently at Clockbrain because he could not get a second's peace. In spite of what his father used to say, Vasyl believed with all his heart that children should be noisy.

He squeezed her hand. "It's all right."

She shook her head and molded to his side. They joined the line of refugees at the gate, waiting their chance to be eyed by the bored Ukrainian soldiers and recorded by harried aid workers.

She looked up at his face. "We don't have to stay."

He picked her up and sat her on his shoulders. A woman with dead eyes, holding a baby in one arm, glanced back.

"Why would you say that? They have food here. Your family might be here."

She pointed her chin at the soldiers. "What about the guards."

Vasyl never looked up. "What about them?"

"You don't like the guards. You're afraid of them."

Clockbrain whispered. *She is smart.*

He chewed at the corner of his cheek. He felt a needle of fear around the soldiers, though not for himself. In a fight, no one would care if a small girl took a bullet to the brain. "You know this how?"

"Duh. Every time a Russian patrol drove by you hid in the crowd."

"Clever girl." Clockbrain's quip echoed through Vasyl's mind. *"Be more careful. If a child noticed, you are lost with adults."*

Vasyl nodded to one of the soldiers. "These are Ukrainian soldiers. Trust me, they won't help the Russians."

"Because of the war." She hugged him a bit tighter.

"Yes. Why?"

"My brother was killed by Ukrainian soldiers."

"That complicates things. Get rid of her."

Vasyl whispered "Shithead."

"Clockbrain's talking to you again, isn't he?"

He nodded. The soldiers walked along the line. A show of force to keep starving and tired people in line. Ivanna hugged is head and buried her face in his hair and refused to look at them.

Two women dressed in stained and worn Red Cross uniforms sat at a table by the gate. "Name." One asked.

Clockbrain whispered, *"Lie to them."*

I'm not stupid.

"Well, that remains to be seen."

FutureTense and the Russian army hunted Vasyl Peternko. He suspected they would place the blame of the deaths of their soldiers on him. They would report his name, and enough men would come for him that even a monster could not fight his way free. His mind spun through memory for a convincing name and latched on a childhood friend long deceased. "Borys Alexandro."

The woman never looked up. "And your daughter's name?"

Vasyl started to answer. He realized that he did not know her last name. Out on the road, he avoided using names, and so had refused to ask. Her head popped up for the first time since the soldiers walked by. "Ivanna."

The aid worker glanced up at the sound of the child's voice and smiled. "Where do you come from, Ivanna Alexandro?"

"She's not my daughter."

The worker frowned. "But you are related."

Ivanna's body tensed, and she squeezed his head tighter.

"I found her on the road. No family. It's dangerous out there. I wanted to make sure she would be safe, so I brought her to you."

"Excellent, Vasyl. You even sound convincing. There's hope for you in this role, yet."

"We are short of resources." The woman looked at her paperwork. If you provide her family's name, I will attach a note to the form that you are caring for her, should anyone look for her."

"They are all dead," Ivanna mumbled into the back of his head.

The woman clenched her jaw. "We need her surname.

Ivanna held him tighter. Hard to believe that a girl her size could cling with such strength. "Petrenko."

"You idiot." Clockbrain sent.

I didn't tell her. He swept her off his shoulder stood her on the table, facing him. He leaned close, placed his hands on her cheek, and whispered. "Where did you hear that name?"

She nuzzled his ear as if kissing him. "You talk with a rat in your sleep. How many people live in your head?"

Vasyl pulled her close in a quick, fatherly embrace. "That is a name that can get us both shot."

She placed her hands over her mouth. "I just want to stay with you."

"I do not want you to die, Ivanna. I can't protect you from the men who hunt me."

She looked sideways into face the aid worker. "Ivanna Stanislavovna Shakmakova. My family died when a rock hit our house. I was in the yard, feeding my dog."

"I'm so sorry." The aid worker said.

Vasyl placed his hand on her shoulder. Ivanna jerked away.

The women led her away.

CHAPTER SIX

No Help

The refugee camp sprawled like an unruly shantytown. A single crossroad marked out sectors. Elsewhere, Red Cross tents, army tents, and hunting tents vied with hovels made from crates, pallets, cardboard boxes, or blankets hung over wires. Tracks, little more than meandering, muddy paths, wound through the neighborhoods of temporary structures.

Everywhere, people shambled through the motions, lined up for rations of food and water, while children played in the mud, and rude, armed men in no uniform stood guard on their neighborhoods and eyed others.

Vasyl took it all in without comment. He felt no surprise when Clockbrain commented on it. *"Biological civilizations always fail. It is their nature. We need to escape from here before we fail with it."*

Vasyl ignored Clockbrain. He didn't give a damn about civilization. The memory of those last moments with Ivanna hurt. Leaving the little girl to the impersonal mercies of a refugee organization had been necessary. Sooner or later there would be violence, and he would kill to survive. He could imagine no worse fate than to open his eyes and discover that he had murdered the girl out of expediency so that he could wear her face. Other than his rat, Schurr, and Clockbrain's infestation of his brain, she had been his first relationship in five years. With the madness gone, he realized how lonely he felt, how isolated.

At a fork in the path that twisted through the camp, Vasyl turned left. One route through misery seemed no worse than another. A line of women stood in front of a circle of tents, Quonset huts, and temporary structures set within a hollow bordered by stacked crates and pallets. Half a dozen wary men with automatic weapons watched from strategic points atop the crates or along the street.

A woman about his age, with brown hair and haunted dark-circled eyes, sauntered up and laid a hand on his shoulder. "You look tired and lonely."

"Just looking for a way out."

She nodded, smiled, and leaned close. "Well, it's the train or the fence." Her lips shimmered candy-apple red.

He stepped away. "I could walk out of the gate."

She put her arms through his and forced him to stop or pull her along. "You haven't heard? The Russian's won't put up with that."

"Listen to the woman." Clockbrain's urgency surprised him.

Vasyl stopped and glanced around. The armed men focused their attention on him. "I saw no Russians."

"You won't see them until they have you in cuffs or put a bullet through your head. The word is that they are looking for a Russian deserter, a blond like you."

"Then I guess I'll take the train. I've heard it travels all the way to Kaliningrad."

She nodded and smiled as if they engaged in small talk over strong Russian Tea. "It does if you can get past the Russians."

"Ask her what she wants."

Shut up. He followed it with a second of regret. He wanted nothing to do with that voice in his head. He had the irrational idea that if he just ignored it, it would go away. His rational mind, which was all he had now that a terrible sanity had taken him, told him that if Clockbrain survived through a meteor impact, he would remain until death took him. "So, do you have a solution for my Russian problem?"

"I have contacts that can help, but I have my own masters who insist I perform certain remunerative tasks. Once I perform my job, I can help you meet a man who knows other ways out of the camp."

"What do you offer?"

She leaned close as if to whisper in his ear and groped between his legs. Vasyl jumped as if she bit him.

"My, it must have been a long time since you were entertained by a woman."

He stepped away, his mouth dry. "I've neither Roubles nor Hryvnia. Sorry."

She moved against him and laid a hand on his arm. "You have food." She tapped on the bag hung over his shoulder. "Money is worthless within these walls. It's getting colder. Governments are falling like snowflakes in winter. A man with food is king while it lasts."

He removed her hand. "I have to leave."

"You'll be back."

A diesel engine idled in the distance, its low rumble felt through his feet.

"Just ask for Sveta. I'm always hungry."

"If she's right about the Russians, this will not work."

Mud splashed beneath Vasyl's feet. *Go away.* He was tired of the voice in his head. He would follow that arrow in his mind to Aranea because he wanted to see her, to apologize for the madness.

He stopped in the shadow of an official UNHSC refugee tent. Orange, green, and blue cargo containers laid end to end formed an impassable wall around the railroad siding and controlled access to the tracks. Refugees lined up at the gate under the eye of nine Russian soldiers in full combat gear. At least one other soldier armed with a rifle lay atop the cargo container. A light tank sat ten meters beyond the gate, weapons aimed at the refugees.

Clockbrain intruded. *"The soldier on the roof is a sniper."*

Vasyl wanted a moment's peace. "And the tank is a teapot?"

"A teapot, I assume, is a device used to brew a drinkable beverage."

"Are you deaf to sarcasm, today?"

"I recognize your humor because I read the emotions and other mental content accompanying the statement. I apologize. Another task distracts."

"What other task could you have inside my head?"

A Lieutenant on the gate called one of the refugees, a blond man thirty years old. He compared the man's face to a photograph.

"They are looking for you." The abrupt change of focus pulled his attention back to the refugees.

The officer summoned two soldiers, who placed themselves behind and to either side of the blond. Vasyl wished he stood in line close enough to hear what they said. The refugee shook his head and walked back to the main camp. Soldiers took him by each arm. He pulled loose from one man and swung at the other.

A single gunshot popped above the noise of the idling diesel and a thousand grumbled conversations. A spray of blood blew out from the side of the man's head. He collapsed into the mud.

"Go back to the camp, Vasyl."

Vasyl stuck his hands in his pockets and eased into the crowd of refugees moving through the muddy paths.

"I'm trapped."

****

Yume floated faced down above herself. She lay on her back in a dense white fog, eyes shut, with leather straps across her forehead, shoulders, under her breasts, across her abdomen, thighs, knees, and ankles.

What do they think I am?

The answer came out of some place so deep in her mind that she never suspected it might hide there.

An alien, of course.

All the old images of terrible aliens that ripped through humans like living knives reran through her mental television.

Okay, Yume, this is a dream state. How come the drugs aren't working?

A 12-inch-tall Stranger climbed hand over hand up the bedpost and ran the length of her body until he stood on the Jugular Notch at the base of her throat. He opened his tiny mouth and screamed, "Yume!" Not a sound escaped his mouth. Cartoon storyboards filled images in front of her. The words fitting inside a tiny white word balloon.

Oh, this is freaky.

160

Stranger pulled out great chunks of his hair and threw them down. The words *"Yume. You have evolved. Fight this"* filled another balloon.

I am silly.

Perhaps Stranger couldn't hear her because his words appeared in a white bubble behind his head with little circles, like thoughts in a comic book.

He raised his hand above his head in an animated stance of a stern father about to rebuke a recalcitrant child.

Her mother's first rule, however, stated that no man ever laid a hand on her, or any woman, for any reason. She grabbed him by the back of his suit and held him at arm's length.

"Hit me, and I will crush you like a spider on a window." Her words hovered in a bubble in front of his face.

Stranger twisted, squirmed, bent his head back and looked up. *"Turn me around. I can't see you."*

"Of course not. I'm having an out-of-body experience."

He continued to squirm. *"You constructed this reality."*

She wanted to laugh at the comical sight. *"This is hard to get used to."*

She sat in a chair beside the bed where her sleeping body lay attached to various medical devices, a chilling image of television shows where anti-social doctors fought against a patient's strange diseases came to mind.

Stranger sat on the other side of the bed, a cup of tea in his hand.

"What is this?" He raised his cup for emphasis.

"Tea, you drink it. It calms the nerves."

"There's no time for tea, and I have no nerves in a human sense."

"You said I evolved."

Stranger picked up the cup and sipped. *"This is good."*

"Thank you. Now, about my evolution."

"The existing design specifications require that your bodies overcome toxins and other drugs. I cannot wait any longer for you to work to specifications. Time grows short."

Yume touched her sleeping face, tracing the shape of her eyebrow, in a mother's caress.

"What am I becoming?"

Stranger set his tea down and crossed his arms. *"Whatever you want to be?"*

She glanced at him. *"When did you become a greeting card?"*

His eyes shifted away from hers. *"When you ask questions that I choose not to answer. We need to help each other."*

She picked up her cup of tea. Even imaginary tea could be calming if she wanted it to be. *"Every time you say that I end up doing all the helping."*

He rolled his eyes. *"Can you make me larger?"*

He grew two feet, just about the height of a six-year-old.

"Better?"

He tapped his foot. *"You're difficult."*

Yume sipped her cup of tea and tasted Earl Gray, hot, Tio's favorite. *"You have no idea."*

"Please, make me look like I am supposed to look."

"How can I when I don't know what that is."

"Tall. White suit, Panama hat. Ring any bells?"

She leaned forward. *"Are you one of the Grays that crashed at Roswell?"*

His head grew, his body thinned, and his skin change to a uniform shade of gray with huge black eyes. *"No aliens crashed in or near Roswell, New Mexico."*

"And you would know that?"

He blinked. *"I will not dignify that with an answer."*

Yume frowned and took another sip of tea. It did not help her case of nerves. She doubted enough tea existed in the world to do that. *"Perhaps you are one of the lizard people."*

The seat of his pants parted with the sound of a fart and a long green tail uncoiled onto the floor. Green lizard's scales grew across his skin. *"You're having fun with me now."*

She sat her cup of tea onto a mushroom table that grew out of the floor and counted on her fingers. *"I'm frightened. I lost my parents. My Tio was murdered. My sister is running from the police and corporate mafia. Worse, I'm becoming a monster. And you pop into my dreams and tell me I'm evolving, but what's happening is that each day I become less myself."*

Stranger bit his lip and plopped down on the floor. *"I am sorry."* He buried his face in his hands. *"I did not mean to hurt anyone. I have lost my home and a part of myself. What can I do except try to put things back together to the best of my programming?"*

"What did you lose?"

He looked at her, shook his head, and once more buried his face in his hands. *"We are a Liveship."*

Her brow wrinkled, puzzled at the unfamiliar word. *"What's that? Do you mean you are an Artificial Intelligence commanding a space ship?"*

"My species is post-biological. Long ago we evolved through ever greater technological enhancements until we placed our minds in more enduring structures. Some remained individuals and others chose existence as communal entities."

"What were you?"

"Oh, we are very much a communal species, or were until--" He pulled his knees up to his chest wrapped his arms around them and buried his face.

"For how long?"

"Time is such a difficult concept. Every biological species develops its methods to measure it. Out in the greater universe, time becomes meaningless. We left our star of origin long ago, and no longer count time for ourselves."

"What happened to you?"

He glanced up at her, and Yume saw it as his way of measuring the information she wanted against his needs.

He must have recognized that she required more. *"In our travels, not far from this system in a relative sense, we encountered something we did not expect, a cloud of dark matter transiting the Galaxy. Its gravity caught us. We orbited close enough to your sun and managed to escape but struck the earth. Friends I have known for all my existence were destroyed. My partner, you could think of her as our captain, was separated from me. I am so alone."* He buried his face, and his shoulders shook.

"What do you want from me?"

"Toss Bonneteau is near. He may be in this facility. His modifications have not advanced to the point that I know exactly where he might be."

"You want me to take you as I did before."

"No, I need to find him. Events accelerate, and soon everything will be in place."

"We walk through the door and explore."

"I need one other piece of knowledge. I must find myself."

What did he mean by that? It sounded like some existential philosophical quest. She did not think he meant that. *"You are here with me."*

He pushed himself up from the floor and shook his head. *"My consciousness cycles between you and Vasyl Petrenko. I have a physical counterpart in the ship. I know it is near, but my link is broken. If we do not find our ship before the others arrive, all this will be for nothing."*

"Is that the sense of direction I feel?"

"Yes."

She leaned back in her chair. Her cup of tea drifted up and took its place in her hand. The fragrant steam curled into the milky air. Yume realized that, for her, this was a rare moment of no return. She had no idea what she was and could not even grasp what she would be, but this was the point when she ceased being an object reacting to the forces around her. If she said no, she would go on being Yume until this set of circumstances led to an ultimate conclusion. Yes, meant she became the impetus for her own change.

The scent of Bergamot filled the air, a scent from her past. She sat her tea on the table. *"Let's go."*

****

Aranea's head thumped against the top of the trunk. Red brake lights illuminated the interior. The car slowed. Jet engine whine drowned the sound of the engine and reduced the voices of the men in the car to a buzz. She rubbed the grit from her eyes. How long had she slept?

No cell, no watch, no way to know the time, but it would be daylight outside because the taillights were dark. When she visited South Dakota, she flew into Sioux Falls and took a rental. The state had other airports, but she could not remember where.

The car braked to a stop and doors opened. "Welcome to Ellsworth Air Force Base. I am Colonel Ellen Abrams." She spoke over the roar of aircraft engines.

The woman Aranea considered the ringleader said, "We have four vehicles and nine passengers bound for Keflavik, Colonel Abrams."

"I need the names for my flight plan."

"No, you don't."

"I don't think you know how this works, ma'am."

"Check your orders, Colonel. We are not here. You are on a routine training flight to Keflavik, flying empty."

"I'll have to check that out."

"We will load the aircraft while you post your flight plan."

The car pulled away and drove up a short ramp. Aranea lay inside, frightened that one of them would open the trunk. They moved around the outside of the vehicle, and by the sound, used chains to secure it in place.

After what felt like forever, the aircraft taxied down the runway.

What was she supposed to do? Madeline Moore was in this mess because Madeline knew her, helped her. How could she rescue her in midair, guarded by overzealous thugs?

One of the men inside the car spoke." Ms. Moore, we have food for you."

"So you feed your prisoners?"

"You are not a prisoner."

"Then what am I?"

The woman answered. "A guest of FutureTense. Until this is over, it is best for your own safety to be where we can protect you."

"Who are you, and what is your position with FutureTense?"

"Margrethe Thorn. At this time, your host."

"What's the difference between a guest and a prisoner?"

"Guests have a room with a wet bar."

Aranea's internal compass that pointed to some distant destination remained quiescent. Reykjavik was northeast, more or less. Could that be where it led or was this coincidence?

She had no way to tell, but she would bet the place that compass led her lay in Iceland.

****

The white fog evaporated, and the real version of Yume's prison cell coalesced. Sandra sat at the foot of the bed, a basket of yarn beside her feet, knitting a blanket.

"I thought that was for show," Yume said.

Stranger stood beside Yume's knee, looking up at her. *"These people do have lives when not torturing you."*

"Grow up, little man."

Stranger expanded to his accustomed size and rolled his shoulders as if stretching out the kinks in his adult muscles. In Yume's dream version of reality, the door slid open, and they walked out into the hall past the two guards. She looked right and left. "Where do you think they have him?"

Stranger spurn right to left. "I have a relative sense of nearness."

Yume smiled. "Relative?"

"He is nearer than Shiso, Aranea, or Vasyl. I think much nearer."

She nodded. "So, he could be a thousand miles away."

Stranger turned in circles, his eyes closed. He stopped and shook his head. "Closer I think, measured in meters."

"Do you think he will be near your ship?"

Stranger shoved his hands in his pockets and closed his eyes. "I don't know."

"Did you ever play warmer and colder?"

Stranger frowned. "What has the temperature to do with it?"

"It's a child's game. One of the children hides something and directs the other children to help the first find it by giving directions, warmer when close, colder when moving away."

"Let's start by following my own sense of direction." She closed her eyes and twisted clockwise until she faced in the direction of her internal arrow.

"This way." She led him down the long corridor, walking fast as she could. Away from her white cell, the walls, floors, and ceilings took on an industrial appearance, with gray concrete walls, ceilings, and floors. Cables and pipes ran overhead. Light fixtures tended toward utilitarian, and the light stark. When she came to a cross corridor while she stopped.

"Warmer or colder."

Stranger spun twice with his arm outstretched, finger extended. "Colder. Do we go back?"

"No, we go left."

"And what of your sense of direction?"

"It is somewhere below us." She pointed in a direction midway between the right corridor and straight ahead.

They passed several intersections with no change. She turned left again, and after two cross passages, he had progressed from cool to hot where a passageway ended in a round room with seven doors.

At the third door, they heard faint machine noises and soft breathing. "This is the one." She opened the door.

Toss Bonneteau lay strapped to a narrow padded bed, his arms straight out to his side. "Looks like he's being crucified."

Stranger walked around the bed, eyes narrowed. "You need to pull him into this reality."

"How?"

"How do you do it with your sister?"

"She's asleep, and she's just there."

Stranger walked to the bench, Toss' eyes open, straps over his forehead and chin immobilized his head.

"Touch him," Stranger said.

"What good does that do?"

"I do not know, but it is better than doing nothing."

****

It's like being Jesus on the Cross. Toss Bonneteau lay naked on a narrow, padded bench, legs together, arms stretched out to his side. Tubes fed fluid into his veins. Sensors glued to his chest, arms, legs, and head supplied a constant stream of data.

He slowed time. The high-pitched chirp of the heart monitor had plunged to a croak before he returned time to its accustomed flow.

"I still got it." He laughed.

The doctor knew the drugs did not make him sleep, hence the rig they used to control him. "What's the point of having a superpower if you can't use it for anything?"

The word shifted, a moment of vertigo as if he sat up too fast, and Yume de Guzman stood beside him with her hand on his shoulder.

"You shouldn't be here, but since you are, how about covering me up and setting me free."

There he stood, like a preacher of the Prosperity Gospel Sunday School about to deliver hell and brimstone to a congregation willing to pay for the privilege. He glanced over his shoulder at the rack where he lay; eyes closed, face slack, with a nobody-home sign scrawled in lipstick on his forehead. "How did you do that?"

Yume glanced at Stranger. "I'm a bit hazy on the process."

"How do I get back inside my head?"

Stranger touched his forefinger to Toss' chest. "This is your consciousness." He pointed at Toss' sleeping body. "That is your physical body."

"This is astral projection?"

Stranger opened and shut his mouth, confused. "I am unsure of your meaning."

"Lived with a fine Cajun girl who performed séances, cast out spirits, hunted ghosts, and ran a Vodouan temple. As part of her con, she projected her soul outside of her body."

Stranger shook his head, and his nose wrinkled in confusion. "There are no souls, no ghosts, no supernatural. Yume projects her consciousness outside of her body."

A white toothed grin opened Toss' face. "What's the difference?"

Yume went to the door. "We don't have time for metaphysical discussions. They will wake me soon."

"She's right." Stranger waved for Toss to follow. "We need to find my ship."

Toss ran to catch up with Yume. He realized that she moved toward that point where the internal compass directed. They ran like ghosts, passing through objects and people. None of the people they passed through suffered chills or shocks or the associated strangeness that went with cons concerning ghosts or other supernatural subjects. They found no stairway down, no ladders, only an elevator going up.

Yume slapped the wall. "It's down there."

"I feel it too if a point of consciousness can feel."

Stranger sat down on the floor and put his back to the wall. "I don't know what to do. I assumed we would be connected."

Toss ran his hand along the wall, poking and prodding.

"How big is the thing?"

Stranger stood and dusted himself off. "It's not a thing. If the ship has recovered fully, a thousand meters."

"That's a mighty big object to stick underground."

"It's not underground." She reached out and Toss pulled her up."

"How would you know?"

"There was a photo of it in one of my dreams. There were all these men around it, with cables strung everywhere. It was in a huge aircraft hangar."

"How can you see it in a dream?"

"Well, Stranger accuses me of creating my own realities."

"Fortunately, you seemed to have learned to control the urge. Now you just open doors."

"If you are just a point of consciousness, why open a door? Why not just walk through it like a ghost."

"It is easier to conceptualize."

"Then why not just conceptualize an escalator down to this place."

Yume laughed and pointed at Stranger. "He told me a sensor addicted to creating its own reality was unreliable."

Stranger laid his hand against the wall as if feeling for a pulse. "It might work."

"So now I can make my own realities."

He glanced back. "Maybe I was wrong. It cannot hurt to try."

For Toss, the world changed. A doorway grew. Beyond the door, rollercoaster cars appeared on tracks angling down into an impossible darkness.

"And this will take us where we want to go?"

Yume shrugged, which he didn't find comforting.

He smiled and patted her shoulder. "I haven't ridden a rollercoaster in more years than I like to think. Let's sit in the front car, hold our hands up, and scream."

****

Stark poured a shot of tequila. The team contact screens displayed blank squares. Writing casualty reports and condolence letters came with job. He dredged through his memories for something to say. He knew these men and women personally and telling their families that the loss of their loved ones meant something to him did not come easy. It was much easier to take gunfire in the field than write casualty reports behind a desk.

The screen on the bottom left flickered on. Two beds lay side by side, Guzman on the left and Bonneteau on the right. Saline drips fed fluid through their arms and machines monitored their heart rate, respiration, blood pressure, and brain waves. Doctor Becker and two nurses stood by.

"Are you ready, doctor?"

Becker's eyes narrowed. "I want to register my strongest objection."

Stark sipped his tequila. "Noted, are you ready?"

Becker walked to the machines beside his two patients and checked the lines hooked to their arms. "A medically induced coma used to control two healthy individuals could be considered torture."

"Are they conscious, doctor?"

Becker glanced at one of the computer monitors. "Brain waves show that they are fully aware, but unresponsive. There are some atypical displays."

"In what way?"

"Ms. Guzman and Mr. Bonneteau's brain waves display an interference pattern."

"And that means?"

"There appears to be a separate brain wave pattern as if third individual's brainwaves bled into theirs. I've never seen anything like this before."

Stark sat his tequila on the table. "Finally. You are monitoring four individuals with only two heads."

The doctor shook his head. "Three. The interference appears to be identical in both of the patients. We delayed initiating the coma because we assumed a malfunction."

"But you are sure this is something else?"

Becker looked at his tablet and nodded. "There is no malfunction in the equipment, and the pattern is strange."

Stark glanced at him. "How?"

"They are not what I expect in another human."

Stark pondered the idea of strange brainwaves. They had spent a lot of time considering the nature of their enemy. Was this confirmation of an alien source? "What will happen to the third individual when you induce the coma?"

"I don't know?"

"Any other objections or concerns?"

Becker shrugged. "Blood tests and a medical exam reveal numerous physiological anomalies. Their immune system attacks the narcotics we use as if they were a disease. Changes in their blood since we first brought them here show that they have developed immunity over a period of days, perhaps hours."

"So how long will they remain in a coma?"

"I have several drugs at my disposal. I suspect we can keep this up for a few days, maybe a week."

"That should be long enough. Initiate their comas."

"Yes, sir."

****

Stranger sat in the back car of the rollercoaster, alone. Yume and Toss immersed themselves in the experience of false reality, lifting their arms as the car eased away from the platform.

After all these iterations of existence, was he finally insane?

He reached out with his mind, following the oldest connection his consciousness had with another, his link to Pilot. It was a conscious act to soothe a phantom pain for a missing part of his physical anatomy.

To be sure, Pilot was not entirely absent. He felt something, a vague presence, a trickle of energy that told him she existed. No, the other parts of their ship died, and their absence led to an absolute void. He compared that void to the tenuous links that existed into the ships core where Pilot's consciousness would reside had she occupied her proper place. Those links were incomplete, but their essential existence justified his belief that his pilot's consciousness existed.

He considered the break with Pilot to be persistent damage that required his physical presence aboard their ship.

He had hoped that a physical passage existed between their prison and the ship, and as a detached consciousness, they could find it.

Stark, it appeared, had allowed no such flaw in his plan to control the technology in Stranger's ship. The prison hospital where Yume and Toss lay was separate from the main complex.

Now, Stranger trusted himself to Yume's insane notion that their traveling conscious minds could wend their way through a false reality back to the real. Experience told him that they were lost, and that separated from Ship, their consciousness would fade, and bodies die.

Logic and grief dictated surrender. It would be easy simply to fade away. Oblivion offered a strange comfort in the face of grief, while fighting extended the pain.

Toss looked back over his shoulder and called. "Hold up your hands, Stranger." Toss waved his hands above his head. "Like this. Surrender to the inevitable."

"This is madness."

"I'm a human ghost talking to an alien ghost on a haunted Rollercoaster. Might as well enjoy it while it lasts."

Stranger returned Toss' smile and reached into up the dark.

****

The screen darkened. John Stark rolled the shot glass of tequila between his palms. A bleak view of a craggy, snow-covered hillside and muddy clouds soured the mood inspired by good news. He sipped tequila and waited for the director of the National Security Agency of the United States.

"Mr. Stark." The pilot called from the cockpit. "We are on approach to Denver International Airport. Victor Wu is on the line, and Margarethe Thorn requests that you call."

"Tell Mr. Wu I will see him on the ground."

The Eagle and Key Seal of the National Security Agency appeared on the screen and faded into the trim figure of the Chairman of the NSA.

"This is not a convenient time, Mr. Stark."

"The world is going to hell in a hand-basket. We all have jobs to do. What is Darknet Oviraptorus?"

The Director's eyebrow lifted. "I have no idea what you are talking about."

"A non-denial denial. I'm impressed. You are interfering with my operation."

"The Russian Event, five survivors, I've been read in, and we have cooperated in monitoring your five targets."

"Why is Oviraptorus warning them?"

She frowned. "I cannot tell you."

"I have a clearance and the need to know."

She leaned back in her chair. As an attempt to appear relaxed it failed. "How important is this?"

"You know everything. We provide regular reports to the FBI, CIA, and NSA."

She laughed, and as far as he could tell it was a genuine display of humor. Experience taught him that anything genuine at her level lacked credibility. "Nobody knows everything or tells everything they know. For instance, that meteorite your people recovered from the Ukraine in 2016 was not a meteorite. We allow you to keep your secrets."

She gave him something, but he wasn't buying the appearance of generosity. He needed to know what she knew. "Oviraptorus has maintained constant contact with Yume and Shiso de Guzman. It warned them. It also warned Doctor Aranea Gekas on at least one occasion."

"That is not our fault."

"It's your operation. We have a working agreement with the NSA."

She pressed her fingers together under her lips. This was the moment she examined the situation and decided if the NSA had more to gain from telling him the truth or hiding it. "Oviraptorus is a rogue operation that piggybacks on our equipment."

So, she needed his help to end it. "Perhaps we can help. Whose operation?"

"We have no idea, but they are good."

"When did it start?"

She looked to the side, checking with an expert. "January fifth, 2017, a hacker broke into our secure equipment and accessed our files on the Russian Event."

He clenched his jaw, an unconscious reaction. The triumph in Director's eyes told him she caught it. "You never told us."

She smiled. "We all have secrets we keep."

"Read Eric Leeds in the program and brief him."

"Is that a request?"

John smiled. "Please."

"And what do we get for the annoyance?"

"Our records on the alien ship we recovered after the Russian Event and the results of our attempt to breach its hull."

"So, you admit that you recovered part of an alien ship."

"You already know that because you have a spy in our organization."

"Everybody spies, Mr. Stark. What is the Breach?"

"January fifth, 2017, we successfully breached the hull and entered the ship. We lost the team inside when the ship repaired itself, and the ship briefly gained access to our computer systems and the World Wide Web."

"Coincidence?"

"I don't believe in coincidence, Director.

"I look forward to working with you."

The screen darkened, and the aircraft touched down. As the plane taxied, Stark picked up his phone and waited for Margrethe to answer.

He heard her phone pick up. "It took you long enough."

"I had a meeting with the Director of the NSA."

"Another woman. I knew it would happen eventually. I'll forgive you if we can meet soon at that little hotel in Bali." She smiled.

"As soon as this is over. I promise."

"What's so important?"

"Darknet Oviraptorus is connected to the spacecraft. It appeared the day of the breach."

She put her fingers together in front of her face. "We knew there was a possibility that something escaped."

"How do we capture an alien program on the Internet?"

She smiled. "You know, that sounds insane."

Of course, he did. Since the Russian Event, insane was the new normal. "What about Gekas?"

"She escaped. Members of my team are staking out Madeline Moore's house. We are monitoring all public surveillance video. We will find her."

"As per protocol, I will escort Moore to Iceland for quarantine until we know she has not been infected."

The jet came to a stop and crewman opened the doors. "I have a meeting with Victor. We'll talk later."

Light snow fell in fits and starts on the tarmac of the Denver International Airport. Stark walked fast beside Victor Wu. Neither man spoke until they eased into the back of a black armored limousine. "So are you sure Shiso De Guzman is in Denver."

Wu motioned the driver to go. "We traced her communication with Oviraptorus to a phone used by the teenage son of one of the police officers in Mesquite. He's traveling with a Church group by bus and will arrive soon."

"It would have been easier to stop it on the highway."

"We don't know what she does. The protocols set up before we began this pursuit does not allow us to endanger three bus-loads of children."

"Let's meet with your team. We can discuss the plan to take Shiso de Guzman where we reduce the risk to other teenagers."

****

Vasyl sat at a table in a refugee soup kitchen, a bowl of cabbage boiled in broth on the table. He ate a spoonful and ignored the taste, a skill learned over five years of lunacy. One of the serving women sat a shaker of salt by the bowl. He threw out "thank you," though she moved on before he spoke.

"Clockbrain," he called. Did Vasyl's mental companion exist, and if so, did it monitor him? No answers echoed through his mind. "Always offering suggestions until I want one," He said.

The man eating stewed cabbage in the next seat did not bother to look. The world had gone to hell in a hand basket. In hell, insanity was a defense mechanism.

The Russians guarding the train killed a man before his eyes. No matter how incredible his newfound skills at killing, he doubted he could dodge a bullet.

"Have you come to your senses?" Clockbrain's thought carried a breathless quality.

"Are you distracted by something?" He spoke aloud because nobody cared.

Breathlessness gave way to fear. *"We're riding a rollercoaster."*

Vasyl lifted a tin cup of weak tea. "Imaginary friends go to amusements parks, now?"

"What is your need?"

"This camp is a Russian trap."

"We established that." Clockbrain's breathlessness shifted to sudden vertigo.

"I need to get out."

"You will have to change. Find another human, not a blond."

"And if they're stopping men?"

"I should think the answer is obvious. Make yourself a female."

Vasyl glanced to the left. The man had put down his cabbage to stare. "I will not kill a woman just to escape."

"Killing isn't necessary. You need intimate contact. Any exchange of body fluids carries an exchange of genes. Intercourse will provide the intimate contact with the targets genetic material."

"If I establish this intimate contact, I will have a woman's face."

"You will be a woman of your height and build."

"Completely?"

"Since you have no more intelligent questions." Clockbrain vanished from his mind."

Bad enough to take a man's face. Perhaps he should attempt to leave. He could kill the soldiers if necessary. No, one shout from the gate to the train yard, and he would be shot.

Vasyl rounded a curve in the pathway. Five women stood by the tents, smoking cigarettes, drinking from cups, or watching passersby with dead eyes. He recognized none of them from his earlier glimpse, except for the brown-haired girl with the haunting eyes, Sveta she called herself.

She wore a short red dress, too much makeup, no nylons. What could he expect in a refugee camp? Anyway, men came for a quick fuck and didn't give a damn about the package.

She checked the bag of food hanging from his shoulder and stepped out of the curve. Sveta spotted him and ran across the street, splashing up mud like a child. She stopped just out of reach. "I knew you would be back."

"You have the best offer in town."

She ran a finger down his stomach to his belt. "Show me what you have."

"Here?" He panted, and burned, and flexed his fingers. It had been more than five years since the last time.

"Your currency, let's see what you can afford."

He felt stupid, and his mouth ran dry. He pulled the bag off his shoulder and handed it over. Sveta counted the boxes of military rations. "For this, you get the special."

She stood on her tiptoes and kissed him, pushing her tongue between his lips and reached between his legs and rubbing his cock. It felt like being fifteen, hard, short of breath, with no real idea of what to do with his hands. He reached around, cupped her ass, and lifted her up.

Sveta pulled away and laughed. "Let's not make a public spectacle."

He eased her back onto the ground. She took his hand and led him toward one of the Quonset huts.

His mind felt like mush. His whole purpose was supposed to lead him to a safe way out of the camp. The feel of her tight round ass in his hands, her lips, and her tongue flashed through his mind like fireworks. She led him through the door. He pushed her against the wall, cupped one of her breasts and pulled up her skirt. On either side of the hall, doors opened in small rooms where women and men fucked in narrow beds.

She kissed him. "I have a more private room."

Something about her words sent up a warning flag, but her firm breast under his hands, her nearness killed his caution. It was sex with a prostitute. What could go wrong?

She led him past a toilet, no more than a hole in the floor with a seat over it surrounded with the stench of stale shit and flies. Beyond the smell, she led him into a room, shut the door, and locked it. Vasyl stepped behind her, wrapped her in his arms, and slid one hand down between her legs. She pulled his hand away, turned to face him, and then pushed him back against the wall beside the bed.

She held up her forefinger. "One minute."

Sveta backed away and stood beside a battered vanity with a mirror where she pulled her blouse over her head. She posed naked with her hands out, palms up. "You like."

"Yes." To his own ears, he sounded breathless.

Sveta pirouetted on the points of her toes, danced forward, and slid on her knees. She smiled up at him while loosening his belt and pulling his pants and underwear down to his ankles. She took his cock into her mouth, sliding down its length before easing back. His legs muscles locked, and he came.

She stood, sliding up the length of his body. That was too quick. I won't hold it against you. He grabbed her shoulders to push her onto the bed, but she danced back and away.

"No. We do it my way or not at all."

He collapsed on the bed and leaned back against the headboard, his prick at attention, ready for more. A worm of worry bored into his fugue state brought on by an extreme case of desire.

Five years! Five years! Shit!

He should worry. What if Clockbrain bailed from the Rollercoaster and popped in for a visit during coitus, an uninvited member to make a *ménage à trois.*

Sveta crawled up his body, kissing him all the way up until they slipped together. She pulled his hands to her breasts and leaned close with a hand propped against the wall beside his head and the other on the bed under the pillow. He leaned back, relaxed, feeling no sense of urgency though he should. Something was happening with his muscles.

"No!" He felt the change, internal twists, and knots in his muscles.

"Yes!" She whispered and leaned close. Something cold touched his neck. A snap startled him, and a sting burned Vasyl's skin above his jugular.

She slid off the bed and held up a jet injector used for inoculations. It will make you sleep. She grabbed the sheet and tossed it over Vasyl's body. She dropped the injector onto the vanity, took a pistol with a silencer and a cell phone out of the drawer, pressed a single number, and waited. "I have your package, Mr. Leeds."

Vasyl did not fall asleep, did not feel anything except a momentary drowsiness and several small waves that convulsed his body.

"The General is waiting across the hall. He has another prisoner, a girl that traveled with your package."

Vasyl sat up, and the sheet fell away. He had breasts, a thinner waist, widening into hips, and pubic hair above a vagina.

"Damn!" He whispered and looked away. If Sveta were 350 centimeters taller and twenty-two kilos heavier, he would be her.

"The plan is to kill your package and ship it to you by air."

Vasyl slipped out of bed and crept toward Sveta.

"I'll take care of the General." She glanced at the mirror and dropped the phone.

Vasyl grabbed her from behind and regretted it.

She slammed her forehead into his chin, reached back around his neck, and rolled her shoulders. Vasyl collapsed against her, pushing her to the floor using his weight and strength. His body burned as the acceleration kicked in. Sveta knew methods of combat that Vasyl never imagined. She used every move, punch, jab, and twist to escape. Through the entire fight, she remained silent. It ended when he kicked the vanity and knocked the jet injector on the floor. He picked it up, pressed it against her neck, and pulled the trigger. After half a minute, her body relaxed.

Vasyl dropped her on the bed. As a precaution, he tore the sheet into strips and tied her hands, feet and gagged her mouth. Hunger wracked his body. Almost mindless he took a box of rations from the bag, tore it open, and ate. After consuming a can of cold, oily meat, Vasyl remembered that the general had another prisoner, a girl.

He had Ivanna!

From the closet, Vasyl took a robe and wrapped it around his body. It was a tight fit, but he needed something to cover his curves.

He picked up the pistol left on the vanity and held it behind his back.

Just outside the room where the general waited, Vasyl took a deep breath and opened the door. Ivanna sat on the bed, eyes puffy with tears. General Lagounov sat by a vanity, a cigar in his mouth. "He glanced back. "Do you have him?"

His eyes widened. Perhaps it was his attention to detail or some other natural caution. Vasyl looked like Ivana, but as Clockbrain had noted, he was taller.

The General reached for his sidearm. The men standing guard outside the whore house would react to a gunshot. Vasyl launched himself, arms reaching. He hit the general in the chest and knocked him backward onto the floor. The two rolled in the dirt, knocking over a chair, and slamming against the vanity, jostling the contents onto the floor.

Vasyl slammed Lagounov with his fist. Sticky blood flowed from a deep gash on the general face and covered his hands. Lagounov stepped sideways. To Vasyl's accelerated senses, the man moved in slow motion. General Lagounov lunged, his hands grasping. A punch to the face drove him back against the wall. Vasyl placed his hands on both side of the General's face and twisted. His neck snapped.

Sweat ran down Vasyl's body. He felt on fire. Ivanna slipped off the bed and threw her arms around him. "Vasyl."

"How do you know?"

"You came in as a woman, and now you are a man, but it's you. Does Clockbrain know you can do that?"

"Yes, he knows." He looked at his hands. His tenure as a woman had been short-lived. Vasyl Petrenko now wore the body of General Lagounov. The danger was not over yet.

He glanced through the door into the hall. It was empty of customers. He carried Lagounov into the toilet and dumped him into the pit.

In Sveta's room, he found two jugs of water, poured one over his head, and drank part of another. By the time he finished another can of oily meat, he had a plan.

Dressed as the general, he picked up the sleeping Sveta and carried her over his shoulder. Out in the open, he met the general's men led by a captain.

"I have Petrenko," He said. He lifted Sveta off his shoulder and handed her off to a soldier. "He killed her and changed himself into a woman."

The captain glanced from Sveta to Ivanna. His hand hovered near his sidearm.

"Are you deaf, Captain?"

The man's head popped up. "No, General."

"Good. I need to deliver the prisoner and this girl to FutureTense in Iceland. Arrange for air transport."

"Who will deliver her, sir?"

"I will take care of that task, myself."

****

Shiso jerked awake. The air brakes hissed. "Rollercoaster," Shiso mumbled, rubbing sleep sand from her eyes.

David smiled, "I wish."

Her head rested on his shoulder, and his arm curled around her waist. She sat up and rubbed her eyes. "Where are we?"

"Denver." He pointed through the window. "The Eleventh Street youth hostel ain't a bad place to stay if you don't mind bunk beds and bedbugs."

"Bedbugs?" It was a stupid question, but her mind did not quite want to work. She dreamed about a Rollercoaster. Yume, Stranger, and Toss Bonneteau were there. It had all the markers of one of Yume's strange dreams but felt more personal. The car rattled down through a dark tunnel. She raised her arms high and screamed her head off.

Was Yume somewhere with Toss Bonneteau, riding Roller coasters, if so, maybe she should have surrendered.

"Come on, we can settle into the dorm and sneak out of the sing-along after the prayer circle."

"Okay."

That was just a placeholder word to save space for what she did not want to speak aloud. Talking on the bus about picking up a package and flying off to Iceland was cool, fun, and made her feel like she had someone, but she had no intention of taking David along. He could get hurt or worse.

The bus driver waited outside the door with a clipboard. Shiso grabbed her purse and stood so she could follow David. On a whim, she called out, "David."

He pulled a backpack down from the overhead bin and glanced back. Shiso popped up on tiptoes and kissed him on the lips. "Well, lead on."

She followed him out of the bus but stood back while he waited in the crowd of kids milling around the cargo door. The bus driver and the adult monitors consulted near the doors of the hostel.

Another teenager tapped David on the shoulder. "Dude."

Shiso slipped around the front of the bus, crossed the street, and disappeared into the crowd of pedestrians. By the time David checked in and finished a prayer circle, she would have her package, whatever it was, and be on her way.

Half a block from the Post office, in the shadow of the 20th Street Rec Center, she scanned the street, cautious. What did Oviraptorus mean when she said the package would be delivered? Did she need to go inside, and who should she say she was? How stupid to trust an app that everything would go as planned.

"Coffee, Ms. Guzman?" A man said.

He was thirtyish, over six feet tall, athletic, and spoke with a touch of a British accent.

"Who are you?"

"You don't need to know." He handed her the coffee and a white paper bag.

"Is this the package?"

He looked past her toward the front of the post office. "No, it's a Danish. We don't have time for breakfast."

She glanced back at the post office. Was this man from FutureTense? "I was told there would be a package."

"I am the package, but you're the one being picked up. I have just one other task."

He stepped around her and searched the street near the post office. A light dusting of snow blew along the surface though it was too warm to stick.

David stopped at the light and crossed when it flashed.

"Right on time," the man said.

"David?" She stepped past the man. He grabbed her shoulder.

"I can always count on young men following their hormones."

A homeless man parked his shopping cart near a trashcan. Shiso noticed he was Asian, with a shadow of a beard and a knit cap pulled down over a shaved head. He must have said something, but she could not hear what.

David looked up.

The trash can exploded, blasting its contents across the street.

The shopping cart whirled a dozen feet, spilling trash, bottles, and miscellaneous objects. The homeless man tumbled through the air and struck David across the chest. They rolled together over the asphalt. Two of the pedestrians drew weapons from beneath their jackets and ran into the street where David and homeless man had come to rest. The remaining three drew pistols from inside their clothes. One of them looked up the face of the buildings. Two of them must have seen her with her Danish.

In a small park across from the post office, four more trash cans blew up like a string of firecrackers, throwing chunks of concrete and burning junk in all directions.

"That should slow them down." He took her hand and pulled her toward a van. Dense black smoke poured across the street from the site of the explosions and boiled out of the storm drains.

"David!" She screamed.

"He'll be fine, probably."

Shiso felt a sting on the side of her neck. The whole world tilted to the left and spun toward the sidewalk.

"Sorry about this." His voice faded into the distance. "I'm being paid to..."

CHAPTER SEVEN

Iceland

A dull, mechanical hum called Shiso out of a dark empty sleep. She opened her eyes; the world spun clockwise one time and righted itself like a compass. Her lips felt dry, and her stomach complained. A curving metal roof with aluminum support ribs arched overhead.

"Where am I?" Her tongue felt stiff as a cucumber, and her unruly lips slurred the questions.

"I'm impressed." The package she met on 20th street spoke somewhere out of her sight. She followed the sound and found him sitting in a seat that folded down from the wall. "The drugs I injected should have left you unconscious for another six hours."

She sat up. Blankets slipped to the side. The air burned her skin. "David?" Her breath steamed.

"He's alive, or was, according to reports and my last communication with my employer."

She chewed on her cheek. What was she supposed to say? Was he a kidnapper or a helper? "Are you employed by FutureTense?"

"Here is the coffee and Danish I offered earlier. The coffee's cold, but the Danish isn't bad. Eat, you'll feel better."

"I'm not hungry."

"Suit yourself. It will be here when you are ready." He folded down another seat and patted it. "Sit. There is a message from my employer that you need to read."

Shiso stood and wrapped a blanket around her shoulders as a barrier against the cold. Her breath steamed. Moisture froze on her dry lips. He handed her a tablet.

She sat. "Why is it so cold?"

"We are flying, Airfreight, at forty thousand feet over Canada. Listen to this."

The tablet screen lit, and the face of Oviraptorus looked out at her.

"I have found you, little bird." Her voice carried the same singsong cadence.

"What I say is as important as your next breath, life or death. You will be dropped on a corner with the necessities of life; clothes, cash, a van, and a phone."

Oviraptorus wiggled her finger from side to side. "Never call, never use it. If you need me, I will know, and I will reach you."

"Okay." She nodded at the phone and felt exquisitely stupid for speaking to a recorded message.

"Your lifeline, your life, is in the hands of the others. You know of whom I speak."

Shiso rolled her eyes in answer to the rhetorical question.

"Use what was given you. Reach out with your gift, and you will find the other survivors. Goodbye." The screen darkened.

"That's it?"

He pointed at the coffee and Danish. "Eat. After that, sleep until we land."

Shiso shook her head and stared at her hands. She reached out. "Yume? Talk to me." Yume's giddy excitement, a rush of adrenaline, and a buried hint of fear suffused through her.

The man watched her, his face as impartial as a Department of Motor Vehicles' attendant. "You're young for this, so I have two pieces of advice."

She glanced at his face and found no emotion, no empathy.

"If you have a moment to eat, eat. You never know when the next meal will come, and you need your strength to face whatever the opposition throws at you."

Shiso bit into the Danish and picked up her coffee.

"Second, sleep when you can." He leaned back and closed his eyes.

Shiso waited for several seconds. Was this a bizarre way to illustrate his silly rules? After a while, she took another bite of the Danish and reveled in its cheesy, cherry sweetness.

She really could not sleep. How can they rendezvous if they had no way to talk? If he had just given her a phone she could use. Of course, phoning would not work. If the others had phones she could reach, FutureTense would find them. How could people stay in contact with no physical link? She took another bite. Yes, she was hungry. How long had it been since that *carne asada* in Nevada, twelve hours, more?

She took another bite. The Danish tasted good. The taste reminded her of her hunger. The damned package was right, not that she would ever give the man the satisfaction by saying so.

She sat upright. "I'm a telepath."

But would it work for her? Shiso had not tried to contact anyone but her sister, but Yume dreamed with all the survivors. If Yume could stretch out to touch the other survivor's dreams, Shiso could reach their thoughts.

She glanced at the mysterious man who had taken his own advice. Even if it was a pretense, it did not matter.

She closed her eyes, thinking she would reach out to Yume. She stopped because Yume had been captured by the enemy. Even without trying, now, she could sense her sister. She rode a rollercoaster, which was wrong in so many ways.

FutureTense would not capture her and take her to a theme park in Iceland if such a thing existed. Something had gone wrong, but that was okay because Shiso had Aranea Gekas.

Shiso picked the crumbs from her blanket and licked them from her fingers. She needed something to drink. The coffee tasted cold and bitter. She gulped it down and sat the cup aside.

Closing her eyes, Shiso reached for the mind of Aranea Gekas.

****

A shrill ringtone ripped Stark from sleep. He sat up and rubbed his eyes.

What time is it?

At this point in his life, he had no idea. Running operations on two continents across half the earth's time zones, 24/7, coupled with constant flights from one continent to another killed his circadian rhythm. After this, if there was an after, he intended to take a long vacation. Let some other sad sack save the earth.

"Hello."

"Mr. Stark," The man spoke with a Russian accent.

Was that Lagounov? No! "Kuvayev."

"You impress me. We've spoken three times, and you recognize my voice."

"That's why they pay me the big bucks. Have you captured Petrenko?"

"Yes, sir." He paused. "I think."

Stark sat up, the vague answer drew all his attention. "Explain."

"The trap set by Agent Gorelova and the General worked flawlessly."

He frowned. In English flawless did not translate to vague. "I've seen Leeds' report."

"The General did not kill Petrenko, as he promised."

Something felt wrong, like a knot in the pit of his stomach. "And why should that be a problem?"

"The General's actions do not make sense. When he called us in, he said Petrenko became Agent Gorelova, completely. Our doctor assures us she is a woman in all ways. Considering your briefing, we are keeping her heavily sedated and under guard."

A woman? How the hell was that even possible without a team of surgeons?

"That is a new wrinkle." His mind ticked over the ramifications of a creature that could become a perfect duplicate of another human being down to the genitalia, and, quite possibly, the DNA. "What else is wrong?"

"General Lagounov is acting out of character."

And that was the source of his discomfort. Lagounov was a useful blunt instrument. He did not change. "How so?"

"The general is bringing Petrenko and the child companion he traveled with, himself. Abandoning his duties and flying off to Iceland to receive payment is treason against Russia. Lagounov is many things, but a traitor is not one of them."

Stark leaned back against the headboard. Lagounov remained useful because he was efficient, decisive, and predictable. A patriot could always be manipulated with an appeal to an idealized vision of his nation. He took payment from FutureTense with the full knowledge of his government, acting as a spy on a possible enemy. He always used the hidden channels FuturTense devised to pay him. He always reported it to his superiors. Taking payment in person implied that he had chosen to go rogue. The man did not have a rogue bone in his body.

"Bring everyone. I will have agents on the plane to keep an eye on Gorelova and the General. Do not allow anyone to be alone with him."

"Yes, sir."

"And one more thing. Send a team to search the location where Petrenko was captured. Let me know what you find."

****

The thump and rattle of aircraft wheels on a runway woke Aranea. She lay in a fetal ball as protection against the icy cold. How long? Her memory reeled out the answer, three thousand miles, about six hours. She felt dirty and would kill for a shower and a bed where she could sleep in comfort.

The nagging fear that someone would open the trunk and find her remained. She shelved the fear under pointless anxiety and shifted her mind to other pursuits. Faint voices spoke inside the car, too soft to make out what they said over the whine of the engines and sound of wheels rolling over concrete.

To take her mind off her discomfort, she searched the memory of her last dream, which had lingered long after most dreams faded. She rode a rollercoaster, screaming, arms in the air, and it wasn't a nightmare. In 2009, an explosion on the Ring Racer in Nürburg put her in the hospital. That damned rollercoaster haunted her memory and her dreams.

Perhaps the changes that made her something other than human also altered her perceptions of memory, or possibly days on the run from men with guns put her fears into proportion.

The plane rolled to a stop. Madeline spoke from the backseat of the car. "My prison with a wet bar is on the base at Keflavik."

"No, Ms. Moore." The woman from FutureTense spoke with proper English accented annoyance. "Mr. Stark will explain everything."

The sound of machinery outside the car signaled a cargo door in the back of the plane. The car engine hummed to life, and after a brief delay, it rolled down an incline and out onto a runway. Iceland was a big country though sparsely populated compared to the US. She wondered where they would take Madeline.

Outside the plane, the car braked to a stop, and the door opened. "Ms. Moore." She recognized Stark's voice as if she had known him all her life.

"You must be Mr. Stark."

"I want to apologize for the inconvenience."

"I would call it kidnapping."

"We prefer to use paid consultant."

"I had no idea that consulting and kidnapping meant the same thing in Iceland."

The car shifted, and Aranea imagined him sliding into the back seat.

"We contacted your university on your behalf. You are now on a fully paid sabbatical."

"Your generous kidnappers, I will give you that."

"About the visit from your friend, Aranea."

"She's more than a friend."

"Through your relationship with her father?"

"Yes."

"A Stepmother, then?"

"Aranea is not Cinderella."

"Mother figure?"

"Oh, that's a ridiculous phrase. I don't think English has a word for it. We both loved her father, and love and respect each other as women and colleagues."

Madeline paused, and Aranea pictured her sitting in the seat, her cheeks sucked in as they always did when thinking about something complicated. "Why exactly did you kidnap me?"

"Because of your relationship, because she came to see you and to make sure that whatever infection she suffers from is not contagious."

"From what malady does she suffer?"

"We don't know. Ms. Gekas was one of five who survived an incident in Russia."

Madeline cut him off. "I know that story. Why are you pursuing her?"

Aranea felt the ridiculous urge to high-five the air. She wondered how Stark would answer.

He surprised her. "As a result of exposure, all five have suffered changes. It started in 2016. Since the impacts, their changes have accelerated. They can do things no human can match."

Why would he say that to Madeline? What did he want?

Madeline continued. "That doesn't explain---"

Stark cut her off, and his voice took an edge. "We don't think she's human anymore. It is necessary that we determine if those who were closest to the five are changing."

Madeline fell quiet. No doubt she recognized the implications. "So how long do you intend to hold me? A week. A year. Forever."

The car shifted again. "I want you to meet, Sandra Jenkins. She will be your companion on the drive to Ólafsvík."

"I know the town."

Another voice, a woman, spoke. "Oh, we have a lovely facility just outside of the town. The view of Snaefellsjokull is incredible. Before all this snow and cold weather, I hiked the mountain every day."

"How long will I be held there."

Sandra Jenkins continued as if she had heard nothing at all. "Oh, and the amenities, five-star all the way."

"How long?"

"And, dear, the dining is the best. Chef Longpre trained at the Academy de France. We even have companionship, if you get lonely on those long Icelandic nights. I've taken advantage of that perk a few times, myself."

"You're not going to answer my questions?"

The door closed, and the car began to accelerate away.

"Do you knit," Sandra Jenkins said.

"What?" Madeline's voice rose to a higher level of frustration. Aranea could not blame her. Sandra Jenkins' congenial chatter bordered the surreal.

"Aranea Gekas?" A girl's voice echoed in her mind, distinct from her own vocalized thoughts.

"What?" She echoed Madeline out of surprise.

"Stop the car." Sandra Jenkins said.

The brakes locked up, and wheels skidded. The deceleration threw Aranea against the front wall of the trunk."

"Fuck!" All sound vanished, but her own faint breathing and heartbeat. She dropped through the bottom of the trunk, though not before the lid opened. The tall agent she saw in Dakota stood with two other men in Kevlar body armor, armed with automatic weapons. They looked down into her face, guns ready, mouths moving in words she could not hear.

She passed through the gas tank. Light bloomed beneath the car. Her head sunk beneath the road. How far could she fall? Could she fall to the center of the earth? What if she became lost? "Don't be silly." The voice in her head spoke.

And, of course, the speaker was right. Light beamed through the walls of her bubble, and she retained her sense of up and down—gravity had an effect on her.

She did not want to remain underneath the car. One of those men might have a shovel.

Aranea willed herself to cease falling and moved perpendicular to gravity's acceleration.

The words came again. "Aranea, do you hear me?"

"Shiso de Guzman?" Aranea knew she was right though she could not say how.

"Thank God. Didn't know if this would work."

"Where are you?"

"In an airplane, on my way to Iceland. You?"

"Keflavik."

"Good. Wait for us."

"Us?"

"Vasyl Petrenko and me."

"Vasyl?" Oh, that name summoned up feelings, memories.

"Way too much information." Shiso sent.

"You can read my mind?" The trip through memory ended.

"If you just put it out there? I'm not looking for it."

"What about Toss Bonneteau and your sister?"

"Stark has them in Iceland. I don't know where."

"How long?"

"I don't know. A few hours maybe."

"Stark took a friend of mine. She's here in Iceland. I can't leave her."

"I know what you mean. He took a friend of mine, too. I think together, we have a better chance of dealing with Stark."

"They have guns."

"We're superheroes."

"I'll wait."

****

Vasyl Petrenko searched his reflection in the mirror of the restroom of FutureTense's corporate jet. A scrim of short gray hair grew in a ring around his face. The stomach was flat, and the shoulder's wide. Was this really him? Had he lost two decades of life to enable himself to live? If he chose to change to a younger image, would he be young again?

So many questions and too few answers.

He relaxed his mind and waited. "*Clockbrain?*" Was Clockbrain real? He could not stop asking that old question. He had no satisfactory answers. Unless he lay in a straitjacket in an insane asylum, existing evidence and experience indicated reality. The evidence did not show whether he liked it.

A knock on the restroom door pulled him away from introspection. "Yes."

"It's the girl." Captain Kuvayev said.

"What about her?"

"She wants out of her cuffs."

What was he supposed to do? He played a deadly game with the highest possible stakes. The relationship he enjoyed with Ivanna on the road could not be duplicated here. Starks men guarded Svetlana Gorelova and kept her drugged. Two of them remained in the cabin, distant and quiet, watching.

Did they know?

"Tell her to sit down and shut-up."

"She's a child. I don't think she knows how."

"Take her to the back of the plane where we left the whore."

Kuvayev paused. Had Vasyl given himself away? How would a Russian General speak to a subordinate? He had met a few, and they all qualified as supreme arrogant assholes. He did not feel comfortable in that role.

"They traveled together. Is that a good idea?"

Of course, he was not speaking as an arrogant-assed general. "Do it!"

"Yes, General."

He gazed into the mirror and whispered. "So old."

A woman called into Vasyl's mind. *"Vasyl? Vasyl?"*

"Clockbrain."

No, that was wrong. The voice was female, and he recognized the woman's mind as readily as he knew the sound of his own mother.

"Shiso de Guzman, how are you in my head?"

"Who is Clockbrain?"

"The being that shares my brain; who talks to me, guides me, who perverted me." Vasyl hadn't meant to reveal that last part. He would never think that to Clockbrain. He trusted Shiso de Guzman better than he trusted himself.

She answered back. *"Sort of like Stranger."*

"Clockbrain is not a stranger."

"No, I mean, I use telepathy to talk to my sister, and she shares dreams with me. We do more than that, now. I can communicate with you and Aranea. Yume can project herself out of her body."

"I do not think that is possible."

"I wish it weren't. What's your trick?"

"My trick? I change myself into copies of the people I kill or those I have sex with."

Shiso fell silent. He felt her in his head, just as he always felt Clockbrain's presence.

"I apologize if I shocked you."

"Do you do that much?" Revulsion and curiosity leaked through like dropped emotions.

"Kill or have sex?"

"Become people."

"Only when necessary, but you did not communicate just to chat."

"I can't reach Yume. When I try, I get images of a Rollercoaster. I'm afraid."

"Where is Toss Bonneteau?"

"They have him too, somewhere in Iceland."

"On my way. We land in three hours."

"Me too, but I don't know how long."

It popped into his mind, like the arrow that always pointed to Aranea Gekas, but now he knew the direction and even sensed distance.

"Sooner, I think. Shiso, you will arrive in approximately two hours."

"What do we do?"

He shrugged into the mirror and laughed at himself.

"What we can."

And she was gone, leaving Vasyl, his guilt, and the mirror.

Another knock sounded at the door. "There is another restroom." He did not mean to be short, but he felt shaken, ripped apart.

I want my mind back.

No, that was wrong. Vasyl did not want his mind back, he wanted his innocence.

"Sorry, General. We thought something might be wrong."

Vasyl pulled his uniform straight and checked his appearance one last time. Of course, he remained perfect. The bits and pieces of memory that came with the change told him that General Lagounov would never appear less than perfect. Fitting the image was necessary.

He pushed the door open, hard, catching Kuvayev on the shoulder and knocking him back.

The four men from FutureTense stood as if a single mind controlled their bodies. They reached beneath their suit coats for weapons. "Why are you all jumpy? Afraid someone will catch your mother's being fucked by dogs?" He marched back to his seat. Sudden sweat beaded on his forehead and under his armpits.

They knew.

"If you are going to be jumpy, go watch the bitch in the back."

In his peripheral vision, he saw Kuvayev motion for them to calm down.

They knew, and somehow, he doubted he would get the jump on these men. Since they boarded, not one of them came close enough to be touched. "Kuvayev, bring vodka."

"Yes, General."

"I am going to be very rich, time to celebrate."

He leaned back in the seat and sent a quiet call to Clockbrain or Shiso.

"They know who I am."

Shiso answered. *"That's Okay. Aranea is in Keflavik. She can help."*

"I know Aranea. She is a capable woman, but what can she do against armed men."

"She walks through walls and bullets don't touch her."

Vasyl felt something, not an emotion exactly, more as if he felt Shiso de Guzman shrug, so he asked. *"How does she do that?"*

"She's a superhero."

Shiso's answer came so matter of fact that all he could return was, *"For my sake, she had better be."*

Kuvayev handed him a glass of vodka. Vasyl swallowed it in one gulp and ordered, "More."

"General?"

"More Vodka, you ass-kissing sycophant."

Kuvayev's mouth opened, but he appeared to think better of it and shut it.

"Surprised."

"A little."

Vasyl lunged to his feet, and the four guards rose, and their hands reached for their guns, but he ignored them. "I'm like any other man, Captain. I piss when I need and shit when I must, and sometimes, my young *protégé,* I fuck beautiful women and howl at the moon. Does that alarm you?"

Sweat covered Kuvayev's pale face. His hands shook. "A little, General."

"Then have a drink with me, and tell the prick flying the plane to land and find us a few prostitutes. I will pay of course."

"We're over the Baltic, General. It's a nonstop flight."

"Vodka now and women later, unless you'd like to have a go at the woman in the back."

Kuvayev shook his head and backed away.

****

Stark rammed a clip into his weapon and checked his other gear.

His cell rang. He checked the caller. Margrethe's smiled up from the screen. He hit 'answer' and continued to prepare for war. "Bring your team home."

"They are on their way. Victor Wu's team will be on the ground in less than an hour."

"What's his condition?"

"Battered, bruised, and pissed off."

"He can join me here. I need you to take command in Ólafsvík. Light a fire under Leeds' ass. We need to find Oviraptorus."

Margrethe frowned. Stark intuited that she was about to tell him something he did not want to hear.

"Oviraptorus has disappeared from the net with no display in twelve hours."

"Any guesses where?"

"Leeds doesn't know what it is. Guessing where it's hiding is beyond us."

His personal weapons were ready and secure; he holstered his pistol and slung an assault rifle over his shoulder.

Margrethe's face softened. "That isn't your fault, John. It's mine. I never considered that she would hide in the car."

"The plan was to isolate anyone we took in until the moment we had them in our secure facility. My plan, my failure."

"We're fighting super villains. You can't plan for the inconceivable."

He stopped preparations and placed the phone closer to his face. "In about two hours, give or take, Vasyl

Petrenko will arrive wearing the face of General Lagounov. He killed Lagounov and dumped his body in an outhouse."

She smiled. "Well, at least, Petrenko knows where Lagounov belonged. Which team is covering the plane?"

"Grackle."

"Good people. Take your own advice, for once. Trust your team."

"Petrenko took down a full squad in an APC. Lagounov gathered the blood evidence. He was shot in the fight, at least once and walked away as if nothing had happened."

"We both have seen extraordinary men and women do amazing things."

"Extraordinary men and women I can plan for. His abilities are superhuman."

"I prefer alien," Margrethe said.

"Thanks."

She leaned back and smiled. Stark touched the screen with a forefinger and traced her face. "Get there as soon as you can."

****

Shiso sipped her cold, bitter coffee. Maybe the package that grabbed her off the street was right. Her back hurt and her eyes wanted to crash down on her cheeks. She could not remember feeling this tired.

Who decided she would be the telepath and act like everyone's cell phone? Yume's work required her to sleep. Aranea walked through walls. Toss either moved fast or made everyone else slow. Vasyl changed into other people.

It wasn't just that those powers were way cooler than telepathy. They did not carry the terrible burden of responsibility to the group. Only Shiso possessed the ability to speak to everyone. Only she could devise a plan that would save everyone's life. That meant that everything that happened was her responsibility.

This wasn't like baking cookies, where the only repercussion to failure was stinking up the house and setting off the fire alarm. People could get hurt, like David, or even killed.

She wanted to rest, to sleep, but Toss and Yume were in danger. No one else could do anything about that. She closed her eyes and reached for Yume.

Yume screamed, held up her arms, and the rollercoaster rattled down an insane incline and up through a loop. Shiso looked through her eyes into a rollercoaster world that faded away into distant blue mountains built with rollercoaster tracks. She felt a jerk as the chain beneath the car caught hold and accelerated them up.

"There you are," Yume said.

Shiso found herself sitting by her sister. "This is a dream!"

Yume looked at her with eyes bright as a car's high beams. "Ride with me."

Shiso pulled back and slumped in the seat of the aircraft. Her blanket lay on the floor, and the air burned her face and hands.

Something controlled Yume, something deep in her eyes.

If she entered her sister's mind again, she might not get out.

Words popped into her head.

Toss, remember him? He's in there, too.

She recognized the voice of Stranger, but not inside her head. The words bled through her link with Yume.

Could she mind speak with Stranger? Did an imaginary friend have a mind? She reached for Stranger and felt her sister.

Stranger was in her head. If Yume went there, she would be trapped on the rollercoaster. No, it had to be Toss. He slowed things down or sped them up. Yes, if anyone could do it, it would be him.

Shiso gulped down the last of the bitter cold coffee and picked up the last crumbs of Danish. Better now than never.

She reached for Toss Bonneteau.

****

The rollercoaster lurched and screamed around another curve. How many times, now? Ten? A thousand? Toss had lost count, God knows how long ago, and it now reached the point where each new curve made him want to toss his cookies.

He could not get off and could not see the beginning or end, only an infinity of loops, curves, rises, and falls.

"Toss?" Shiso's voice stood inside his ear.

"Hold on a moment, I need to lose my lunch." He leaned over the side of the car and vomited, bilious and green, that splattered away with the slipstream.

He glanced back at Shiso, who he did not remember starting the ride with him, and she wasn't there. "I must be getting old."

She sent back. *"No, I'm talking in your head, using telepathy."*

"When did you learn how to do that?"

"Today. I need your help."

"I'd love to help, but we are stuck on this ride. If you look out through my eyes, you'll see there is no end in sight."

"You're in Yume's dream."

"I know. Wonderful isn't it." But it wasn't, and he knew it. On the surface, his ghost body accepted the whole damned experience as a lark. But Toss knew it was wrong, though only in the first few moments after a vomit session did he question the mad joy.

She continued, and that comforted him. *"I need to talk to Stranger."*

He leaned back and pretended to put his arm around her as if he were a teenager and she was his date at the world's largest amusement park. *"He's in the seat ahead of me. Just jump out of my ear and into his."*

"I can't talk in his head right now. You have to do it for me."

What a damned nuisance, bothering him in the middle of the most fabulous carnival ride in the history of the universe, but something about Shiso's urgency and the fact that she saved his life pushed him to act. Toss Bonneteau owed her, and he always paid his debts. He lowered his arms. Ghost pains shot across his back and down to the ends of his fingers. It felt like he'd held those hands up for a solid month of Sundays.

His muscles burned, and his arms wanted to fall and leave his hands to sleep in his lap like a lazy cat. After a quick breath, he reached out and tapped Stranger on the shoulder.

For the first time, he noticed Stranger did not like the ride one bit. The man clutched at the bar across his lap as if the whole universe attempted to throw him into the void, and his hands were all that anchored him.

Stranger looked back over his shoulder. Tears streamed down his cheeks. The screaming slipstream tore them away. Far worse, a deep fear boiled inside his eyes that threatened to tear what sanity Toss retained.

"Shiso wants to talk with you."

Stranger stared deep into Toss' eyes, uncomprehending. Then, he changed. Stranger swallowed his fear and grief. His eyes brightened. He released the bar and grabbed Toss' hand.

"We have to wake up!"

The wind ripped at his hair, and the rails screamed. He did not understand how Stranger heard him, but he spoke anyway. *"She doesn't know how. Yume almost pulled her into this dream."*

Stranger nodded. *"Where is she? I don't see her."*

"In my head. She says she's a disembodied spirit haunting the granddaddy of all rollercoasters. Can't do anything here."

"Toss, you can get us out."

He felt Shiso's attention pique. *"Ask him how."*

"How do I get us out?"

"Your consciousness and your brain are entangled. You can still command it."

"How do I do that?"

He took her question and ran with it. *"Command it to do what?"*

"They must be using drugs. Speed up time, and you speed up your metabolism. The drug will wear off. You will wake up."

"Thanks."

He slumped back into his seat. His body heavy, as if he carried his own corpse over his shoulder. He had noticed that before. It must be his living body, of course. The link remained while his consciousness immersed itself in the dream. He imagined that connection like the silver cord mystics believed tied a living body to its soul.

Across that cord traveled vague sensations, pains, itches, and an impression of weight and substance. It wanted to sleep, to lie like a headstone in a cemetery. He fought the lethargy and performed his mental trick.

Toss lay naked, quiet. The steady beep of a medical machine had slowed to a long deep moan before it dropped below his ability to hear though he fancied he could feel the sound as thumps in his ear. He could not see anything.

Am I blind?

No, someone placed a bandage over his eyes. His arms lay like dead branches at his side. He forced them to rise and rip away the tape.

A nurse sat at a desk, frozen in place by the speed of Toss' time stream. Beside him, in another gurney, Yume lay with eyes blinded with bandages. Tubes and wires ran to various sensors on her nude body.

He eased out of bed. The wires and tubes ripped free. The Heparin lock feeding a saline drip and drugs to his arm pulled out, and blood ran down his arm. No moment to think. He touched Yume's arm, she took a sudden, deep breath. She did not wake up, but she would. He had every confidence in time.

Wires and sensors ripped free of her body. They whipped in slow motion and froze in place as they lost contact with her skin. Toss lifted her off the table and placed her on his shoulder. The door slid opened in slow motion. The nurse started to twist around. In half an hour of Toss' time, he suspected they might be a problem. He bashed the door with his shoulder. The energy transfer blew the door off its hinges. A guard who stood with his hand on the doorknob flew to the side as if hit by a car.

A crisp snap followed by a sudden flare of pain in his forearm said something was wrong. It reminded him of the tenth birthday when he broke his wrist while taking a dare to jump off the roof.

Where to go? This was not the same hallway where he first woke. He did not understand the layout of the building, but it was best to move where fewer people stood in his way. To the right, several guards charged in slow motion toward the door. He took the first left and ran through the halls, avoiding doorways that would announce his presence to everyone inside.

Ahead, a nurse stood with her foot lifted, frozen in mid-step as she passed through an automatic door. She walked toward them with a tray of food in her hands. Toss took a chance and slipped around her and through the door crawling through the process of closing.

In a small kitchen used to serve the needs of patients, he placed Yume down against the back wall. She moved, which told him that she was, at last, waking up.

As always, his whole body screamed for food. Moving at human speed, he opened a cupboard and found boxes of cereal. Toss tore off the top of a cereal box and began to eat.

****

Yume twisted around. Everywhere the rollercoaster receded into the blue distance. She whispered, "All wrong."

Something familiar stirred in her mind, and the sense of herself, Yume, separate from her dream construct, forced the sense of wrong into retreat. Her recognition of personal identity, apart from her existence as a giddy flesh bag of joy, began to return. She recognized that as the beginning of the process of waking up.

Good. Time to get off this damn rollercoaster and deal with life outside the dream.

Stranger called out of that vast howling space behind her head. *"Wait."*

She glanced over her shoulder. *"You look like crap."*

"Don't wake. We have to get to the ship, and this is the only way."

She noticed that somehow Toss Bonneteau had escaped the rollercoaster. *"Where's Toss?"*

"He's awake. I believe he rescued you, but I do not see into his mind or dreams."

"Why do we need to get to this ship, if it is even possible?"

"To regain my physical body and its resources."

"Why?" Her mind crawled from thought to thought, refusing to follow at the right speed.

"Your sister is coming with the others. We must try one more time to reach the ship at the end of the rollercoaster. Only you can construct that reality."

She nodded and closed her eyes because she wanted just one more minute. The rollercoaster rocketed downhill. The memory of the past hours, days, or years told her of another rise and another after that. It went on forever.

She heard Shiso in her head. *"It doesn't have to be that way."*

Yume reached into her sister's mind as if it were a lifeline. *"Help me. Come into the dream."*

"Not in the dream." Shiso's panic and fear bled through. *"I was almost lost the last time. Safer inside your head. That should be enough."*

Shiso visualized the track ahead, pictured it leveling out and driving through a pool of water, slowing their headlong flight.

The sound of rushing water drowned out the noise of the wheels and tracks, splattering water on her face. The air smelled of moisture, cold oil, and steel. Water tickled down her cheek.

"You did it," Stranger said.

The cars rattled and clashed to a stop. Smiling clowns stood by to help her out and pointed the way to an arch that opened into a warehouse. An enormous object with a triangular, organic shape sat in the center. It bore a vague resemblance to a manta ray the size of an ocean liner.

Men moved back and forth around the object. Some wore white lab coats and operated machines. The men in that vast space did not notice the carnival arch, the clowns, or Stranger. He walked right through one of them as if flesh and bones contained no more substance than air.

"Follow me!" He grabbed her wrist and pulled her along.

She felt a hand touch her face but saw nothing and realized that wherever she lay someone touched her, Nurse Sandra perhaps, or Toss.

"I'm being pulled." She struggled against that touch. The rollercoaster dipped, whirled, rose, and lurched. She could ride this forever or until her separate consciousness decayed. Stranger's hand proved the stronger force as he propelled her across the floor through men dressed in white lab coats, their eyes observing streams of data on computer screens.

"Do I need to make a door?"

He shook his head. The ship will accept us.

They reached the edge of the wall of dull gray metal. The skin of the ship flowed around Stranger and Yume and absorbed them.

Yume felt her distant heart race. Sudden darkness and silence after an eternity of light and noise unhinged her. It lasted only a moment, and she found herself in a familiar place.

She dreamed here when she first met Stranger.

He answered her. *"I helped you create that reality from my memories. This is real."*

She scanned the gray walls. *"Could use some color. Did you just read my thoughts?"*

"This is home, my link to all of you. From here, I can access all surviving functions of the ship."

He pulled her down long twisted corridors and entered a room like a sphere. A bipedal, humanoid, two and a half meters tall, give or take, floated in a translucent sack of amniotic fluid near the center of the sphere, linked to the wall by twisted organ cables attached to the base of its skull. The body showed no sign of nipples or genitalia.

"Is that you?"

"Yes, I've healed here without a consciousness since the crash." Stranger dropped her hand and drifted up through the fluid.

"Are you male or female."

He passed into the body but not through it. His eyes opened, luminous, black orbs.

****

Stranger looked out through the amniotic fluid in his healing chamber. Yume's consciousness had fled, which delayed the necessity to answer her question concerning their gender. Biological species required gender or an equivalent system for reproduction. Their species chose long ago to evolve beyond the biological.

Thinking of Yume initiated a routine within their body. Through the umbilicus, he sensed the request for information routed through systems to the healing cell of her predecessor, a consciousness snuffed when Ship crashed. Ship's body had regenerated, but vast sections of internal equipment remained twisted dead scar tissue.

They required time and energy for healing. Stranger signaled Ship, a handshake after a long sleep, and found Ship structurally complete, but without a present command consciousness. A tenuous link existed through a conceptual feedback routine, the essential connection between a conscious being and its shell housing. Ship lived, but without the necessary prime connection that allowed her consciousness to reattach to her physical body.

After numerous detours, the command routed to an identical healing chamber and returned the message, Crew member deceased, seeking a conceptual link to a replacement node.

Yume's presence, a combination of thought, sensory data, and wellness information trickled back through the feedback link. Of all his recruits, she evolved the quickest. The rest would require time on the ship to reach their full potential and come to grips with what they had become.

Ship read his grief in the flood of *corticotropin*, a hormone released to promote healing and help the brain deal with emotions. Stranger had not shared in the project that evolved their species to a new level, making them near-immortals. In retrospect, he wished they encouraged expressions of grief rather than overcoming it. Stranger's personal consciousness had survived five years within Vasyl

Petrenko's mind, and he had come to appreciate human expressions of grief.

Useful or not, he needed his eyes. Yume de Guzman existed for that purpose, able to shift her consciousness anywhere within reasonable limits. Being conscious, she focused all her abilities on seeing with mortal eyes, which left him in the dark about many things.

Had Ship functioned at full potential, he could move from mode to mode, using them as necessary through Ship's interface. With the primary functions offline, and much of the ship inoperable, waiting remained the only option. The umbilicus detached from the base of his skull, an autonomous response initiated by his movement. He swam to the film wall and passed through it.

Recognizing his presence, Ship fed fault data, damage reports, and launch checklists directly to Stranger's mind. Under normal circumstances, only Pilot could initiate a launch sequence, but Stranger possessed command authority to all functions in her absence.

He reached out with his mind and caressed Ship's conceptual feedback stream. Stranger's mind slipped from the neutral. How he missed her, sister, mother, lover, self to his brother, father, lover, self. The humans he converted to replace nodes would feel scandalized. Their gendered framework clashed with relationships of post-biological species.

It struck stranger that back in Ship, where the bodies they assumed knew no grief, that he carried pain with him. He missed Ship, missed her grace, the touch of her mind, her presence. Though they came so far from the bare fragment that had remained of their Liveship, there existed no guarantee of success. Uncomfortable tears trailed down his cheeks.

Time to go to work.

Yume gasped and propped herself up on elbows. Toss knelt beside her, wearing only a plastic, disposable chef's apron. He leaned close, face twisted with alarm. "You need to wake up. They're searching for us through the halls."

Her apron slipped. She pressed it against her breasts. *I don't remember taking my clothes off.*

Conversations with her aunt came to mind about what to do in such situations. Did that apply when a woman was captured and held against her will by shadowy figures?

Toss pulled back. "Thought you'd feel better if I covered you."

No woman ever wakes up naked, in a strange place, feeling better. Ashamed and angry, yes, and though it wasn't Toss' fault, more than a little annoyed at his banter. She hugged the opaque, gray apron close, and fantasized killing John Stark. "What happened?"

"They drugged us, placed us in an induced coma."

She glanced around at a small kitchen. "How did we get out?"

Toss offered her his hand. "Your sister and Stranger figured it out."

She pulled the neck strap over her head. "Clothes?"

"Woke up in a hospital room dressed for my first birthday party. I didn't think to ask politely to get them back."

She sat up. "We reached the ship after you woke."

He glanced left, toward a blank wall. "Where is it?"

She pointed the same direction.

"Yea, I get that too."

Quick footsteps pounded through the halls. Toss huddled beside her. The doorknob jiggled. A distant shout echoed through the walls. The movement ceased, and footsteps pattered away.

"We have to get out of here."

"There's another door over there." He motioned the direction. "Didn't hear any sounds on the other side so it might be a broom closet, a pantry, or an office. Don't see an easy way out."

She wrapped herself in her arms. "It may be necessary to surrender."

Toss nodded. "Yea, but they may shoot us for our trouble."

"I'd rather try that room first."

"We agree." He stood and offered his hand to help her up. "Ladies first."

She tied the apron strings behind her back. "I don't think so."

"All right then, follow me."

Beyond the door, they found an office with all the usual furnishings, a desk, stationary, posted schedules for work, posters warning of the hazards of food contamination, and a wall clock. Two filing cabinets flanked a small electrical room with circuit breakers and boxes of supplies. Better than all that, there was a window.

The sight of a muddy sky and scudding clouds provided a glimpse of heaven. How long had it been since they took her? She had not seen the world outside white walls with her real eyes since that van in San Diego. The office overlooked the side of a mountain with stretches of snow broken by twisted lavascapes and a few green treetops piercing through the surface of the snow, and in the distance, a sliver of ocean. A helicopter pad sat in front of the building, and a road twisted down the mountain toward the sea.

"Damn, but it seems like forever." The light, snow, and the bright, free horizon danced a number through her emotions.

"Prison's like that," Toss said.

She peeked up at his face. "You've been in prison."

"A year in Louisiana, and three in France."

"Were you guilty?"

"Of making a living in the wrong line of work."

A clump of footsteps penetrated through the walls but no voices. Toss held a finger to his lips. Yume chewed on her cheek waiting. Other than footfalls the searchers acted with stealth.

After a while, Toss sighed. "You have any suggestions, or do we surrender."

"I need to dream."

"Don't we all, kid."

"No, I need to dream. I can talk to my sister or to Stranger or to someone. If I only knew where we were."

"I'd say we're on Mount Snaefellsjokull, looking west over the Atlantic."

She looked up at him. "How do you know?"

"Been a fan of Jules Vern and *'A Journey to the Center of the Earth'* since I was a kid in New Orleans."

"You'll keep an eye on me."

"Oh, I have a better idea."

She didn't like the way he said that. "What are you going to do?"

"Teach John Stark how to chase a goose." He opened the door to the electrical room. "You can curl up here on the floor."

"What if they--?" She left the last word hanging.

"Don't worry about me. I'll give you all the time I can."

She started to answer, but he was gone.

****

Shiso woke huddled in the closet with her arms wrapped around her knees, head down. Oh, she so wanted sleep, but it was all on her, the lives of five people, including her own. All of them loose in the wind following a freaking compass in their heads, all of them with superpowers.

Why am I in a closet? She glanced left. Ah, *Yume is dreaming me again.*

Yume lay fetal on the floor, eyes closed, dressed only in a plastic apron.

"And why are you naked?"

Yume poked her head through the door without opening it. "That is me sleeping. This is me dreaming, and technically, I'm not naked."

Shiso glanced at Yume's body, barely covered by a gray plastic apron. "That's a pretty thin technicality, and don't you usually open the door first."

"I'm so past that. Now, come on, I need to show you something."

Shiso stood and fought the urge to brush the dust off her pants. She wasn't really in a closet, but her mind wanted to run with the dream. "So, we're dreaming?"

"Jesus, get up to speed. We are seeing or viewing or having an out of body experience. I don't know how, but that is how Stranger explained it. Same as when I came to see you in Mesquite. What you see is real. They just can't see us."

She ran her hand through her hair. "Oh, god, I just want to sleep."

"We don't have time. Toss is dressed in an apron, running through the halls, and playing tag with armed men."

"Both of you are dressed in aprons?"

Yume's arm came through the door, and she rapped Shiso on the forehead. "They drugged us, and I spent hours on a fantasy rollercoaster."

"Hate to tell you this, sis. It was more than a day."

"Oh shit." Yume stepped inside the closet. Her dream body wore the same panties and tank top she wore the first night this whole nightmare started.

"Don't you ever change your clothes?"

"It's a dream, so I don't have to, and you should talk."

Had Yume dressed her in ratty panties again? No, she wore the same pair of old jeans from Mesquite. "I changed clothes."

"Not in my dream. Come on."

Shiso held out a hand because her eyes would not allow her to walk into a wall. She passed through like a ghost, following Yume to the window. Yume stepped through and dropped. Shiso ran to the window. Yume hovered mid-air, her hand outstretched. "We have to get down."

"Why."

"I managed to return Stranger to his ship.

Shiso pushed her hand through the window. Reality felt like syrup. So long as it did not stick to her fingers, she supposed she would be fine. "Thought this was a dream."

"He called himself a disembodied conscious. I know the ship is downhill."

Shiso grabbed Yume's shoulder, terrified. They hovered five floors above the snow. "If I fall in a dream will I die?"

"I won't let you fall. You're outside, so it's your job. Bring Aranea and Vasyl here. I hope this will help."

Shiso stood in the air beside Yume. She kept one hand on the smooth side of the building as a brake against gravity. Her head told her this was a dream. Her eyes reported reality. A road, mostly clear of snow, curled around the front of the building and entered a parking structure. Their view took in a folded landscape of valleys and ridges receding to the ocean.

Yume pointed down-slope toward the distant ocean, grabbed Yume's hand, and walked through the air. "It must be over there."

"Could we walk on the ground?"

"Quicker this way."

They walked through the air much faster than on foot. Shiso kept her eyes on Yume or the horizon, so her mind embraced the weirdness. She found the changes in Yume more difficult to accept. Yume and never been this focused or disciplined. Her sister had changed in the days since they fled Suki's Paradise. Shiso wondered how much she had changed.

A warehouse half hidden beneath the snow in a valley opened beneath their feet. *"That has to be it. Don't you feel it, the compass in our heads?"*

Shiso glanced sideways. *"I think jail agrees with you."*

Yume glared. *"I haven't been in jail."*

"Well, captivity or whatever you want to call it. You take charge now."

"I think we've all changed."

"Come on, we have to find another mark of reference."

Yume followed the road, and their bodies screamed through the air as if they wore jet engines on their backs. The route followed the twists, curves, rise, and fall of the landscape until it entered a small town named Hellissandur if the sign at the city limits meant anything. Snow drifted down from dirty clouds, and a few locals strolled down icy streets or shoveled fresh snow off the sidewalks.

"This is it. Now you can find us?"

Shiso squeezed Yume's hand. "What do you suppose is going to happen when we get there?"

Yume glanced over her shoulder. "Oh no!"

Shiso's hand evaporated into mist and drifted up in the cold. Something firm touched her shoulder. She opened her eyes.

The Man from Denver stood over her. "We're here."

****

Vasyl Petrenko swallowed another shot of Vodka. Kuvayev had passed out half an hour back. The four men from FutureTense remained alert, positioned well apart, drinking water although Kuvayev had given each of them a bottle.

Men relaxed when returning home, drank, talked, read magazines, or slept. These men remained alert, on guard. *"They know."*

"Of course, they know. Stark is no fool." Clockbrain's thoughts felt different, louder and stronger, as if he sat in the next seat drinking Vodka.

Vasyl slumped lower, pretending to settle into the dead sleep of a colossal drunk. *"You've changed."*

"I reunited with my body."

"Wonderful." He didn't mean that, of course. The word filled the space that understanding would have taken. *"I thought you existed in my head."*

"A figment of your imagination, you mean."

That remained a possibility. Perhaps all of this was no more than the lunatic fantasy of a madman, and he lay in a ditch talking to his rat.

Before he organized his next comment, Shiso's voice broke in. *"The ship, it's in a warehouse near a town named Hellissandur, near Snaefellsjokull."*

Vasyl recognized the name. *"Jules Vern's volcano in Journey to the Center of the Earth. Is that where we are going?"*

Clockbrain answered, *"We most certainly are not."*

Vasyl felt Shiso's sudden surprise flood into his mind. *"Why is Stranger in your head, Vasyl?"*

"Stranger? His name is Clockbrain."

"Please, I answer to both names."

Stranger? Clockbrain? He wondered if they all heard voices. *"So, which name is correct?"*

Stranger bristled at the question, his emotion feeding into their minds like a mild electric shock. *"Both."*

Shiso pushed in. *"Your name is Stranger and Clockbrain?"*

Stranger receded, his presence all but disappearing. Whatever the truth, he did not want to discuss it. *"Those are names given by the de Guzman's and Vasyl."*

"And your real name is?" Shiso transmitted confusion and concern.

"Not important. Shiso, find Aranea and be prepared to act when we arrive."

"But--" she began.

"Go," Clockbrain ordered. She vanished.

"You sent her away."

"We have much to do, Vasyl. You will have to kill these men."

"Not drunk enough to do that."

Clockbrain's emotions slid into the annoyance of a faint, angry static buzz. *"Your body has changed. You cannot become intoxicated with alcohol."*

"What makes you think I could kill without being drunk?"

"Do you want to die, Vasyl Petrenko?"

What a question. Vasyl hated the killing, wanted it to stop. He wondered if serial killers ever questioned the voices inhabiting their heads that told them to kill.

"You are not Schizophrenic."

Vasyl laughed aloud. *"Yes, yes, I'll bet all the voices say that."*

"Do you want Aranea to die?"

That question clenched his resolve. *"No?"*

"It took five years to bring you all to this place. All of you are necessary. If you do not act, we all die."

"Why me?" He wondered why he had not asked that before.

"It is the role you accepted."

"A role? Is this a theater play that Clockbrain directs?"

"So to speak, it was offered to thousands. Only you survived."

One part of him wanted to say no, wanted to refuse. If it were just Vasyl, Clockbrain could pound sand up his ass if he had one.

This was for Aranea. He owed her. *"What do I do?"*

"Do not let them shoot you in the head?"

"That's useful."

"You heal at an incredible rate, can turn off the pain from your wounds, and move at roughly twice a human's speed. But we have yet to create a copy of your consciences. A bullet in your brain would be permanent."

An announcement from the cockpit pulled his attention away. "We are coming in for our final approached. We should be on the ground in Keflavik in half an hour."

"You have to do this now."

"Any other suggestions."

"Visit the toilet. One of the men is stationed near there."

CHAPTER EIGHT

Rescuing Vasyl

Vasyl pushed himself up and pretended to hold onto the back of the seat in a desperate attempt to keep from falling on his drunken face.

"Shet there," He said to the unconscious Kuvayev. "I can piss all by myself."

He stood and swayed while reaching for his zipper as if he intended to whip it out and spray the floor but reconsidered the urge. He walked with the extreme care of a drunk attempting to hide the booze, one hand always holding something until he came alongside the guard nearest the restroom.

The man stood; his hand under his jacket. The other visible guard eased to his feet and pretended to stretch, ready either to come to the aide of the first guard or to shoot.

Vasyl pointed at the bottle of Vodka and added a tremor to his hand. "You want that?"

The guard's eyes shifted to the bottle.

No matter how often this happened, Vasyl's mind boggled at his speed. He grabbed the man's hand and jerked. The agent's shoulder cracked, separating from the socket. Vasyl pulled the body close like a shield and spun around to face the next agent. Two gunshots fired close together. The first bullet struck Vasyl's shoulder, and the second caught the agent he wielded as a shield in the chest.

Vasyl held the corpse up for a shield and met the second agent half way. Another bullet drilled into his side. He wrapped his hands around the pistol and bent the hand back. Bones shattered. The man screamed. Vasyl fired a round up into the agent's brain from beneath his chin.

The third guard ejected a clip from his pistol. Vasyl fired, and a bullet blew through the hollow of his target's collar-bone. The man grabbed his neck and choked, spraying blood. He locked gazes with the last guard. The man raised his pistol aiming at Vasyl's head. Their weapons discharged. A bullet tore a gash along Vasyl's temple, knocking him onto his back beneath the corpse of his first victim. He struggled to rise, unsure whether the guard took a bullet or ran through the intervening space to fire the coup-de-gras.

Rising to his feet, he saw the fourth man dead—a bullet blew through the bridge of his nose and out the back of his head.

A roaring filled the passenger compartment. Bullets had taken out windows. However, the aircraft had descended low enough so that they did not suffocate.

Kuvayev struggled to rise.

Vasyl raised the weapon and pointed it at Kuvayev's face.

"Kill him," Clockbrain's thought sounded like a shout.

"Lay down, comrade."

The Russian nodded and fell back into the seat. Vasyl tore seat belts free and tied the man down.

"You should have killed him."

Vasyl checked the knots. *"He is not a threat."*

"An exceptional justification."

He sat down, dizzy, stomach screaming.

"You need to eat. When detached from the ship, you convert your body's natural reserves. You are not an infinite source of energy."

He grabbed another bottle of vodka and swallowed half down. Kuvayev, awake if not sober, watched him.

"What now, Mr. Clockbrain?"

"Just think the words."

"I tire of that. Sometimes it's good to hear a human voice."

Vasyl wiped the blood from his face on a towel. He envied Kuvayev's opportunity to sleep off his colossal drunk.

Clockbrain interfered again. *"We have to get into the cockpit."*

"I don't think even this body is strong enough to do that." Vasyl ambled to the front of the plane. Clockbrain's presence felt like lightning in his head. *"Bulletproof, steel reinforced, designed to keep everyone out, just in case someone wants to take over the plane. For better or worse, I have to wait to land."*

Clockbrain's rage and frustration burned like a fever. *"You are not immortal."*

"Fortunately."

"One shot to the head and all this is for nothing."

"Don't sound so bitter. I'm not dead yet."

****

Shiso sat behind the wheel of a white van, the cargo area filled with a few boxes that her rescuer said, "You might find useful, or you might not."

"You never said who you are!"

He walked away. Shiso half opened the door? Who was he? What was he? Why did he save her life? She needed to know. A woman's voice spoke out of her pocket. "Let him go."

Shit, the phone.

Shiso pulled it out of her jeans. Oviraptorus' face filled the screen. "Who are you?"

"The woman that looks after you and fulfills your wishes."

"That's a fairy godmother, which you are not."

"The little bird has a sharp beak, but stationary is not safe, only flight, unexpected, random, provides cover. I cannot teach you the song of my life if we are not safe. Start this vehicle. Drive. We will talk."

Shiso shook her head. "I need to know."

"Spread your wings and fly or I will return to storage and wait for someone who wishes to live."

Shiso started the van, glanced in the side mirror, and accelerated past large warehouses. Clouds hovered overhead, and snow clung to the roads.

Oviraptorus' head swiveled to the left as if she tried to look out of the screen of her phone. "Faster would be good."

"I've never driven on snow or ice. Driving faster is bad. Now, who are you?"

"For the moment, I'm Homeland Security."

"What does Homeland Security care about me?"

"Stark and FutureTense care about you."

"What have you done for us?"

"We have burned agents for your benefit. We spent enormous sums saving you from capture, flying you here. Drive, little bird."

Shiso held the steering wheel with her hands at the ten and two O'clock positions, afraid the tires would slip. In that eventuality, she would need to remember which way to turn the wheels if she went into a slide, her memory hazy on that subject. "Really? Homeland Security has an App on my phone? Why does Homeland Security give a damn about us?"

"FutureTense Incorporated is a powerful multinational corporation with its fingers in everything of importance to the earth."

"They're the bad guys?"

Oviraptorus put her finger on her lips, a dramatic pause. "They are powerful. Power is of interest to us. Who has it? Who they give it to? Who uses it? Good and bad are subjective concepts, irrelevant."

"What does the great Homeland Security want us to do?"

"Go where you are being led."

"And that is."

"That would be telling, now, wouldn't it?"

Shiso almost stabbed the brakes. It would feel so good to throw that phone through the window, turn around, and go home. Suki's Paradise and her Tio were gone, so she had no home, no choice. "How do I get there?"

"You feel the arrow in your head. Rescue your friends and then follow it."

"But how do I do that?"

"Ah, they are about to find me. Goodbye, for now, little bird."

The phone switched itself off.

An oppressive silence made her thoughts more alarming. She turned on the heat. Warm air blasting through the vents felt like a breeze from summer. The radio came next, and she found a station playing Björk's Hyperballad, a song her mother had loved.

With music and warmth, she thought about Aranea. A woman who could walk through walls and not be touched would be useful.

She did not know why, but Aranea was all she had.

****

Aranea waited inside a wall, well away from the car with its bouquet of agents, a scene she would have considered surreal two weeks before, but now not even worth remarking on. She could not see their faces but read their body language. Some agents held hurried conversations over their cell phones, others fanned out and waited at some distance from the center of the group, guns at ready, eyes on everything. Military police arrived, blocked the road, and widened the perimeter. The number of men used made her out to be a deadly enemy who demanded heavy weapons and overwhelming military force to hold her at bay.

She felt flattered in a vague sort of way, flattered and frightened.

Aranea closed her eyes and searched for calm while breathing the stale air in her sphere. Madeline never left the car. Its dark windows made it impossible to see inside. The directive from Shiso tore Aranea in half. Orders from a sixteen-year-old would once have galled. Now, they just made sense. She wanted to charge in and rescue Madeline like a white hat cavalry. Those men with their guns could not touch her unless she stepped out of her warp bubble.

She could position herself under the car and come up, but if someone else occupied the space inside, she wasn't sure if she could exclude them. In a movie, there would be no obstacle. She could get in, kick ass, and rescue her friend. Aranea did not have the skills.

A helicopter landed on the road. Stark and other men in camouflage body armor moved in under the protective watch of the military. They held a brief, disciplined conversation.

The car doors flew open, and two men ushered Madeline from the car. Six of them surrounded her. She walked fast, pushed by men with a constant hold on her as if they expected a beast would rise out of the earth and swallow them all.

As the helicopter lifted, she whispered, "Sorry, Madeline."

Once the helicopter disappeared into the west, the military fanned out from the car. Soldiers searched everything, careful, methodical. Aranea pulled her face back into the wall. She needed to move away, get something to eat and drink, find a place to think.

She needed to prepare for Shiso's call.

"Aranea?"

"Speak of the Devil."

"Uh, I'm not the Devil."

Aranea laughed. *"A figure of speech."*

"Vasyl is arriving soon. He will need to be rescued."

"They have military here, hundreds, maybe more."

"They can't touch you."

"Not until I open up the bubble. I'm not bulletproof."

"You are inside the bubble and have nothing to worry about."

"Look, I don't think I'm equipped to ride in like the Cavalry."

"Cavalry?"

"Cowboys, Indians, John Wayne; did you ever watch old movies?"

"Pop-culture reference fail."

Aranea could not see Shiso de Guzman, but she felt her laughter. The tension broke, and they both laughed. She ran her hands through her hair. "I needed that."

"Me too. Been a while since I laughed."

"Where are you?"

"Driving down an Icelandic street with a long and difficult name, Valhallabraut, I think."

"That's not difficult."

"Says the Greek lady."

"Try driving around in the Ukraine, different language, different alphabet."

Shiso's mind quieted. Aranea felt her presence, and a distant sorrow, but no real communication. She wondered if Shiso knew that she communicated more than she verbalized, that emotions slipped through the mental link. That would make her what, an empath as well as a telepath?

"I'm sorry."

"Me, too." Her acceptance felt real, but the moment of personal connection had passed.

"How do we rescue Vasyl." Her voice caught when she said his name. After all these years, she still felt something. What if she failed? What if she killed him?

"There has to be something I can do."

"What about Stranger? Can he help?" Aranea paused for a moment. *"What does he do?"*

"I don't see how. Stranger returned to his ship."

"Ship."

"He's an alien, and he made us."

"Yes, I understand that."

Aranea poked her head out of the building wall to see if there were soldiers. Even if they couldn't hurt her, she did not want to be seen. A United 737 dropped out of the clouds, angling down toward the runway.

"I wonder how fast I can fly?"

The question was for Shiso's benefit. The airplane followed a predictable glide slope. If she drifted to the right altitude, it would fly through her, or she would pass through it.

Shiso's frustration bled through. *"I don't know what you are talking about."*

"I need to talk to Stranger."

"He isn't here."

"You have telepathy. You can link us."

"Give me a minute."

****

Stranger ran a hand over his bald scalp. For the first time in a remarkably long life, he wished he grew hair. He could if he wanted. Since the leap to a non-biological life, form followed function and desire. His ship, his mate, was female. The crew, all dear friends until the crash, had chosen shapes the Ship required or on a whim.

As Stranger, he took a form dictated by Yume de Guzman, but he had become accustomed to the hair, and

238

understood how helpful tearing it out as an expression of frustration would be.

For five orbits of a star, he had lived in the head of a madman. Ship healed and grew without its consciousness according to a general design template. Left without a guiding conscious, personality, or guide, she regenerated in chaotic ways.

Tracing nerve conduits through the core of the living ship left him grimy and frightened. Could Ship fly? If Ship did not sit in a hangar surrounded by hostile humans that would use whatever force necessary to breach her skin, he would test fire the drive systems. If successful, half the humans working to plumb her secrets would burn, but he would know.

The consequences, however, would be severe.

"Stranger?" Shiso de Guzman's voice emanated from speaker nodes in the walls.

He closed his eyes and looked inward. In a tiny room, Yume de Guzman searched for her sister. Because Shiso called, and Yume saw, he gazed out through Toss Bonneteau's eyes. Toss ran down a passageway with bullets frozen in the air. Turbulence from his passage knocked heavily armed and armored soldiers aside like toys. While glancing in a mirror, Vasyl washed the blood from his face.

"You have linked us, Shiso. How you have grown."

Vasyl dried his face with a towel. *"Six people in my head is not an improvement."*

Toss ran around a corner and sagged against a wall. *"Can't keep this up much longer. Nice to talk to you all one last time."*

Shiso's thought twisted and united the five. *"This is what I'm supposed to do. I don't know how long."*

Stranger clapped his hands but calmed himself with a breath. *"You will grow with each use."*

Through Aranea's eyes, he tracked her view as she shifted her gaze and caught sight of another aircraft descending through the ceiling of ash clouds. *"I have a question?"*

Everyone else quieted save Stranger. *"Go ahead."*

"I can rise up and intercept Vasyl's flight, but they are moving fast. How fast can I fly?"

"As fast as thought, as fast as you need. You guide by mind."

"What about the guards?"

Vasyl answered, *"They are dead or captured, koxána."*

In his head, Stranger translated the word to sweetheart, and the meaning passed through Shiso to everyone.

Shiso did not want to know that. *"Way too much information."*

Stranger ignored her. *"They may open fire rather than lose their prisoner. How close are you, Vasyl?"*

"We are on a glide slope, but still in the clouds. Soon I think. Can you stay in my mind, Shiso? Soon as we drop down, you will know."

"I can."

Stranger eased away from the ship's nerve conduits. He had a team, now, and needed to look after all of them. *"Toss, can you return to Yume."*

"Maybe, won't be easy." Stranger felt him move away, and his thoughts compressed.

"Stay there. Stay safe. We rescue you next." Toss' manipulation of time made his answer an unrecognizable whine.

Vasyl said. *"I'm beginning to see more light."*

Aranea locked eyes on the plane emerging from the clouds. *"Time to go."*

Stranger's tenuous link with them remained. He wanted to sing one of the ancient songs of his people, but it required more voices than he could command.

"Where is she?" he wondered. *"My captain, my mate. The Ship, She, lives and grows, so her consciousness remains."* He had hoped that she would recognize when the ship became functional and return. Somehow FutureTense isolated Ship. He hoped that if they managed to escape this location, she would find them.

****

Well beyond the far end of the runway, an aircraft dropped below the ash clouds, a stylized FT marking the tail. Aranea flew the sphere out of the wall, flying up toward a point above the center of the runway.

"I see the light." She caught Vasyl's message

"Be ready."

Gunsmoke and movement from the north side of the field attracted her eye. Soldiers fired automatic weapons. Tracer fire marked the paths of bullets. They touched one side of the bubble and appeared on the opposite with no discernible effect.

"They're firing at me."

She accelerated toward the nose of the plane. In the last seconds, she saw two men in the cockpit, eyes terrified. After passing between them and through the door, she willed herself to stop. Aranea traveled half the length of the plane before coming to rest.

Two dead men sprawled in pools of blood. Another two corpses slumped in seats. A fifth, a conscious man in a military uniform tied down with torn seat belts, jerked at his restraints.

"Where are you?"

"In the back, hurry."

Windows blew inward, and chunks of the wall ricocheted among the seats. Bullets tore jagged holes in the metal walls.

She flew through a wall and entered a conference room. A woman lay handcuffed to a gurney. A little girl in handcuffs sat beside the woman. Vasyl unlocked the girl's cuffs.

Aranea dropped her warp bubble and fell half a foot to the floor. The aircraft shuddered. Explosions rocked the plane as windows in the back section blew out.

Vasyl unlocked one of the woman's cuffs. "You have to take us all."

"I don't know if I can."

"I tire of killing people. Try, for me, please."

She took an envelope of air in the bubble, so she knew she could carry other things, but the mass of the woman strapped to the gurney increased the effort by orders of magnitude. Aranea grabbed Vasyl with one hand and the woman's knee with the other.

The warp bubbled expanded around them all. Aranea gasped and almost crumpled. A force tapped her heart. She felt herself flowing away. Warping alone left her exhausted and starved. Three people and most of a gurney? Her vision wavered as if she saw the world through a drifting veil.

Fire bloomed around the sphere. The little girl in Vasyl's arms screamed, providing a soundtrack for the disintegrating aircraft.

"It's breaking up," Vasyl said.

Aranea drifted with the fire and debris to the ground and continued into the earth beneath the fireball. She whispered, "Have to get away."

Vasyl handed her something cold and smooth. "Drink the Vodka."

Aranea thought south and hoped that would be enough. She glanced at Vasyl's frowning frozen face. "Wonder how time is affected inside a warp bubble."

The little girl wrapped her arms around Vasyl's neck and spoke in Russian. "She doesn't sound so good."

"Shh, she's working."

Aranea hoped she had traveled far enough to get out of sight of soldiers. Her head spun, and her stomach ached. The top of her head rose above the ground in the middle of a road running between warehouses. She passed through the wall of the building, rose above the floor, and dropped the bubble. Aranea landed in a heap on the concrete floor between long rows of shipping containers. Light collapsed around her.

****

John Stark rode the lead fire truck toward the rising column of smoke. Two ambulances and a second vehicle followed as a precaution, not that precautions mattered in the burning debris field. He stepped down onto the tarmac and raised a hand to catch the attention of the fire crew's scene leader. "How many escaped?"

The man glanced sideways at the fire spread over half an acre of the runway. "No one walked away from that crash, Mr. Stark."

Stark did not doubt the team leader's scientific assessment. The fuselage of the plane lay in four pieces, the wings detached and broken, and fire covered everything. No human walked away from the crash. A series of explosions, the result of damage due to heavy automatic weapons fire, had torn the plane apart and left a remarkably compact debris field. The man could not guess that something alien traveled inside the plane. Stark had no idea where to place the limits of the powers of Gekas and Petrenko. "I need a positive count of fourteen bodies. When you find them, deliver the remains to the Snaefellsjokull facility."

The team leader took off his helmet. "The Icelandic government will not--" he began.

Stark cut him off with a brief shake of his head. "The Icelandic government will stay out of this. Do as I say."

The crew chief climbed down from the truck and joined his team using fire hoses and water cannons to hose foam over the wreckage and the runway. "The NTSB will be all over this site within eight hours."

"I can handle the NTSB. Do your job."

Stark left, seeking out the members of his team who had formed a perimeter around the burning wreckage. Always professional, they knew their jobs and performed them without the need to await orders.

His phone buzzed, and he answered without looking. "Stark."

"We have yet to apprehend Bonneteau or Guzman." Becker's voice registered anger and disgust.

Stark wondered if he had assigned the right person for the job. He shut down the concern. It was his policy to never second guess himself. Mistakes were a natural part of any undertaking. If it proved disastrous, he would make a different choice, next time. "Did they escape?"

The Doctor grimaced. "No. We maintained complete isolation of the prison hospital floor. After sustaining seven casualties, I pulled my teams back."

"Have they killed anyone?"

"Two are in critical but stable condition. When Bonneteau moves, he creates enormous turbulence. They were too close when he passed between them."

The situation had gone off the rails, and his intent to control the five and learn from them had failed. Too much had gone wrong, and he suspected he was one mistake from losing everything. "Kill them both."

"That's not my job."

"You're fired. Ms. Thorn will land within the hour turn control over to her and return to your position as chief medical officer."

"Yes, sir."

"Once you confirm they are dead, put a watch on their bodies, especially during the autopsies."

"You think they are going to come back to life?"

"One of the survivors can kill people and become them. Another one surrounds herself with an intangible, impenetrable bubble. Bonneteau moves faster than anyone alive. I don't know what they can do."

"This is unexpected."

"We were tasked to capture them alive if possible. That is no longer possible."

"Yes, sir."

"Double the security on their ship."

"Do they know where we have it?"

"I don't see any other reason for them to be in Iceland."

"Anything else, sir?"

"Attach charges to the hull of the ship. If we can't keep it safe, we destroy it."

****

Toss poked his head around the corner. He expected a squad of men advancing in close order, a moving human wall. With even a narrow space he could slide sidewise through a group, they flew like bowling pins against the walls.

Colliding with a soldier had the same effect as if he hit a man with a car. It hurt him a bit, but the amount of energy transferred to the soldier was sufficient to put a man in the hospital. A group of men in a solid wall might retain enough inertia to slow him to the point where they could catch him.

He saw no one at all, and that surprised him. Stark's men must have pulled back. He suspected that meant something wrong, but the notion of being alone, even for a while, lifted his mood. He ran to the rooms where he left Yume and slowed to a reasonable, human pace.

Hunger gnawed at this stomach, and thirst parched his mouth. He drank three bottles of water without a pause and looked for food. A gallon of cooking oil occupying a high shelf with other dry ingredients drew a laugh. "Man, this is going to make me run like Usain Bolt."

He took two long swallows, and once he passed the oily feel, it went down as smooth as a fine whiskey. He moved through the back door, looking for the closet where he left Yume. It hit him. When was the last time he felt the urge to take a whiz or even squat?

He had been hooked up to catheters, of course, and probably cleaned by nurses, but a man his age did not hold water or anything else with the efficiency of the young.

Yume looked up when he eased into the closet, terror flashed across her face before she recognized him.

"Didn't mean to scare you."

"I know." She curled up tight and patted the floor.

He shook his head. His eyelids must have weighed a ton and wanted only to close and stay that way. His legs and arms ached from the exertion. He took another swallow of cooking oil, and it felt like speed straight to his snake brain. "You don't feel a need to visit the ladies room, do you? Maybe take a tinkle."

Yume's eyes scrunched up. "I think that is the weirdest question anyone ever asked."

"It just occurred to me that since I woke up, I haven't felt the need. After all that exercise, for a man my age that ain't normal."

She hugged herself. "Two days ago, I think."

"Is that normal?"

She shook her head. "Not at all. In fact, I should have started--"

She stopped herself, but his mind pounced on what she didn't say and understood.

He sat beside her and put his feet up against the door. "I wonder what we are like on the inside."

She leaned against Toss, and he put his arm around her.

"I don't think we're human anymore."

Her head popped up, and he caught her fear.

Toss patted her shoulder. "Oh, we look human, but I'd bet that the human is just skin deep. Whatever we are under the skin?" He shrugged because he knew no words to express this fear.

"What are they going to do to us?"

He did not want to say, but Yume did not sound like a young woman who wanted a comforting lie. "I think they are going to kill us and then cut us into pieces to see what makes us tick."

"Then we have to get out of here."

Toss sighed. "I know where the doors are, but they're locked, and I'd bet a lot of unfriendly people wait on the other side."

Yume chewed on her lip, thinking he guessed right. "I need to look below."

"Going ghost and dropping through the floor?"

She nodded. "Yes. Let me talk to my sister."

Shiso's voice echoed through Toss' mind as if she had been eavesdropping just to hear her name. *"I hear you."*

"Shiso, I need to see the floor below. You have to help."

"A lot going on here, sis. I Can't drive and sleep at the same time?"

Yume laughed aloud. *"Since when?"*

"It only happened once."

"I can't think of anything else. You'll have to translate what I see for Toss."

Shiso's frustration and fear translated into dynamic tension. *"Stranger should have made another radio operator."*

The overwhelming sense of Stranger fed through the telepathic link with Yume's mind. *"One is quite enough, thank you very much. I will join Yume. Perhaps my observations can help. I have done all I can until the Captain and Her crew return."*

Yume touched Toss' arm. "Take care of me while I'm gone."

"This sounds pretty desperate."

"You have a better idea."

Toss stood and offered her his hand. "Can't say as I do."

****

Shiso glanced into the side mirror. A police car careened around a corner with lights and sirens signaling an emergency. Her stomach clenched, and she pulled to the side. "I'm caught," she whispered.

The screen on the phone lit. "You're fine, little bird. The Police are tasked with guarding the parameter of the airport," Oviraptorus said.

"And you know this how?"

"Remember, I'm the Homeland Security App on your phone?"

She pulled the van back onto the road. "I've been thinking about that."

"Thinking is a dangerous thing."

Shiso felt the presence of Aranea and Vasyl away to the right, arrows in her mind that pointed like the other that had been there since the beginning. She followed their arrows, keeping what she hoped was a discrete distance from the police.

"You're too quick and smart for an App. You're a living human."

"Well, you are fractionally correct. Consider yourself to have earned fifty points."

"Dead humans don't talk. Did you survive the Russian event in 2016? There were only five of us."

"Clever girl, there are only five of you. Keep guessing."

"Stranger, is that you?"

"I'm neither Stranger nor Clockbrain nor any other version of himself."

"Clockbrain and Stranger are the same."

"True, but I'm not another fragment of that consciousness."

Sirens wailed in every direction. How were they going to get out of this?

"You're Ship." That had to be it. Stranger lamented that his ship was missing its consciousness.

"Very good. Pilot would be a more accurate word. You've increased our chances of escaping alive by 1.3%."

A line of police cars and ambulances came into sight behind them. Shiso pulled to the side again and parked between two warehouses. "We're going to get caught. I can feel where Aranea and Vasyl are hiding, and I'm getting warmer."

"What's the temperature to do with it?" Oviraptorus said.

Shiso hated overly literal aliens. "I meant closer."

"Ah, you referenced the children's game." Laughter peeled from the speaker. "Call them. Tell them they have to come to you."

"Then what?"

"Got to go."

The phone switched off. "I'm tired of that. Hope Aranea and Vasyl can think of something."

****

Aranea walked heel to toe atop one of the toppled ionic columns in the National Gardens. Today, she is just seven and perfectly happy with that, thank you very much. Mother and father are still together. Men, heartbreaks, and Russia are years away, and the memories that sit on the edge of her consciousness are shelved under, go to hell.

"Aranea."

Who could that be? It sounded like an adult woman's voice. Why couldn't it be a faun or even Pan? They could dance.

A Satyress stepped out of the trees, her goat legs awkward. She recognized Shiso de Guzman though the Satyress and the young woman looked nothing alike. "Aranea, please, I get enough of this from my sister."

Aranea sat up. The little girl from the plane smiled and spoke in Russian. "What's your name?"

The other woman, the one handcuffed to the bed, rubbed her chaffed wrists. Something about that woman felt familiar, as if she knew her, though not from the plane. Aranea, let it go. "Where's Vasyl."

The little girl shrugged. "Hmm-mmm."

The child-speak needed no translation. With effort, Aranea summoned up Russian for "Starving."

The girl handed her a bottle of Vodka. "He said drink this."

Aranea gulped half the bottle in three long swallows. She felt the slight alcoholic burn, but otherwise, it acted like water. She held the bottle up and checked the label. "I haven't chugged Chopin vodka since the university."

The little girl nodded. "I'm Ivanna."

Aranea's hunger vanished.

I'm like a machine, and I run on alcohol.

"Aranea Gekas."

Her face screwed in a small frown and she balled her fists. "You're Vasyl's girlfriend."

"Was his girlfriend." She felt ridiculous talking to a child about an adult relationship.

How do I explain old history to a child?

Vasyl stepped around the end of a pile of crates. "I can't find a way out, police everywhere."

Aranea knew Vasyl, but not because she recognized the face of a middle-aged Russian. She felt it in her head. Something about the change gave her a new organ for recognition. "What are we going to do?"

The link to Shiso opened. *"Thank God you woke up. I hate goat legs. You and Vasyl must get out of there. Bring him to me. I can't get any closer."*

Vasyl placed a comforting hand on Ivanna's shoulder but gazed into Aranea's eyes. "She's right. Give me a minute."

"Take as long as you want." Aranea swallowed another mouthful of vodka.

Will we get out of this alive, and would that be a good thing?

With each escape, disaster squeaked closer. What would they do when they reached the ship or whatever it was? She looked again at the label. At least, the vodka was good. Too bad, she could not get drunk to save her soul.

The other woman watched Vasyl approach, hesitant. Something had passed between them. Sex, of course. She felt it through her link to Vasyl's mind via Shiso, not the memory just the fact.

Oh, this just keeps getting better and better.

Shiso answered, *"Welcome to my world."*

The woman sat up. "Why didn't you kill me?"

What? Do I want to know this?

"I didn't have to. I assume you've killed people. Why do you do it?"

"It's necessary."

He glanced back at Aranea. "We should go."

The woman continued. "How did you change into Lagounov and me?"

Vasyl took a deep breath and his body tensed. Aranea had known him well enough to read his body language. He did not want to talk with this woman or about the subject.

He didn't look back. "I don't know. Please take care of Ivanna."

"Sure, why not."

He stalked back to where the woman stood and poked into the small of her throat. "If she is hurt, I will hold you responsible. You will never know who is coming to kill you, or when."

Aranea placed her free hand on his shoulder, and the warp bubble expanded, shutting off all sound before they sank through the floor.

In the darkness underground, she oriented on Shiso and took another swallow. "You can change into a woman?"

"Yes." His tone was final.

"Completely?"

"We had sex, all right? I require intimate contact."

"What about the guy you are wearing now."

"I killed him and stuffed his corpse down an outhouse."

"Oh."

"Your thoughts are creepy, right now." Shiso sent.

Vasyl laughed. It was his laugh, exactly, with its accustomed touch of hysteria and fear. "You have no idea."

"*Oh, I do, I do.*" Shiso answered.

CHAPTER NINE

Cocoons

Aranea sipped Vodka and ignored Vasyl, who stood as far away as he could. His fear fed through Shiso's mental link and threatened to wall off that arrow in her mind.

"Vasyl, why are you so afraid?"

Vasyl glanced over his shoulder. "What makes you think--of course."

Shiso spoke in his head without invitation. "Sorry, I don't mean to. It's getting harder to remain separate."

Vasyl shifted until his back touched Aranea's. "The changes are accelerating. I thought--"

Shiso picked up his thought and finished it. "That the changes had stopped because we do what we do."

Vasyl laughed, and Aranea heard his laughter and felt his bitter sarcasm through the mental link. "I would much rather do what you do, Shiso," he said.

Shiso sent. "Can't blame you. Changing to a guy in the middle of sex would be, embarrassing."

For a second, Aranea's concentration faltered, and she felt the earth begin to press in. "What?"

"Koxána."

She focused on the invisible wall, and it expanded once more. "I'm almost there."

Vasyl shifted and brushed against her back. He answered Shiso with his mind. *"I'll thank you to stay out of my head."*

Shiso sent. "I can't, not entirely. It's like all the stuff in your head is leaking into mine."

"We're here." Aranea drifted up through the ground and the bottom of the van. She moved to the back and collapsed the bubble.

Shiso's eyes widened. "That was, wow."

"I know what you mean." Aranea walked to the front of the van and eased into the passenger seat. Vasyl sat on the floor. They drove in silence, no one speaking. Aranea tried not to think anything and found it impossible.

Shiso turned the van onto another road, and Aranea felt the compass in her head point home. "You feel it too."

Shiso nodded. "Yeah."

She welcomed the sound of words. *Will I ever get used to hearing voices in my head?*

Shiso glanced up in her mirror and tapped Aranea on the shoulder.

"I think we're being followed."

****

John Stark watched the van through a rifle scope. "The driver is a positive match for Shiso de Guzman."

He placed the rifle on his lap. "Wasp, close the roadblock. Thrush, take your shots. No survivors."

"Yes," Manquoba said.

"Yes," Thomas Wu echoed.

Stark changed channels. "Thorn."

"Are you in position?"

"We have Bonneteau and Guzman isolated on the hospital floor. I'm waiting for a report from Leeds that all personnel are clear of the building."

"How long?"

"Ten minutes. It'd be easier if we could set off a fire alarm."

"We go in five. Manquoba will call it. We cannot risk a survivor escaping."

****

Vasyl collapsed against the seat.

God, but I'd love to sleep.

He hoped Shiso would not transmit or repeat it to everyone, but he didn't care. He wanted to sleep, but not from exhaustion, just to be able to close his eyes and drift away for a while.

"There's something up ahead."

He craned his neck until his head topped the dash. A large truck blocked the road thirty meters ahead. "You said you thought we were being followed?"

"Yes."

The screen of the phone that sat on the center console displayed a woman's face.

"It's a trap. They're going to kill you," Oviraptorus said.

He grabbed Shiso and Aranea by the shoulder and jerked them down.

The windshield and side window blew out. Bullets blasted through the walls of the van. Something burned through his shoulder and wrist.

Aranea screamed as a hole appeared in her shoulder. Blood and flesh sprayed around them.

"My phone!" Shiso called. She groped for the center console where Oviraptorus looked out from the phone. A bullet blew through Shiso's hand. She screamed.

A part of Vasyl's mind demanded that he vomit and curl into a ball. It felt normal. He accelerated, his muscles flushed. Falling glass slowed, and he grabbed the phone, hugged both women close and pulled them to the floor beneath him.

The uncanny silence of Aranea's warp bubble surrounded them. Outside the bubble, bullets blasted through the walls, sunlight angled into the interior. Shiso sobbed beneath him. Aranea, pale and sweaty, held the broken neck of the vodka bottle in her hand. They passed through the back of the van, floating in air. Guns blasted without sound. Nothing touched them.

"Into the earth," He whispered.

Instead, they accelerated in the direction of the compass in their heads. Vasyl sensed that place, whatever it might be, rushing nearer.

A small bullet hole in the front of Aranea's right shoulder ballooned in the back to a gaping crater exposing bones, muscle, and torn arteries. Blood covered the front of her blouse, but the bleeding had stopped.

"Dead," He whispered, and his heart twisted on itself.

"No." Shiso gasped.

Red filaments grew out of Aranea's flesh over the wounds. A few drops of blood seeped through.

The process duplicated over the exit wound. Pale skin and cold sweat of shock. Vasyl laid Aranea down as much as possible over the lower curve of the sphere.

"Vasyl," Oviraptorus said.

"What?"

"She's cocooning, healing herself. Aranea will be fine."

"How?"

"Slow down your acceleration, and do not allow yourself to adapt her form."

Her blood covered his face and chest. He noticed that his fingers had lengthened and the skin smoothened, hands that once touched him. He closed his eyes and remembered an image of himself, just before their first date. In that memory, he wiped the condensation from the mirror in the shower room, a straight razor in his hand.

"That's a good look for you," Shiso said.

"It's my default shape." He glanced at his hands, expecting to see the straight razor that had once belonged to his father.

Shiso held up her hand and watched the fibers grow over her own wounds with an expression between horror and amazement. "You mean your real shape."

"I don't have a real shape, anymore."

"Vasyl!" The phone lay on the bottom of the bubble.

"What?"

"Hold her. Put your hands on her skin?"

Shiso shook her head. "This is creepy."

"She needs energy and can use yours."

Vasyl didn't ask how. He pulled Aranea up on his lap, cradled her, with one hand on her shoulder and the other on her side. Fiber, like the cocoon around her wound, spun them together.

Shiso took one of Aranea's hands and joined.

"Little bird, reach inside her mind. She is acting by instinct. Direct her to a place close but not in the middle of the conflict."

"I don't know Iceland," She remembered the last dream with her sister. "Hellissandur is north of Snaefellsjokull."

"I doubt she can hear you," Oviraptorus said.

Vasyl heard Shiso as if she sent it to him. "Aranea, change your direction."

"Where?" Her pain bled through the communication.

"It's--" she began and realized that she did not know exactly where the town sat. She recalled the memory of the dream.

"I'll try," Aranea answered.

****

Yume dreamed a trapdoor with a ladder down through the floor of the closet. She climbed through the hole but stopped halfway to the bottom and laughed at herself.

Making doors and ladders and other things were unnecessary. Yume could go ghost, walk through walls, and sink through floors. Mentally, adding objects to reality made it easier to visualize the impossible.

Everything she did should have been impossible. She eased through the wall into another office, and called, "Shiso?" No answer, of course. Why couldn't she listen now? Did the change mean she did not need to sleep? Yume sensed the tenuous link with her sister, but as usual, Shiso wasn't listening.

"Stranger!"

After she had drifted halfway across the office, he appeared beside her. "What is your purpose?"

"Reconnaissance. Waiting up there in that little room is killing me."

"Waiting does not kill you, otherwise--" He didn't finish.

They passed through the wall into the corridor. Men and women wearing combat gear and gas masks fidgeted, checked their equipment, or leaned close to speak in low tones.

She glanced at Stranger. What were they doing?

He didn't answer, so they ghosted down the hall, passing through men and women with no resistance, and only a vague disappointment that they did not shiver from some supernatural chill.

They rounded a corner into the lobby near the elevator banks and the emergency stairway. A woman, her gas mask loose, held a cell phone. Her mouth moved. Yume read her lips. "Now." She pulled on her mask and cinched it tight.

"Oh dear," Stranger said.

"What's wrong?"

"They're using gas."

"They're putting us to sleep."

"Or killing you. There is no way to know."

"We have to get out."

"Wait," Stranger said.

Yume woke and pushed Toss' arms away. "We have to get out now. They're pumping in gas."

****

Stranger smashed his fist against the wall. "No!"

261

Why couldn't she wait just a moment? He could fix this if she just gave him a chance to speak. She was awake now, and he did not have a link.

"Shiso! I need you." He sensed the open communications link, as a door through which came sensations of pain.

"Vasyl!"

"You don't have to yell. I'm just hundreds of miles away in a warp bubble with three of my best friends."

His communication felt hazy with distance, almost disconnected. *"Shiso, you must contact your sister."*

"Don't know if she can. We're feeding Aranea. It's-- I don't know."

"Put the food down and tell Shiso. Yume and Toss will die if I cannot reach them."

"Not feeding her that way. We touched her skin and cocooned. It's like being a glass of milk, and she's drinking me through a straw."

Stranger rocked back, and a chair grew from the deck and met him. "I don't know how you learned to do that, but she has to pull free or Yume and Toss will die."

"I'll see what I can do."

****

Shiso imagined herself as a pool of clear, lucent water. Everything within the pool drained down a narrow channel and over a precipice. At the edge of sight, she glimpsed an ocean called Aranea far below where her water splashed and mingled with deeper, darker waters.

An earthquake shook her. She pulled her tree-lined banks close, protecting her water from turbulence. Who knew what sediment would boil to the surface.

A clear image of David sipping soda and watching her flashed through her senses. She felt warm all over and opened her eyes. Vasyl leaned close, his eyes half closed. "Clockbrain says you need to talk to your sister."

"About what?"

Vasyl closed his eyes and settled close to Aranea. Wherever their skin touched silken filaments bound them together.

Did I do that? She looked at her hand. *How did that work, and why am I so hungry?* Outside the bubble, ash clouds drifted close. *It must be snowing below.*

"Stranger? You needed me to--"

"Call your sister, now. Tell her to wait." His fear fed through with his words.

Yume's intimate presence wrapped her, inseparable. She felt the others as if they all took up real estate in her head. *"Yume?"*

"Not now." Yume shut her off. Panic and fear in equal portions bled back.

"Toss, Yume, Stranger needs to speak with you."

****

Toss placed his hands upon Yume's shoulders. Panic oozed through her like hot tar. Fear of death drove her. He felt the same fear, but it felt more like a meeting with an old acquaintance, one he did not like much but could not deny entry. Being over fifty, well, death did not bother him quite so much. He did not want it but recognized its inevitability.

"We don't think we have a lot of time, here." Toss pushed his own fear out of his mind. With Shiso in their heads, far closer than any lover ever could be, emotions percolated from Yume to Stranger to Toss and magnified with each change of mind. He needed to stop it, so he allowed other feelings to permeate up from where he kept them under a con man's leash. He pushed calm soothing, elevator music emotions to Shiso.

He felt Shiso's mind echo his calm. "Stranger, talk to them," she said.

"I can save you if you listen!"

Toss laughed, a low deep rich sound that pushed away panic. *"You might want to take the whip out of your thoughts. It will work better."*

Yume took a deep breath. Her shoulders slumped, and she relaxed him. Her fear eased from a tsunami wave to a rough chop.

"Please listen." The fear vanished from Stranger's thoughts.

Yume released the door handle. "Stranger, how do you control our minds? Is it because you are an alien? Do you just not live in the same way?"

Toss felt a presence as Shiso moved into his head. A thousand flickering images came through the unexpected nearness along with snatches of memory and shifting emotions.

"I can see out through your eyes." Toss' lips opened and spoke the words, but they weren't his.

"And you're speaking through my mouth," He answered in what was undoubtedly the weirdest monologue he had ever heard.

Stranger spoke again, and the cadence and sound of Toss' voice changed. *"I'm sorry. I have never done this before."*

Toss smiled. "Fortunately, there's no one here but us aliens, so only we can think we are crazy for talking to ourselves."

Yume stood with her back to Toss, hand on the door. She wore only the plastic apron.

"You should put clothes on," Shiso said with Toss' mouth.

"Well, that's not creepy at all," Yume said.

Toss felt her embarrassment and blushed with her.

Stranger followed Shiso into his minds. "You, I mean we, can cocoon, wrap ourselves in a protective barrier. We use it to repair our bodies when damaged, but it will protect us from the gas, force, or even from hard vacuum of space."

Toss pushed a hand through his hair. His mind felt like a crowded subway platform. "How do we do that?"

"Think about protection," Stranger said.

"Sort of like a condom," Toss said.

None of the people in his head listened to his joke. He forgot it himself when thin, transparent filaments pushed out of his skin. "Better come close, Yume."

Stranger slipped from his mind, and Shiso trailed away like a kite at the end of a long, long string.

****

Margrethe Thorn took the stairs two at a time, an assault rifle cradled in her arms. Her night vision goggles picked up all her people, and the Infrared ID marked them as friendlies.

So many unknowns, so many mistakes in assessing the strengths of the survivors left her pessimistic concerning the efficacy of the poison gas. Four of her people lay in the hospital, and she would not be surprised if Bonneteau or Guzman put some of them in the morgue.

Desperation brought the killer out in people. She suspected that was true even with aliens.

Her people moved by the numbers, covering each other, leaving nothing to chance. She pulled aside her command group and led them toward the back of the building. Internal cameras picked out that suite of offices as the hiding place.

With Bonneteau active doing whatever it was he did, they never made it within sight of the door. With them dead, there should be no surprises.

She led the way, taking up positions that offered protection, leapfrogging from one place of concealment to the next. The night vision goggles picked up heat sources through the walls. The heat signatures of desktop computers and other electronic equipment gleamed. The kitchens where the two survivors hid displayed heat from a refrigerator and some associated electronics, but no human heat signature.

If they had died, their residual body heat would not have vanished in five minutes. Thorn pointed two fingers at the door, and her team moved in to clear the room.

"Thorn, you need to see this," Jensen said.

She walked into the back office. Open cabinets and empty food boxes provided evidence that Bonneteau and Guzman had occupied the room. The two men waited behind the desk by the door of a small utility room. White fibers extruded beneath the edge of the door.

One of them shook his head. "I can't open it."

"Take the door off."

A demolitions team moved into the room and planted small charges on the hinges and lock. A muffled thump blew the hinges off the wall and shattered the locking mechanism. The door remained in place. It took another four men with pry bars and sledgehammers to remove the door.

White filaments filled a third of the utility room. The fibers resembled a butterfly's cocoon, but that resemblance ended with the appearance. Bullets fired into the fibrous mass blasted small divots from the web but penetrated no more than a few centimeters. While they watched, fibers grew around the slugs and sealed the holes.

"They're like silkworms," Hyde said.

Rollins shrugged. "What do you think they will be when they come out?"

Thorn hung her weapon over her shoulder. "I want that mass moved to a holding cell."

Hyde prodded the fibers with his finger where they touched the walls. "The fibers are stuck to everything."

"Tear down the walls and pull up the floor if you must. I need to talk to Stark. Call me when it's done."

CHAPTER TEN

The FutureTense War

Fresh snow swirled through the parking lot outside FutureTense's headquarters. Margrethe stripped off her mask and handed it to an armorer. She removed the yellow, hazmat coverall, took a towel from the man, and wiped the sweat and grime from her face before the cold froze the moisture into a scrim of ice on her skin.

"The Perimeter teams report no unusual activity," the man said.

"Tell each of the squad leaders I want them to report everything; birds, rabbit, arctic foxes, if it moves, report it. If they see it, report it."

"Yes, sir."

"I'll be in the command van if I'm needed."

Half a dozen men sat at communication consoles, attempting to manage the worldwide FutureTense Network.

War in Africa, religious and ethnic issues in the Middle East, whole nations sinking beneath the rising oceans in the Pacific required constant attention to ameliorate the human suffering. They were the reason she started working for FutureTense at the point when either

her conscience ate her alive or she flushed it down the toilet. "I didn't sign up for this."

The man at the nearest console glanced up, eyebrows lifted in an inquiry.

"Nothing. Just talking to myself."

"An occupational hazard," he said before he returned his attention to South America.

She entered the secure conference chamber in the back and opened a private communication channel. "Stark."

"Report."

Oh, but she could curl up and sleep in the sound of his voice. "We screwed it, John."

"Explain."

"They wrapped themselves in a fibrous material, looks like cotton, feels like Kevlar. The mass is being removed and placed in a cell until we can decide how to kill them."

"Well, that's new."

He did not sound surprised or angry, just tired. "What happened with Gekas, Petrenko, and Guzman?"

"They escaped in their bubble. Two confirmed hits, one critically, or would be if she were human."

"They're evolving faster than we can keep up."

"The bubble was last seen flying your way. The damned cloud cover makes them impossible to trace, visually. We cannot pick them up on the radar."

"They are coming for the two we have or the ship?"

"Both. I don't know what they've become, but they work together like parts of a machine."

"I'll put everyone on watch."

"My helicopter lands in twenty minutes. Set up a meeting with all team leaders."

"Yes, sir."

"And Marg?"

"Yes."

"Thanks for everything."

****

Stark ended the call, and his phone chimed, again. He glanced at the screen. "How does the Director of the National Security Agency intend to screw up things more than they have?"

The woman ignored the insult, her face unreadable. "It's about Oviraptorus."

Stark sat up, guessing what she was about to say but needing to hear it.

Oviraptorus used NSA assets to break into your secure communications and warned your targets.

"That explains a lot. What is Oviraptorus?"

She sat back, fingertips touching, the expression of a woman trying to decide just how little she could say.

"If you have things you will not say, I will call the Board of Directors and tell them the NSA has assumed control of this operation and evacuate my personnel. How long will it take you to get teams on the ground in Iceland to control the situation here?"

"You've fucked things sufficiently that, as much as I would like to take over, I must refuse."

"I take full responsibility, so I need to know everything."

"Oviraptorus is an Independent Artificial Intelligence using distributed systems to move around the Internet."

"Who on earth devised such a program, Director."

"No one did. We traced Oviraptorus back to FutureTense's secure storage facility in Iceland."

"The Breach."

She smiled. "Something escaped, and it's living on the Internet. It's your fault, and I will nail FutureTense for that error."

"If we survive, we should expect the FBI and Congressional investigation?"

"Of course. Someone must take responsibility."

"Anything else?"

"I'll send all our data to Mr. Leeds."

"How will you explain that to the Congressional investigation?"

"I won't have to. We are the NSA. No one will know."

"Except Oviraptorus."

****

Aranea rolled her shoulders, no pain, no stiffness. An hour before, a bullet blew out most of her bicep. She must have lost half her blood volume. Now, she felt fine. Pink, unscarred skin grew over the hole torn by the bullet. "We're getting close."

Shiso let go of Aranea's arm and flexed her hand where the bullet passed through.

Vasyl released her and stood. His eyes searched her face.

"I must look like hell," Aranea said.

"No. Small dark circles under your eyes and you've lost all your body fat, so I've never seen you so thin."

"You still know the right thing to say to a woman."

Shiso laughed. "Why don't you two get a room?"

Vasyl rubbed his forehead, and it was Vasyl's face, now, and his clothes hung loose, so it was his body under everything.

Damn, but it has been a long time.

She blushed. Internal monologues were no longer secret. "It is nice to see you back, Vasyl."

"I'm not sure about that." He turned his back to them. He wasn't pushing her away, exactly, but she saw from the way he stood that a thought percolated through his mind that he did not want to speak aloud, and it wasn't about their old relationship.

Aranea needed to change the subject or get a room for real. "How close are we?"

Shiso pulled at her blouse where dried blood splattered across it. "I just feel hotter and colder, but we are quite warm. Vasyl, you know."

He closed his eyes and swiveled his head as if searching for a direction. "At this speed, we are five minutes from Toss and Yume, seven minutes from the ship."

The phone lit up, Oviraptorus appeared on the screen. "You cannot walk in and take them. They have set up a secure perimeter, are heavily armed, and expect you."

Vasyl nodded. "We'll need guns. Get me close, I'll take care of that."

Oviraptorus' face moved so close to the screen that only one eye was visible. "Shiso, call Stranger. He needs to know about me. Aranea, move down into the mountains below; you will need to find a safe place to open the bubble."

Aranea dropped out of the clouds. Layers of snow and ice covered the lava slopes of Snaefellsjokull. "It's cold and steep."

"There." Vasyl pointed down a slope less steep than nearby cliffs with a few trees growing in tall green spikes out of the snow. A black oval hole appeared in the face of a cliff wall.

Aranea nodded. "It's a lava tube." She drifted to the entrance. Small prints, no larger than a cat's paw, marked the pristine snow.

"I'll take us inside. We can plan there."

****

The globe drifted through the entrance. Two meters inside it widened, and Vasyl dropped a few inches to the ground. The scent of earth, of cold water, and something else blew with a faint breeze out of the cave.

"There's something here." He held up a hand, warning everyone to stay put and walked deeper into the lava tube. A high-pitched yowl followed by brief yips echoed from the walls. A white animal charged him, larger than a cat, with long pointed ears.

An Arctic Fox.

The fox leaped, jaws open. Vasyl raised his hand to protect his face. The fox bit deep into his flesh. His metabolism accelerated, and muscles heated. He could snap its neck, could rip it in half if he wanted.

Instead, he allowed it to bite while he changed. Dropping to his hands and knees, his limbs thinned, a tail sprouted from the base of his spine, and white fur grew from his body. His uniform shredded as his body adapted to a new shape, and he met that with a sigh of relief.

That difference in the air became the scent of five individuals, three females and two males.

He felt a presence in his head and scratched his ear with a hind paw.

Clockbrain's thoughts echoed in his brain. *"Keep your human mind, or you lose yourself again."*

That must have been what happened when Vasyl became a rat, and only a threat to his life changed him back. In the fox's shape, he saw in shades of gray and touches of infrared, but his sense of smell told him more than he could determine with human eyesight.

"You also need to speak."

His muzzle shortened, closer to his human organ. "So why didn't you tell me this before I became a rat."

"No time."

Shiso crept close and reached out a hand to offer him her scent. "You changed into a rat."

"Just once, and I can smell both of you from across the room." Aranea stepped out of the gloom. "Not bad I hope."

"Interesting, yes. I smell blood, sweat, and female scents. Interesting."

"Why did stranger show up at just the right time."

"Oviraptorus told me to call him," Shiso said.

Strangers thoughts echoed in all their heads. *"Who is Oviraptorus?"*

Shiso waved the phone in her hand. "She's my NSA app."

"Oh, so much more than that, dear."

Shiso broadcast, *"Can you hear her?"*

"I hear and see through Vasyl. Shiso allows me to glimpse into your minds."

Vasyl felt Clockbrain moving through him, his mouth opened and Clockbrain asked, *"Who are you?"*

"Zhashour," Oviraptorus said.

"My love."

Shiso giggled. "I wish I could upload that. An arctic fox calling a cell phone 'My Love' would be an instant hit."

"I need to use your voice, Vasyl."

"Who's stopping you?"

"Zhashour is us, or our ship, the consciousness that drives it. Why did you not contact me?"

"After the breach, they shut down all digital communication. I could not return. I protected my consciousness as best I could."

"So, what are your orders, Captain?"

"You must get me on board the ship. Fly it out of reach of the jamming signals in the hanger."

"I am not an adequate pilot. Look at what happened last time," Clockbrain said.

"You will operate it well enough."

"They have set charges on your skin. If we fly without Aranea Gekas, we will be destroyed."

"Then rescue the others first."

Aranea knelt beside Vasyl and touched his fur. "We need to get Toss and Yume."

Vasyl rubbed his muzzle against her hand. "She is going to be guarded. We will need guns."

Shiso walked to the front of the cave. "Where will we get them?"

Vasyl stood on four legs and shook himself. "Leave that to me."

****

A helicopter dropped out of the clouds, circled once, and set down onto the landing pad atop the FutureTense headquarters building. John Stark stepped out onto the platform and ran with his head bent beyond the reach of the rotors to the spot where Margrethe Thorn, Eric Leeds, Thomas Manquoba, and Victor Wu waited.

"How close are they?" Thorn asked.

Stark shrugged. They walked down the stairs to the top floor. "They could arrive at any moment. We have no way of knowing how fast they are."

Manquoba glanced at Wu. "How do we stop them?"

"We separate into three teams. Manquoba and Wu will take the detention center. When they arrive, they must drop their bubble. Kill Gekas. When she goes down, everyone else is vulnerable."

"Thorn and I will cover the parking lot and the road to the hanger. We take down any survivors, starting with Bonneteau."

Eric Leeds looked up at Stark. "And my team?"

"You will man the control in the hanger below. If the survivors get inside, set off the charges and blow the ship."

"The ship can repair itself."

"We can worry about that later. Get your teams into position and be ready."

****

Vasyl padded through the snow, moving from shadow to shadow. In the shelter of a tree, he lifted his muzzle and tested the air. The scent of trees and bushes mingled with the traces of small lives hidden in the remnants of the unseasonal storm. A strange euphoria spread through his lean muscles. Instincts of a fox, he supposed, of a hunter.

He caught a scent carried on the wind, the spoor of fourteen humans, mixtures of gun oil, sweat, fear, and mingled salts that marked each as a unique individual. Twelve of the scents carried from some distance. Two of them occupied a ridge north of the lava tube, positioned where they could see any human activity.

He chose a path up the hill that passed from snowbound trees to boulders to snow mounded up over bushes. Those patient watchers did not speak or move. Their patience and silence made them professionals. Vasyl repressed a laugh. He had killed professionals, ripped them apart.

"Vasyl?" Shiso sent. *"Are you Okay?"*

"Shh, Hunting."

"It's just that your thoughts don't feel like you."

Clockbrain bloomed in his mind. *"He expresses the instincts of the hunter. Careful, Vasyl, do not lose yourself as you did with the rat."*

"You both assume too much. Back away. I cannot hunt and host a convention in my brain."

Clockbrain vanished while Shiso receded until he only felt her presence as a faint heartbeat, which he thought must be her burden. A woman who heard thoughts would never have a moment of personal privacy and could never grant such a moment.

The human species evolved alone. Sure, they organized into sexually compatible pairs, families, tribes, nations, and in ever larger groupings, but they remained isolated in their minds. He supposed it just possible her curse might be worse than his. Humans had always murdered for food, mates, survival. His change made him a better killer than most. He could grieve that difference in solitude.

His circuitous path brought him to a position where he could see the men. They wore white camouflage, and in the dull eternal daylight of the Arctic, they kept night vision goggles pushed up on their heads. Patient killers, they pointed rifles into the canyon.

He bunched the muscles in his legs and sprang, landing on the back of the nearest man. Vasyl closed his jaws on the man's spine and bit deep. Bones crunched, and hot copper blood gushed into his mouth.

The second watcher rolled onto his side and swung his assault rifle around. He never brought it into line with his target. Vasyl landed on his chest, drove his claws through the soldier's clothes, and lunged at his face.

They rolled over the steep side of the ridge and tumbled through the snow. The soldier grabbed Vasyl's fur and attempted to push him away. If Vasyl had just been a human-sized Fox, it might have been an even fight. The sudden heat of acceleration and doubled strength overpowered his prey. Vasyl caught the throat in the vice of his jaws and tore it out.

And, oh, but he loved the taste of the flesh. He sat on the dying man's chest, ready to feed.

Shiso pushed into his thoughts. *"Vasyl, don't."*

"Leave me alone, bitch."

"That's the Fox thinking for you. Ask Aranea."

Shiso pushed Aranea into his mind. *"Vasyl, please."*

"Leave me alone."

"We can't, Vasyl. We don't belong here, anymore. Bring the guns. We need to get to the ship."

He stepped back from the warm corpse and plunged his muzzle into the snow to clear away the scent and taste of the flesh.

"All right," he growled. They would hear the thought and speaking even in this voice pushed a wedge between the mind of the man and the hunter. "I'm coming."

CHAPTER ELEVEN

Ship

Vasyl backed into the cave, dragging several weapons and a pack. Would have been easier to move the loot as a man. With the taste of the blood in his mouth, he could not bring himself to change. He left the bag and the weapons on the floor and padded to the back of the cave where he sat on his haunches.

Shiso searched through the disordered heap of weapons and opened the pack containing water and food before discarding it and retrieving a weapon belt. She snapped open the holster, drew the pistol, and ejected the clip.

Vasyl licked clean a spot on his fur. "You know how to shoot?"

Shiso pulled an assault rifle from the pile. "My Tio taught Yume and me to protect ourselves, about a year after we returned from Russia." She dragged her sleeve over her face, excising the tears.

He felt an urge to pad over and lick her face in shared comfort but resisted the animal urge. "I guess everyone in America uses a gun."

She glanced sideways at him. Her scent changed with expression. Both his human and animal minds read it as sadness or grief. "Not everyone. He told us that young women needed to protect themselves. The night he died, he told us that FutureTense watched us."

Aranea picked up the other assault rifle, found the safety, and clicked it off. "You should change back. I need to shift to the Warp so we can find Yume and Toss."

Vasyl shook his head. "No! The fox shape is better for this. I feel more comfortable in this skin for what will be necessary."

Clockbrain slipped into Vasyl's mind, and his mental contact with Shiso and Aranea vanished. *"Tell them how you feel, Vasyl?"*

You can turn off my link with Shiso and Aranea?

"Of course, sometimes a private conversation is necessary. Tell Aranea and Shiso. They can help you with your problem."

Can they make me feel less like a serial killer?

"You are a soldier, Vasyl, not a killer."

I'm an insane, murderous, astrophysicist. Now, leave me alone.

He padded over and sat beside Aranea's feet. Her bubble appeared around them, and they drifted up toward the cave's roof and into the stone.

****

Aranea stopped the warp bubble's upward movement. Vasyl's muzzle brushed against her hand, and a static jolt jumped between them. She stroked the side of his face, enjoying the feeling of the soft fur. "How close are we?"

Vasyl lifted his muzzle, following the link that united them. "They are above us, thirteen meters give or take. Stark knows we are coming, so this must be a trap. Perhaps we should consult Oviraptorus."

Shiso pulled the phone from her pocket to a 'No Service' icon. "We're underground. I don't think she can reach us this deep."

Aranea glanced along that invisible line that linked them all. "Can you reach Yume or Toss, mentally? If they know we're coming, perhaps they can tell what's waiting."

She watched while Shiso performed her trick. Shiso shrugged. "It's like they're behind a wall. I can feel them, but there's no contact. Maybe they're drugged."

Aranea inhaled. "It makes as much sense as anything else. I'm taking us up. No point waiting here."

They passed through a floor into a large room awash with whitish fluorescent light. Crates, cleaning equipment, rows of storage racks, and the anonymous medical equipment sat back along the walls. They rose through the ceiling into the foyer. Armed men stood at the doors. Their weapons vomited gun smoke and fire. Tracer rounds drew angry red lines to the edge of the bubble then reappeared on the other side.

They ascended another floor into a cubicle space, without office workers. The bubble climbed through the ceiling and into a cell occupied by a cocoon of white fiber.

Aranea did not know what would happen if she dropped the bubble in the center of an object. She passed through the cell wall into a hallway lined with more cells and terminated by a heavy steel door. She clicked off the safety on her assault rifle and dropped the bubble.

Something sharp exploded on her shoulder and spun her around. A second blow struck her right breast, and she collapsed, unable to breathe. A white animal shape leaped on a man standing near the wall and tore his head off.

She blinked.

Two men lay in pools of blood. Guns blasted, smoke swirled, a man screamed.

Blink.

Vasyl stood on two legs, his shape half-man half fox. He jerked a man off his feet and snapped his back over his knee.

Blink.

****

Shiso grabbed Aranea under the arms and pulled her toward a wall. A bullet buzzed passed her head like an angry insect, and she crouched low as she could, pistol in hand. Blood drenched Aranea's blouse. Shiso forced herself not to stare at the gaping wounds. A human could not survive that kind of damage. She wondered if Aranea remained human enough to die.

The men concealed along the walls ignored her. After taking Aranea down, they had focused their fire on Vasyl. His speed must have surprised them. He hunted them, ravening among the soldiers, tearing out throats, ripping off limbs.

Shiso took aim. She could fire a pistol and was a deadly killer of targets. Humans were not supposed to be targets. Before she needed to kill, Vasyl picked up the fifth man and slammed him against a heavy door. The man's bones cracked, and blood sprayed from his mouth. Vasyl stopped, blood dripped from his muzzle and paws. His chest heaved.

One soldier slipped out of a cell, raised a pistol, and fired. The bullet tore a bloody gouge along Vasyl's side. He sprinted across the floor. Shiso knew he would not make it. The man would kill him before Vasyl ripped out his heart.

She took a deep breath, held it, and pulled the trigger. The bullet hit the man just below his nose. He fell back.

She felt the recoil, corrected her aim, and fired again, hitting him dead center in the chest.

Again, blood mist sprayed from his abdomen.

Again.

When the hammer clicked on an empty chamber, she realized that she had fired nine rounds. Shiso vomited onto the bloody floor.

Vasyl knelt before her, blood dripped from his muzzle. He took the pistol. "Let me have that."

"Aranea's been shot. You have to help her."

Bubbles flowed with blood from Aranea's chest wound. Fibers grew over the bullet holes. Shiso looked away, and her gaze froze on the body of the man.

Vasyl took her chin between his fingers and pulled her face away. "You do not need to look at that."

She pulled away. "I need to..."

"Contact Clockbrain or Oviraptorus. We need to know how to wake Yume and Toss."

The fibrous tissue spread across Aranea's wounds, and the blood slowed to a drip. Vasyl picked her up and held her against his chest.

He's giving her his energy. Shiso looked away because something about the way he held her hinted at intimacy and demanded privacy.

"Stranger," she called. As if she just woke up and decided to check for messages. She felt his presence, but caught nothing of his thoughts, until, "Not now!"

"Aranea's hurt, dying."

"Come to me soon as you can." His mind retreated behind a wall. It didn't disappear. She felt every mind in their little group except Oviraptorus.

Her phone rang and answered itself. Ovraptorus appeared. "You've sprung their trap. They are coming."

"Who?"

"Stark."

"How do we wake Yume and Toss?"

"Touch the cocoon and call them."

"That's all?"

"It is a lifeboat programmed to release at your touch." The screen went blank and the "No Connection" icon displayed.

Shiso reached through the bars of the cage and sent. "Yume, Toss, wake up!" The cocoon resembled silk but felt tough as an old canvas. Beginning at the place her finger touched, it evaporated into a whitish mist. Yume's eyes opened. Toss helped her stand before he pulled himself up.

He glanced over her shoulder, his eyes hard. "How is this better?"

****

Outside the cell, Toss counted six bodies. Bullet holes pocked the wall, and Shiso held Yume's hand through the bars. "Anybody have a key?"

Shiso shook her head. Vasyl turned in a slow circle to scan the room. "The cells are locked electronically, but not from in here. I could try and force them open, but I doubt that I have that kind of strength."

Shiso pulled her hand back and jabbed at her phone. "Oviraptorus?" it remained dark.

Toss shrugged. "We're on our own."

Aranea shifted in Vasyl's arms. "Put me down. I can get us out. Toss, Yume, stand as far apart as you can."

Vasyl shook his head. "I don't think you have the energy."

Machinery hummed in the walls, and the steel door lock thudded open.

Shiso placed her hand on Aranea's shoulder. A bubble grew around them, and it moved through the bars as if they did not exist. Inside the cell, the bubble popped. Shiso grabbed Yume, and Toss placed a hand on Vasyl's shoulder. He wanted to ask when Vasyl became a werewolf, or whatever animal donated the white hair and ears. Someone fired a weapon through the partially open door at the end of the room. Deep pain drilled Toss' arm. Before he could reach for the wound, another bullet grazed his ear and pain flared on the side of his head, followed by profound silence.

I'm deaf. Blood flowed over his cheek.

Shiso touched her head to his, her voice a soft and pleasing sound. "You're fine. It's Aranea's bubble."

"Of course." Accepting the impossible came that easy. The door opened, and men sprayed the cell with automatic weapons. Not a bullet touched them.

The phone in Shiso's hand chimed. The same woman Toss saw in the casino restaurant appeared. "Stark is going to blow up the ship. Damn!" She disappeared.

"We have to get there first."

Aranea's eyes fluttered open. "I don't think I can get that far?"

They drifted through the front of the building, their movement halting. Groups of men behind cover at the edges of the parking lot fired automatic weapons. The warp bubble accelerated and dropped down to a level a few inches above the road that twisted out of the parking lot and down a hill in the direction that arrow in his head pointed.

The fiber covering her wounds extended from her neck to knees. Halfway down the hill, two trucks blocked the road. A dozen soldiers hid behind the Trucks.

Aranea's lips moved. "I need to sleep."

Vasyl pulled her close. "Just a few more seconds."

"Try..."

He caught Toss' eye. "You move fast?"

"Yes."

Vasyl eased her into Toss' arms. "She will drop us on that Truck. You take them. I'll stop Stark."

Toss pulled Aranea close. Wherever their skin touched, he felt a current flowing out of him. "Shiso, Yume, grab hold."

****

Vasyl kissed Aranea's forehead. "Let go."

They dropped two meters. Vasyl twisted in the air. *A fox is better.* He shifted, again, to the desired shape.

Toss, Shiso, Yume, and Aranea. Stretched away and vanished.

A bullet clipped his side. A man, his face hidden behind a gas mask, fired a burst from his weapon. Vasyl felt stiff Kevlar under the man's uniform resist his claws. He ripped off the mask and the man's face.

Something vast, organic protruded through the warehouse door, it's curves and contours cloaked by snow. Half of the soldiers aimed their weapons down the road and fired on the object.

Which of these men was Stark?

Vasyl smelled gun oil, sweat, and fear. Eleven combatants remained ten men and a woman. He ignored her. The nearest man dropped his rifle, half drawing his pistol before Vasyl drove his claws and teeth into the man's leg. The bones shattered, and an artery gushed into his mouth.

A bullet struck his hip. How had Clockbrain shutoff the pain in that other fight? Vasyl spun, and all sensation fled. He clamped his jaws on the man's wrist above the pistol, jerked his head to one side. The man collapsed, holding a stump. Vasyl swallowed the hand. The woman fired striking one of her own men. Bullets raked Vasyl's flank, their touch jarred him, though they caused no pain. He clawed the weapon out of her hand, mauled at her legs and abdomen, and drove her back over the edge of the cliff.

Surging through the remaining men, he ripped at legs or arms, whatever came within reach of his claws and teeth. In a dozen seconds, they all lay on the ground, bleeding or dead.

Vasyl's body burned. The accelerated muscles, the speed, the strength threatened to roast him from the inside. He counted seven bullet wounds, though none fatal. He ran into a snow bank. The ice melted against his fur. He bit the snow to slake his hideous thirst.

From the canyon along the edge of the road he heard breathing. The woman hung by one hand, her mask torn away, and blood on her face. She closed her eyes.

Vasyl lunged. At the last second, he changed his mind. He bit her shoulder through the fabric and the flesh. She hung in the cold air, her weight pulling them toward the edge. He dug in with his claws and backed away, dragging her to the side of the man whose hand he devoured.

Several of the soldiers lived, crying, gasping. Clockbrain must be too busy to speak. Otherwise, he would say, kill them.

Vasyl considered the wisdom of murder. These men and women tried their best to kill him, to kill Aranea and everyone else touched by the Russian incident. Why shouldn't he kill them? They would do the same if he lay at their mercy.

The woman struggled to sit up. He shook his head, a warning. "I'm leaving now."

Her eyes widened.

He walked along the road. Steam curling from his shoulders. Snow gleamed like the pillows of heaven. Why not cool down. What did it matter? Though tempted, he embraced the heat and ran for the ship.

****

Stranger probed the walls of the ship with his mind, spinning along nerve cables until he found a node where the organic conduits terminated in knots of synthetic polymer and raw nerve ends.

He pulled energy from the heart of Ship, teased the knots open, and touched the bare ends together. The motionless drive purred to life. In the hanger, men died and machines vaporized. It would not matter unless he could bring the pilot aboard and stop the explosives. But it should destroy whatever system FutureTense used to seal them away from the World Wide Web.

"Where are you?" He pushed out a thought tendril and touched Vasyl's mind. Heat, fear, and profound grief bled through the link. The raw emotion threatened to rip Stranger's consciousness from his constructed body. He shut down the link with Vasyl rather than leave his work.

Toss touched the ship with an outstretched finger and Stranger felt it like a gentle poke in the ribs. Through that touch, he pushed in along nerve endings linking Ship's mind to those of his crew. His nervous system and those of Aranea, Yume, Toss, and Shiso meshed. At the center, he found Aranea Gekas. His systems cataloged her injuries and estimated the difficulty of repairing her body.

Damage so severe usually ended with the transfer of the Consciousness into a new form. These recruits remained psychologically addicted to their human biology.

He opened Ship at the tip of Toss' finger. "Bring her inside."

He hollowed out a sphere around them and Ship transported them through the walls and other physical structures to the core. Stranger slipped into the wall and exited the bubble. Quicker to lead than teach them how to transit through Ship.

The others bore wounds, some small, some grave, but none life-threatening.

Yume stepped away. "Stranger."

"Of course, who would you expect?"

"You're not exactly how I remember."

He spreads his arms and bowed. "Your subjective thoughts gave me form. This is the objective reality."

"What now?"

The sphere opened into a larger area with smooth walls and six pillars shaped like butterfly chrysalises.

Stranger waved them in. "This is the control room."

Toss spun around. "Where do you hide the controls?"

Each pillar split along a line and opened. Stranger reached for Aranea. "You are the controls. Help me place Aranea inside."

Stranger touched the cocoon, and it sloughed away into dust. Her wounds oozed trickles of blood.

Toss carried her to the chrysalis. "She doesn't seem to be in any shape to do anything."

"We don't have a choice. I promise Aranea will survive."

Shiso crossed her arms. "You are lying. I feel it."

"Search my mind. I told no lie, but it was not exactly the truth. We must escape, or none of us will survive."

He stopped and lifted his head as if testing the air.

"Vasyl has arrived. We must hurry."

A section of the wall altered to a transparent square window that displayed the outside of the hangar. Blocks of C4 with attached wires covered the hull like a fish net. "The ship is rigged to explode. Toss, take your station and manipulate time. We must give her time to arrive."

"Her?" Toss asked. "We're all here if a little the worse for wear. Who are you talking about?" A fireball curled into the sky.

"Oviraptorus." Shiso pulled out the phone. The screen remained blank.

Stranger nodded and winked. "Think of her as the Captain. She integrates all systems. We must get away from FutureTense interference and give her time to download."

Yume crossed her arms. "We are machines."

Stranger buried his face in his hands. "Yes, we are machines."

Shiso shook her head. "I am alive."

Stranger chewed his lip. They had no time for philosophical conversations concerning the meaning or reality of life. He considered several ways to approach it and decided on the most straightforward. "Life is a machine."

Shiso raised both her hands and held them palm out as if pushing the ideas away. "Humans aren't machines. We think, breathe, love."

The wall opened, and Vasyl padded in.

Stranger nodded in his direction. "What is human life, what is any life but a self-aware, self-fueling machine?"

Vasyl glanced at the others. "Animals are not self-aware."

Stranger rolled his eyes. "Says the homo-egotisitian who spent five years talking to a rat and now occupies the body of a Fox."

"In my defense, I was insane. What type of madness leads a self-aware, self-fueling machine to tinker with other living beings?"

"Survival!" His spoke with greater vehmeanance than he intended. He did not have time for this. "What would humans not do to survive?"

Toss chuckled. "As a conman, I can't speak with authority as to what all humans would do, but we don't turn other people into monsters."

Stranger pointed at the inside of Aranea's chrysalis. "We don't have time for this conversation."

Aranea opened her eyes. "I will not go into that machine until I know."

Stranger rubbed his temples. "You manipulate the genes of whole species and devour them. You shred entire ecosystems and slaughter the living creatures that rely on those systems. You grow slave species for food."

Toss nodded, and a little smile crossed his lips. "You have a point. We are the same."

Stranger gestured around them at the ship and her structures. "Our technology operates on a higher order, but all beings are human when forced to survive."

Yume stepped away from the others and turned away. "Just stop it. What difference does it make? Toss, can you take us back before the crash in 2018."

He glanced at Yume, and his face eased to a softer expression. "Like a machine, I slow time. I can't turn back the clock."

Stranger laughed. "Once performed, a sequence of events cannot be undone."

Yume rolled her eyes. "You mean time."

Stranger's brow wrinkled in thought. How to explain to his crew concepts that they did not have yet. "Yume, time does not exist. There is only sequence and entropy. Information once created cannot be destroyed, the universe grows older, colder, more homogeneous, and systems degrade."

Shiso crossed the chamber and threw her arm around her sister. "Of course, time exists. We measure moments by the second and time by the minute. We have calendars and clocks."

Stranger walked to his chrysalis. It opened for him. The interior appeared smooth and inviting.

Aranea glanced at Toss. "Put me down."

He put her down but remained at her side.

"Stranger, do you have a different name. I hate that word."

Vasyl walked to his chrysalis. It did not have his name or any identifying mark. He recognized it the same way he knew his own hand. "I call him Clockbrain."

Aranea pushed her hands through her hair. "I would prefer Stranger to that."

"Well, it doesn't matter unless we leave. Shiso, hand me the phone."

****

Yume closed her eyes and opened her mind. The interior of the control room remained the same, though her point of view shifted. Her vision expanded. Vasyl limped into a chrysalis that resembled a womb. It closed behind him leaving not even a seam.

Toss eased Aranea into her chrysalis, sealed her in, and slipped into his. Shiso waited before she moved into Yume's thoughts and became a comforting presence.

Yume said, *"Take me somewhere."*

Shiso led her through the minds of the others, calm and quiet. When they finished, she entered her Chrysalis and disappeared.

Yume took a final glance at the room.

Is this how Aliens sleep?

A chair extruded from the floor and Stranger sat. He placed the phone link to Oviraptorus into a receptacle in the arm of the chair.

Outside the ship, she saw in all directions. Nothing moved inside the warehouse, and even the fires refused to flicker. Wires crisscrossed the hull linking thick bundles that she assumed were charges set against the shell. She had no idea how much explosive would be required to destroy the ship. She did not doubt it was enough.

With the phone safe in its place, Stranger said, "Yume. I need to see outside the building. Show me immediately beyond and above us. Please enter the chrysalis. It will be easier."

The chrysalis sealed itself shut but brought no sense of claustrophobia. It became part of her and extended her sense of self to the entire ship. Her view shifted. She gazed out through the open hangar door and down a long valley toward the sea.

"Now, Shiso, monitor everyone. Should you or anyone suffer physical distress communicate those sensory inputs to me and, I will, as best I can treat any ill effects."

Shiso filled her accustomed place in Yume's mind and then popped into existence beside Yume. They held hands.

"Aranea?"

"Yes." Aranea's voice wavered.

"Extend the warp bubble. It will now conform to the skin of the ship. That will protect us from the rigged explosions."

"All right."

Stranger sat in the chair, staring at the phone. He touched it. "Launch."

A fireball curled into the sky. Pieces of the roof and the doors blasted away, careening off the canyon walls and tearing through the crowns of trees.

The Ship shuddered and swayed.

The phone screen lit. Oviraptorus smiled. "I'm home."

CHAPTER TWELVE

Five Days Later

Yume De Guzman had a thousand eyes, no, a million, and she saw through them all.

She sat in a seat in a hospital room. A young man of about sixteen occupied the bed, eyes closed, his right arm covered with a cast from his shoulder to the wrist. Contusions and abrasions colored the right side of his face. A woman with the young man's hair sat beside a man with an older version of the young man's face.

His parents, of course.

The woman opened her mouth to speak, and Yume cursed the drawback of her power. She could see but not hear or touch.

Why here?

She built realities in her mind and shared them with other survivors.

Was he asleep or in some more profound unconscious state? Could she read the dreams of someone who wasn't what she had become? She touched his forehead with her index finger and pushed it into his skull. The quick firing of his neurons tickled her skin, or so she imagined. They created a web pattern that pulled her in.

She drifted through his forehead and touched down in his dream.

The young man occupied a room with a door in each of its walls. He walked from door to door and pulled them open and found behind each door another door.

He didn't notice her standing in the corner. The logic of his dream dictated that no one else witnessed his search for something.

"You're going nowhere fast."

He spun around, mouth open in comical, archetypal, surprise. "Shiso!" He ran, arms open.

She held out her hand. "Stop!" He froze in place like a cartoon character.

"Shiso?"

"I'm Yume."

His lips twisted into a frown, his eyes unbelieving.

"Shiso's twin sister. Who are you?"

"David. I met Shiso in Mesquite. We rode the bus to Denver. Where is she? I followed her to a post office, and I don't remember anymore. Why are we in here? What is this place?"

She held up a hand to slow him down. "It's a dream. You are in a hospital. I think your parents are there."

"Am I alive?"

What was she supposed to say to that? Perhaps it was the dream enforcing its logic. "I don't think dead people dream."

He shook his head. "Of course, they do, at least in heaven. Hell, I guess, has nightmares."

He shivered and glanced around with panicked eyes.

"So, you think you are in hell?"

He glanced from door to door. "Doors that open on doors, what would you call that?"

Yume did not care to answer or talk about heaven or hell. As kids, they went to church, but after her parents died and they moved in with their Tio, attendance faded to holidays. She smiled a little. "It was nice to meet you, David, but I think I need to go."

"No!" He grabbed her shoulders. His eyes changed to dark holes where nightmare things flitted among shadows.

She pushed his hands away.

He collapsed onto the floor and buried his face in his hands. "I'm sorry. I'm sorry. I'm frightened. It seems like forever, and I can't get out. You have to help me."

She examined his dream, the doors behind doors, and imagined them empty. When she glanced up, they remained closed.

Yume was just a visitor. Could he have altered her with his dream? No, she didn't think so. There was a better, more straightforward answer. "Your dream. Your reality."

He chewed his lip and watched her. The panic faded.

She knelt beside him. "I have an idea."

"Yeah?" He looked up at her.

"You need a symbolic act, something that shifts the paradigm of this dream. Do you understand?"

He chewed on his cheek, and his eyes narrowed. "No."

"I'm going to kiss you."

He rolled to one side and looked up at her. "Like sleeping beauty."

She laughed. "Exactly like sleeping beauty, but I'm Princess Charming. Get it."

He sat up and reached for her. "I think so."

"Just lay there. You're supposed to be asleep."

"Okay." He put his arms down by his sides and closed his eyes.

Yume placed her hands on his cheeks and kissed him. It wasn't bad. His lips felt warm and his breath sweet. He pushed his tongue between her lips. She tasted peppermint.

She appeared back in the hospital room.

David started up and rubbed his eyes. "Oh, this is so weird."

****

Shiso floated in a chrysalis. She remembered the last moments of the fight on the mountain, Toss, naked except for a plastic apron, and blood everywhere, pain.

Vasyl lived as a monstrous, white dog-fox. She saved him but refused to remember how. Under no condition should she remember looking down the barrel of the pistol Vasyl gave her, the roar when she pulled the trigger. She could not stop the memories. She aimed for the center of the man's body, just as Tio taught her on the range, pulled the trigger, and watched him die.

So why am I here? Why?

Yume floated with her. An umbilicus ran from the base of their necks, which seem stupid since her navel was on her stomach.

"It's Okay." Yume kissed her on the forehead.

"No, it isn't."

"Come with me." Yume took Shiso's hand and pulled her out of her body. She saw herself, naked, adrift in the sphere.

"This is one of your dreams."

Yume waved a finger in front of her face. "I keep telling you."

"Yea, I know, this is a reality."

"Oh, but this is something else. You have to see this."

The illumination stuttered as if all light blinked out for a fraction of a second. Shiso stood beside Yume in a hospital, fully dressed. David lay on the bed, a tray of food on his lap.

"He's alive." Shiso sat in a convenient chair.

David stuffed a wobbling cube of green Jell-O in his mouth.

"But that's not what's cool." Yume poked her forefinger into his forehead up to the second joint. She pulled David out of himself.

He glanced from Yume to Shiso while the David that occupied the bed fell asleep in the middle of a bite of Jell-O. The David she pulled out of his own head, said, "Oh, this is weird."

"How is this possible? He's not--"

Yume finished her sentence. "A survivor. Go ahead, talk to him."

Shiso rolled her eyes. "Hello, David."

"No, use telepathy!"

"David," she sent.

"Now she's in my head." He glanced at his hands and then the person on the bed. "One of my heads."

Shiso buried her face in her hands and looked out through her fingers. "How is that possible?"

"You could do it with Tio, a little."

"Yea, but that was only in the last few months before." She refused to say before he died.

"We have to tell the others."

David smiled. "So, where you girls going?"

Yume looked sideways at David. "Orbit."

"I've never been there. Is the food good?"

"I need a moment," Shiso sent.

"What for?"

"Closure, to thank him, I don't know."

Yume disappeared. Shiso could sense her, but that was true all the time. She didn't know if sensing Yume was part of being twins or something that they developed from surviving.

"Thanks," She said.

He smiled. "You're welcome. I almost died for you."

She grabbed the front of David's hospital gown, pulled him close, and kissed him. He tasted like lime Jell-O.

****

Toss sat at a table in a room in a spaceship. A door opened in the wall and Oviraptorus or Captain or Pilot came in.

What was her name?

She sat down across from him on a chair that grew out of the floor.

"Zhashour, but I answer to Oviraptorus and others. What would you prefer?"

"Zhashour has a lovely sound."

She caressed the back of his hand with her fingers. "You look lost."

She had beautiful long legs and the tight body of a woman well out of her teens but with plenty of time before grandchildren.

"I'm a conman on a spaceship with no marks. I guess I'm searching for a purpose."

She squeezed his hand. "You deal with time; our propulsion system is your purpose."

"That wasn't a job I chose for myself."

She smiled, and her nose wrinkled. "You chose to trick people out of cash."

"Lots of excitement, more than a few women, and I'm always moving. Now, I don't even have my cards."

Three cards appeared face down on the table, their backs bent in an arch, colors faded and worn from use.

He caressed the back of the nearest card with his forefinger. "Is that illusion?"

"They are synthesized, as real as you are."

He picked up the cards and rolled his hands, one over the other, dropping them into place. It felt like home.

"Am I synthesized?" The question popped. One minute he had not intimated that concern, and in the next, he stopped dealing because no answer could ever be as important as what she said.

"We made minor repairs, healed your wounds, and corrected the effects of age."

"Really," He placed a card face down on the table. What Zhashour said blew him away, but he wasn't surprised. The way his body reacted to her took him back to his 20's. "So why the gray hair?"

"Appearance is a choice. You appear whatever age you desire. Think about it. Your chrysalis arranges it.

He ended the deal, picked up the middle card and revealed the queen. He whistled out of amazement. "Eternal life."

"No," She answered though it had not been a question.

"Then how long do we live?"

"You can die from a catastrophic accident to the ship."

"That's what happened to our predecessors?"

She nodded. "The crashed destroyed the portions of storage where copies of their consciousness resided."

"And if that doesn't happen."

"Everything in the universe decays, eventually."

"How long will that take?"

"Before the heat death of the universe."

He lost himself in the Monte. Moving the cards helped him cope with the words, which was a good thing because he had no idea what to say.

She smiled. The joy in her eyes shone up out of her soul if such creatures had souls. "How do you play this game?"

"I'd be happy to teach you. Do you have any money?"

"We have no need of currency."

"Well, we would need something to bet."

Her eyes sparkled. "I know what you want, and we are physically compatible."

"What if I lose?" Toss winked.

"We are physically compatible."

****

John Stark opened his eyes. A plastic feeding tube fed through his nose and another fed down into his throat. His left hand itched.

Margrethe Thorn leaned close. He caught the scent of her perfume and antiseptic. Puffy bruises surrounded both eyes; a cast covered her right forearm. Cuts split her lips, and the way her hospital gown settled over her shoulder hinted at other bandages.

He tried to speak, but only "Yuuu," made it through his dry throat and past the endotracheal tube.

"Try not to talk for once. I've called the doctors and told them to get in here and remove the damned thing."

He held up his right hand and made a scribbling gesture. "Questions? I was told not to answer any, not that you could ask with medical equipment filling your mouth."

How many dead, five, fifteen, more? He dreaded the duties of contacting the families. Of course, FutureTense could take care of that. The families of the dead would receive a generous insurance payment and college tuition paid in full for surviving children if they chose to go to a university.

He felt a higher duty to write the families and tell them what he could about a lost child, husband, or mother.

As sad as that duty would be, he felt happy. On the face of that mountain, after they shot that beast five times after it tore his hand off and swallowed it, Stark had lain bleeding to death unable to save Margrethe. His last memory was of that white monster lunging, jaws open, about to tear out her throat.

He gazed into her eyes, unable to ask how.

Doctor Becker entered the room with another physician and several nurses. "Ms. Thorn, it's time for you to go."

She leaned close, brushed her lips against his ear, and whispered, "You need to know. Vasyl Petrenko saved my life and yours. He bit into my shoulder, pulled me up, and dropped me beside you. I applied a tourniquet, but without him---" She left the rest unsaid.

"Now, Ms. Thorn."

Stark laid back and ignored the medical team. Becker turned off the ventilator while nurses changed his gown, checked IV fluids, and a hundred other little tasks involved with staving off death.

His head spun as if on gimbals, vertigo caused by the influence of drugs. Pain in his arm and elsewhere felt distant, divorced from his body. His thoughts smeared like words on a chalkboard.

After a while, he felt himself drifting off, perhaps sleep, perhaps death. It didn't matter. He felt tired, and either would do.

Margrethe lived.

That mattered.

Margrethe lived because a monster saved her.

What did that say about monsters?

****

Vasyl Petrenko crossed his paws and licked an imagined speck of blood from his white fur. The act catapulted his mind back six years to the Cambridge Shakespeare Festival. They had visited England to attend a National Astronomical Symposium, and Aranea insisted they see "Titus Andronicus, A Midsummer's Night Dream, and Macbeth." Macbeth felt particularly appropriate. He snarled in a mangled Scottish accent, "Will these paws ne'er be clean."

Clockbrain squatted beside him. He wore a white, ivory mask, and plates of ivory skin slid over coiled clock springs, spinning gears, whirling cogs, lava lamp globes, steam pressure gauges, small computer screens, and clock face eyes with hands whirling madly.

Vasyl lifted a paw and pointed. "Why do you look like that?"

Clockbrain spread his arms and looked down at himself. His eyes widened in surprise. "This is how you imagine me. We thought you would be more comfortable with this image."

"You do know that I'm afraid of you?"

Clockbrain sat cross-legged on the floor. "We know you think you are mad."

"I became a werewolf, tore off a man's hand, and ate it."

Clockbrain stroked Vasyl's face. "Technically, you changed into an Arctic Fox, Vulpes Lagopus, I believe."

"An Arctic Fox does not weigh 185 pounds, and eat humans, or think with a human brain."

Clockbrain leaned close. "You mean a human consciousness."

"In your Lexicon, what is Consciousness?"

Clockbrain leaned back against a wall that molded itself for his comfort. The clocks in his eyes counted the time. "An intrinsic part of the universe that manifests as the sum of memory, experience, knowledge, hopes, dreams, and personal awareness."

He laid his head on his paws. "Well, I would like to lose some of those memories."

Clockbrain stroked his head. "Then how would you learn from them?"

"I don't need to remember murder and cannibalism to know that it's wrong."

Clockbrain's head tilted to the side, and his cogs whirled. "Surviving is wrong?"

"Surviving at the expense of others."

Clockbrain fingers chased an itch behind Vasyl's ears. "You would have died when we fell to earth in 2018."

"Yes, but."

"You would have died again when the asteroid fragment struck Aparinsky if we had not saved you.

"And when the Russian soldiers took you, or in the APC, or the refugee camp. You chose to survive, to defend your consciousness."

Vasyl covered his head with his paws because he could not bury his face in his hands. "I must live with those memories."

"Which was the choice you made each time."

Vasyl looked up. "What did you do to me that I would have chosen such a crime?"

"We gave you the power to change. The drive to live is all your own."

"Because I'm a monster?"

"Because you live. What is it that motivates you, drives you? What do you want?"

Vasyl shook his head. "Why did you drive me from place to place for all those years? What did you have me look for?"

Clockbrain laughed, a sound made by meshing gears. "We lived in your head. I shared your mind but never drove you. Remember the notebook you kept?"

Vasyl hunched his shoulders in a doggish shrug. "It's gone."

"Why did you keep it? What did you observe?"

"Stars," Vasyl whispered. "It was always the stars."

"Your own desires drove your restless mind. Your father's actions left deep cracks in your memory. Stars were the glue that held your mind together."

"I drove us to watch stars?"

"Before I saved you, you pushed yourself to see stars. Why would that change, even in madness?"

And Vasyl remembered, not the days of his mad wondering, but being a boy. He remembered escaping to the roof after one of his father's nightly visits and wiping away the tears to see fields of cold, bright stars. A child's mind can be resilient; can hold together against beatings and worse if he has something. Some children he had known, died of bitterness and grief. Others, twisted by their experience, visited pain upon the people in their lives and echoed the crime of their fathers.

Vasyl studied stars, burying himself in knowing cold and unloving physics.

"I would like to see them again."

Clock brain stood. "We can, anytime. Of course, your experience may not be as you remember."

He lifted his muzzle and followed Clockbrain's movement. "Why, has your technology shattered the stars?"

"Energy manipulation on that scale is beyond us."

Vasyl's jaw twisted into a fox's smile. "I was joking."

"Of course, human humor is a tricky thing."

"Why would experience pale when compared to memory."

"You have the eyes of an Arctic Fox. They are excellent for differentiating grays but recognize only green at 550 nanometers and dark blue to purple between 430 and 440 nanometers."

Vasyl laughed. "Dichromatic vision, of course."

Clockbrain winked a digital eye. "Humans call that colorblind."

"I would rather not see gray stars."

"Change, adapt, it is what you do."

Vasyl shook his head and twisted to the side so that he could not see Clockbrain. "It is easier to remain a fox."

Clockbrain laughed. Vasyl found it such a genuine expression of humor that he jerked out of his dazed self-reflection.

"Your evolution is complete. Within Ship, you do not need to sample the DNA or share body fluids. Here changing will not tax your energy. Here you only need to think about who you want to be. But you must want it."

"I want to be myself."

Just like that, he lay naked on the floor of a dawn colored room, his hands clean.

Tears streamed from his eyes. Before he could wipe them away, the walls faded. He lay naked in the heart of space. Below and behind him, the sun burned. Above, the earth and the moon hung side by side and at almost the same apparent size. His mind, without any hesitation, calculated the exact position where such a view was possible.

Beyond earth, moon, and sun, he saw stars.

****

Aranea ran her fingertips along the wall. The Ship lived. It's flesh, warm beneath her touch, responded, a pleasant shock, a minuscule orgasm, reciprocated by the Ship as her way of saying good morning.

Aranea marveled at her hands. They had changed, grown longer. Whether as part of the healing after the battle or the process that began to alter her from that moment on the Don River in Russia she could not guess.

The door opened. She stepped into a round chamber, its walls a pleasant shade of rose. The Iris door closed to a seamless wall. "You painted the walls?"

The wall extruded a human shape, Hamilton North, dressed in a pinstriped suit and matching baseball shoes, stepped into the room.

"What will you wear today?"

"No!" She collapsed against the wall and fancied it cradled her.

"Not Ham. No, please, not him, he's dead."

"I apologize." Ham faded into an androgynous humanoid the color of the walls. "We dreamed him last night." Zhashour stopped speaking and shifted to Oviraptorus in the tight leather costume of an action hero. "I am not used to human minds, and the link is new to me."

"We dreamed him," she blushed, because her dream had been vivid, sexual, everything a human can express when alone in her own mind. "What about privacy?"

Aranea shivered and stepped away from the wall's embrace. She felt the arms that must have grown to cradle her fade back into Ship.

"Privacy is a human concept."

She shivered. "Human? Surely there must be times when your species needs a moment alone."

"We are never alone except in nightmares."

"You never walk alone in the forest, never enjoy a private thought, never defecate." Her formal, almost medical terminology fit the context. Aranea did not want to use the word shit or the euphemism, go. She wasn't quite sure she would be understood.

"Of course, I comprehend your meaning."

Oviraptorus surprised her. Aranea's thoughts had been her own.

Oviraptorus or Ship? Which name should we use?

"We are never alone, never apart. We are all parts of a single whole."

"Your species?"

"*Our* species."

"That's what I meant."

"No, you think of yourself as separate. You are not. You, Toss, Yume, Shiso, and Vasyl are us."

Aranea gasped and sat on the floor. That was wrong, so fucking wrong. "I'm a member of the human species."

"No. You survived to become us. The correct designation is *Our Species.*"

CHAPTER THIRTEEN

Afterword

John Stark sat at his desk, wrist bandaged, arm strapped to his chest. First day back, against doctor's orders, but back at work anyway. The world continued to unravel, to shift to a new paradigm. The first of the internal reports warned of a little ice age. Northern nations desperate for food and clean water eyed southern countries. Wars for power or energy gave way to wars for food.

Reports from teams active in almost every nation on earth revealed how they pried, poked, and prodded governments and transnational corporations in what FutureTense considered a better direction. For the first time since they recruited him out of the US Marines, he had doubts about their methods and goals, though not enough to tender his resignation, yet.

He opened his laptop and faced the first test. A man without a left hand could not type. He needed to write letters. He needed to tell the families of the dead that their sacrifice was worth it, even if he didn't believe it. The empty screen frightened him more than fighting monsters or aliens or failing to save the world. He knew other soldiers who faced amputation with the same courage they found in war. That empty screen mocked his best intentions.

Determined not to surrender, he opened a file on his phone and prepared to dictate the letter. A knock pulled his attention away, and Doctor Becker stalked through, face set in a frown.

"Doctor, don't you get enough of me on the ward?"

Becker pulled a chair up to the other side of the desk.

"I don't like you, Mr. Stark."

"Is that your medical opinion?"

"No, that's personal. It is inappropriate to say things like that to a patient on the ward."

"I admire your honesty, and Doctor, you are an over qualified dick."

"Good, we understand each other. I think that's important, considering what I have to say."

He almost set down the phone, but an ember of the fire he often felt in the face of other overqualified dicks stopped him. "I'm busy, Doctor. If you've any more personal comments, perhaps we should meet for coffee."

"The medical tests on all the survivors are complete."

Stark turned the phone off and tossed it on the desk next to his laptop. "You have my attention."

"There were thirteen deaths. All things considered, I believe it is critical that we cremate the remains. Fourteen other employees suffered wounds. They will need to be watched, perhaps for the rest of their lives. It is my opinion they be quarantined here along with the medical staff."

Stark looked into the doctor's face, attempting to read his body language for a hint. He hugged his wrist closer to his chest and wondered what it meant to him.

"As I remember, we reached a conclusion that the survivors of the Russian incident were not contagious."

Becker looked down at his feet and then back. "We were wrong."

Stark pushed himself up. He knew what the doctor had to say but refused to take it sitting down. "Go ahead."

"Ms. Thorn and you were bitten after Vasyl Petrenko changed into a wolf."

"It was an Arctic Fox."

Becker ignored him and continued without admitting Stark had said anything. "While in the refugee camp, Svetlana Gorelova had intercourse with the target."

"It was necessary to gain his trust. What's the problem?"

"He left cells behind, not unusual in a bite, sex, or any exchange of body fluids."

Doctor Becker's face remained flat and unemotional, with his eyes on the medical files on the desk. "The autoimmune systems ignore the cells. They do not react to any antibiotic and have spread through your bodies."

"Is that it?"

Becker glanced away as if he lost the courage to face what he needed to say. "Spit it out."

"You're changing. It's not quick. It may take years."

Stark leaned on the desk. "So what will we become?"

Doctor Becker closed his files and left the office.

The End

Frank Darbe

A resident of California since 1970, Frank Darbe writes Science Fiction, Fantasy, and poetry. He won the Mesa College Creative Writing Contest for a short story titled "Resurrection Man. He published "Dark Under the Sun" and "Walking the Blade Road" with the Webzine AnotherRealm. The Short Stories, "Training Session," "Ironheart," and "The Last/First Halloween appeared in Whortleberry Press. His short story, "Parcel Post" was published in Burial Day Books, Gothic Blue Book IV. Frank Darbe holds a Masters of Fine Arts in Creative Writing from National University.

You can check out more of Frank's work, as well as other authors with JaCol Publishing, online at www.jacolpublishing.com

www.ingramcontent.com/pod-product-compliance
Lightning Source LLC
Chambersburg PA
CBHW070758190726
48292CB00002B/572